PRAISE JAMES R. Wendell & Tyler

"IF YOU COULD MIX David Sedaris with Maya Rudolph and add a pinch of J.D. Salinger, you'd get something like **Wendell and Tyler.** Kincaid's novel has all the open-ended fun of a great vacation, but the travelers turn out to have brought serious baggage as well. Wendell and Tyler are great characters, fresh and unexpected, and it's a joy to spend time with them."
— Nancy Glazener, author of *Reading for Realism* and *Literature in the Making: a History of U.S. Literary Culture*

"A TALE OF STAR-CROSSED, ill-matched potential lovers as contemporary teenagers thrown together on the American road, this terrific read takes Kincaid to new places—in various senses of both national and emotional "place." The gradual if resistant disappearance of distance between two highly attractive denizens of what counts as the country of the young these days is managed with Kincaid's habitual wit and antic quirkiness—but also with a persuasive, attractive honesty about the difficulties of emerging self-knowledge."
—Gerhard Joseph, author of *Tennyson and the Text* and *Tennysonian Love: The Strange Diagonal*

"JOYFUL ALL THE WAY! If you know a late teen, or have ever been one, this book's for you. In this well-written treat, Kincaid portrays the world of the "new adult" with humor, sympathy and passion."
— Arline Chase, author of *Killraven, Ghost Dancer,* and the spirit series, *Spirit of Earth,* etc.

Annoying the Victorians

"VINDICATED. Finally, a book that explains why I didn't go to grad school to "study" literature. This entertaining book pokes fun at the academic system's "publish or perish" rule, whereby faculty are expected

to write something, anything, no matter how ridiculous, to prove they are studious... My advice to anyone who feels tempted to pursue an academic career in literature is to read ***Annoying the Victorians*** instead."
— books4parents , *Amazon Reviews*

"*WAY SMART* and Way Funny. Why isn't this book a huge best-seller? Probably just because it's too amazing. It's both a terrifically smart piece of literary criticism, AND a laugh-out-loud,snort-your-orange juice-out-your-nose funny FUNNY book. Do you like P. G. Wodehouse? Or Terry Pratchett? Or . . . ? Even if you aren't a literary critic, you'll be amazed by this book."
— Anonymous, *Amazon Reviews*

Erotic Innocence

"*MR. KINCAID* has written a very disturbing, yet highly important work. Perhaps the next time a mother or father decides to dress a nine-year-old girl up in a skimpy bikini, they will think twice before doing so. Cute? Maybe... But what message are we sending, anyway, when we show as much young flesh as we tend to do? Remember Jon-Benet Ramsey?"
— books 4 parents, *Amazon Reviews*

The History of the African American People: Proposed by Strom Thurmond
(as told to Percival Everett and James Kincaid)

"*I BOUGHT* the book because I'd heard it was funny...the book is indeed quite funny. It's also a relatively light read — the language can be a bit dense, (but always amusingly so)."
— Jeffrey Gordon, *Amazon Reviews*

WENDELL & TYLER: WE'RE OFF

OPEN ROAD SERIES, VOL.1

by James R. Kincaid

Cambridge Books
an imprint of
WriteWords, Inc.
CAMBRIDGE, MD 21613

© 2015 James R. Kincaid All Rights Reserved
First Print Edition, February 2015

Publishers Note: This is a work of fiction. All characters and events portrayed in this book are fictional, any mention of real toueist attractions are used fictionally,and any resemblance to real people or incidents is purely coincidental.

All rights reserved. No part of the book may be reproduced in any form or by any means without the prior written consent of the Author or Publisher, excepting brief quotes to be used in reviews.

𝕮𝖆𝖒𝖇𝖗𝖎𝖉𝖌𝖊 𝕭𝖔𝖔𝖐𝖘 is a subsidiary of:

Write Words, Inc.
2934 Old Route 50
Cambridge, MD 21613

ISBN 978-1-61386-343-5

Fax: 410-221-7510

Bowker Standard Address Number: 254-0304

Dedication

To my deareswt Nita

*She hears the grass grow,
the squirrel's heart beat ---
endures the roar which lies
on the other side of silence*

Into my heart an air that kills
   From yon far country blows;
What are those blue remembered hills,
   What spires, what farms are those?

That is the land of lost content,
   I see it shining plain,
The happy highways where I went
And cannot come again.

— A. E. Housman

CHAPTER 1

We're Almost Off

This is about a trip Tyler and I are going to take, a record we'll keep. First, I'll tell you about me, though I wish I didn't have to and think it's a bad idea.

Sean Jackson tells me I'm the only virgin in school, gotta be. That says more about Sean than me, since he's a virgin for sure and says that just to mock the stupid competition boys have, where you might as well kill yourself if you're still a virgin at sixteen. Which I am — both, today being my birthday. Sean Jackson, I'll call him Sean 1 for reasons I'll explain, says stuff like that a lot.

My mom once told me I should have sex about now. What she said was, "Have sex when you're sixteen or it'll loom too large in your mind; and, heavenly days, Wendy, it's not that important." She doesn't say that now, and she doesn't call me "Wendy," including in front of other people. What she now says is I should keep my body pure, for reasons of my spirit. I don't want to know what she means.

I have my own computer. I also have some online subscriptions my mom supposes are to scholastic sites. My mom's not all that bright. That's my opinion.

I like looking at cheerleaders on some of these sites, not real porn exactly. Not very good porn would be the way to put it. The real live in-the-flesh cheerleaders I've seen, at our school for instance, are generally hot. The cheerleaders they have on www.alt.binaries.erotica.cheerleaders.com you don't want to look at real close. I won't get explicit here because that sort of thing kind of disgusts me. I kind of disgust me.

Just to enthrall you, I'll talk about my reading habits. Ms. Barnes-Romans, my English teacher, says you can tell about someone by knowing what they read, though only a dork would talk about that, so here goes: *The Perks of Being a Wallflower, The Virgin Suicides, The Stranger*, and my favorites, *Revolting Youth* and *Youth in Revolt*, two different books but with the same character, Nick Twisp. I wish I was Nick Twisp.

Nick Twisp is cool and smart and has lots of guts. I'm not cool, or smart. I do have lots of guts, though. I really do. I don't mind too much getting beat up, and I ought to know what that's like. I'm not all that tough, never won a fight. To be fair to me, I never had a fight I started, and all were with guys who knew they could beat me up, and they were right, which is a big reason they hit me. I'm not so stupid I can't usually avoid fights, especially at this school I'm at now, where fighting is frowned on. It's frowned on everywhere, but this school is snootier, which means kids care about what's frowned on.

Cartwright Princeton Academy is the worst place I've been, easily. That's the truth and not some personal bitterness speaking. My mom keeps sending me to different schools, trying to find one that will match my needs. I tell her there's no school going to match my needs; I'm just kind of dumb. She hates it when I say that.

I get interested in things, and try to find out about them. Not many things but some. I don't blame schools for not teaching things I get interested in. It's not that I'm not interested in what they do at school, either. That's what Mom thinks. She thinks I'm bored. Truth is, I like a lot of the stuff there, even some of the science. I like the classes better than the kids, in some cases.

I'd like more kids if more kids liked me, but I'm not super-depressed by not being the best-liked kid in school. Not that I'm close; I'm a long way from that. I'm not the worst-liked, but take away a couple of sad cases and maybe. There's others in my boat, so it's not all that depressing. You might start thinking I'm one of those Columbine youths, ready to shoot up the cafeteria. For one thing, our school has dining rooms, not cafeterias, if you can believe it, though the food's no better than at any of the other schools I've been at. The point I'm making is that I have it okay, not so great, but I'm not all wound up tight inside, ready to explode.

I'm not trying to explain myself. I'm talking to get going so I can tell the story without dropping it on you out of the blue, like a truck running over your toe. I'm not being honest. I don't have a high regard for honesty. That's one thing I've thought about. I think honest is something people believe they want other people to be. Like my mom. Mom has strong feelings, and she mistakes that for honesty. I don't mean nobody's honest. "Honest" doesn't mean what people think it does, in my opinion. Not many people make things up out of nothing, like lies; and if they do, it's for a good reason, like not insulting someone or making a story more entertaining. It's not something you'd say was so bad. Some people see what's going on better than other people and that's what counts.

Which isn't moving our story along. I just wanted to get started without you thinking I was some rebel kid spilling his heart out to you.

I don't have a clear goal in life, not even losing my virginity. My mom would like my goal in life to be getting in touch with my spirit. I resist agreeing but not because there's some things I won't say. There's nothing I wouldn't say to not be bothered. I won't say that about my spirit because she'd be pleased and want to get close. I spend a lot of time avoiding being close without feeling too guilty. It's an ongoing struggle, as the school counselor says about not giving in to peer pressure, which is a bunch of bull. But keeping my mother from being too close really is.

I have a paper route, just for example. No I don't. I get up every morning, take my bag and go out. That's to be mysterious. I head to my friend's house, Sean Jackson that I mentioned. I have a good many friends, three really, and one, Sean, gets up early and he and I hang out. Two of my three friends are named Sean, just by accident, and the third is named Terry. I have other friends too, but they come in and out of focus. If you're lucky, you have one friend who stays there. I have three, so I'm super-lucky.

Sean 1 and I hang out every morning. His parents think we're starting up our own Internet Company. They're smart people, but they are like my mom in having feelings. They're so happy we're being business boys, or that Sean 1 is, that they never stop to ask why we got to do it at six in the morning. We hang out in his bedroom and play video games and stuff, "stuff" being looking at porn, like you knew.

I can tell you something about Sean 1. Sean 1 and Sean 2, to make matters more confusing, are good buddies with one another, though seldom with me around; I hang out with both and they hang out with each other. Terry is not buddies with Sean 1 or Sean 2, not an enemy just not a hangout.

As for Sean 1 and Sean 2. One way to keep them straight is to think of Fat Sean (1) and Skinny Sean (2), Dork Sean (1) and Cool Sean (2), Computer Sean (1) and Jock Sean (2). And then you'd know all about them, only you wouldn't. Which Sean do you suppose gets dates and which one sits home Saturday night, and which one gets elected to office and which one doesn't dare run, and which one plays old video games and which one is in a garage band? Well, you'd think you'd know, but you wouldn't.

Actually, a lot of what you'd suppose from those cliches would be true, all of it. I just wish it weren't.

It's hard to say why Sean 1 accepts a dork role like he was in a movie. Puts it on when he goes out of the house, almost.

Next thing he'll be wearing tape on his glasses, only he has rich kid contacts. He doesn't have zits, doesn't have a high-pitched giggle, doesn't wear his pants up by his shoulders, doesn't snort. But the other dork things he has down like he's practiced. He was cool in the sixth grade: at least, that's what a girl who went to school with him in Santa Barbara earlier told me. I can believe it. Sean 1 has blue eyes and dirty blond hair that would make him look good now, if he'd lose twenty pounds — but I don't think he would.

Here's what I think. Sean 1 doesn't want to take the chance. He puts on the loser stuff like a costume because it takes the pressure off. I can understand that. It's not like I do it myself — don't get me wrong. I try to be cool like Nick Twisp and fail. That's why I can see why somebody might not want to get in that race, keep coming in last.

Sean 1 is nice to me, without making a fuss about it. Once I was sick — I'm almost never sick, only missed two days in the last three years — and Sean 1 went around and got all my assignments. And all he said was, "I didn't want you enjoying yourself, Wendell, wearing out your wand when you should be reading *Death in Venice*. You can read *Death in Venice* without getting a boner, I think; even you can." I thought that was pretty witty. And it's just like Sean 1: he'll do a nice thing and make it into nothing.

Here's what it is: Sean wants me to feel good. I noticed one day that he never criticized anything about me or made fun, except in an easy way, like that about wearing out my wand, which I joke about too. Might as well joke, though it does worry me. Sean 1 is relaxing, as good a friend as anybody could have. Except — you knew there was more. He seems almost dangerous. Like a Venus fly trap. Being a lot with Sean 1 might be like being married for sixty years and be enjoying it, except.... It's not Sean 1; it's me, that's the problem. Every time I start having a great time with Sean 1 and wanting to be around him more, I get scared. Hanging around with Sean 1 isn't the best way to make yourself cool.

That's the crude way to put it. The crude way is the best in understanding me. I wish it weren't. Sean 1's a better person than I am by forty miles and I'm down deep ashamed to let people know he's my friend. The worst thing is that he knows that, which is why we get together so early. I wish he wouldn't put up with it.

I've been caught shoplifting three times. Twice at Wal-Mart and once at Macy's. I tried to rip off Wal-Mart because I object to their labor practices, but then who doesn't? Macy's I went after because it's a very annoying store. I can't go back into Wal-Mart again, any Wal-Mart in the world, banned for life, as a result of getting caught, but I'd only go in one to shoplift anyhow. Macy's asked me please not to do it again, only they were sure I wouldn't: they knew I'd simply made a mistake, peer pressure, we won't bother your parents, ha ha. I was supposed to regard that assistant manager as some role model, like he alone understood what it was to be young.

All the times I shoplifted I was with another kid: Sean Durbin, Sean 2. But I didn't do it just to impress Sean 2. Yes I did. I mention me being picked up for shoplifting not because it's some key to my character. I thought of it because it illustrates what I said about having guts. I just picked up stuff, even without a dare. Okay, showing off, but I wasn't scared, just grabbed the goods, stuffed them in my clothes and left. Tried to. Almost made it the second time at Wal-Mart. Got Sean 2 to schmooze it up with the security guy who checks your receipts at the exit. Then I flipped these two basketballs over the electronic hoop gate things. I was aiming for a big box of scrap paper on the other side, but I missed and the balls went bouncing around like mad right there at the exit, where the 114-year-old greeter was. Hit her right in the head, one of the balls did. It was pretty funny, especially when the security guy nabbed me. He was pissed that I kept laughing as he was lecturing:

"Shoplifting is a major felony in this state, punk."

"No, it isn't."

"I advise you to listen to me, Mr. Laughing Boy."

"Yes, sir."

But the security guy was not much older than me and pretty pathetic, sort of, and he was running out of impressive lines, so I stopped laughing, started feeling bad.

"I wish I could help you kid," he said, all at once on my side, "but we have to call the fucking manager. I'm sorry."

And he was sorry. "What kind of guy is this manager, anyhow?"

"Ah, he's a real dick, kid."

"I'll bet he is. How come you work here?" Dumb question.

"Only job I can get. I don't have many qualifications. I'm going to PCC, though. Trouble is, Wal-Mart, the same manager who's going to jump your bones, keeps changing my shift. Screws up my classes."

"Jesus, Bob," from his name tag, "I'll bet they do that just to keep you from improving yourself — and escaping."

"I think you're right, Wendell." I told him my name earlier, being too dumb to give a fake one. I wasn't sorry, though. I liked Bob.

The manager, the shift manager, was another story. I tried to be a smartass but wasn't quick enough to make it worth reporting. He wanted bad to scare me, and at least didn't do that. I wasn't exactly crushed to be banished from Wal-Mart. The reason I included this story is to illustrate what Ms. Barnes-Romans calls "the salient parts" of my character. I'm pretty sure I don't have "salient parts" in the way Ms. Barnes-Romans means when she's talking about Hamlet, but as far as I can see I have guts and I'm not too smart. I've been illustrating those

The other point of this story is to let you know a little bit about Sean 2. Sean 2 is one of the most popular kids in school. Unlike some, he deserves to be. He's the star of the football team, or some team. I don't pay attention, as sports aren't that big an item here at Cartwright Princeton. It's not being a jock that makes him popular: he's handsome, smart, fun to talk to. I don't think Sean 2 is modest, but he seems to be. It works. Not to be cynical, but I think he's adapted, the way a successful bug does. He's found he gets all the attention in town if he doesn't ask for any. Everybody loves him if he seems like he doesn't need love. When you talk with him, it's like he's inside you, obsessed with your problem. There's no way not to love that. It's like loving yourself.

Odd thing is, he doesn't mean to do this. It just works for him. He really is kind and considerate and very sensitive. That's because he's so self-centered and completely indifferent to everybody. But so what? Nobody can resist Sean 2. I know I can't.

But why does he spend time with me? He's not indiscriminate, and he's not a moron. Who knows? Of course I wish I knew, but I don't want to think too hard about it. Obviously. Here's a conversation with Sean 2, as well as I can remember it:

"You been working out, Wendell?"

"How'd you know?" I had been but hadn't told anybody.

"It's obvious."

"My huge muscles." This was a trap to catch his insincerity. My working out hadn't made a bit of difference in the size of any muscles. I'd measured.

"No." So much for that trap.

"What then?"

"It's the way you carry yourself. Your balance and thrust. The tilt of your head. I try to study these things, buddy."

He did too. All that about balance and thrust is odd, but of course I fell for it. Sean 2 calls me things like "buddy" a lot, sometimes "best friend" or even "honey." Once he called me "love," pronounced it like it rhymed with "move" and said it was an English term of affection when I asked. I'm sorry I asked, since he's not used it since.

You wormed my secret out of me, which I needn't spell out. Not that I'd get in a situation where anything would happen, but I have thought about it. I'm not homophobic, but I can't imagine I'd fool around with Sean 2. I'm gutsy, but not that gutsy.

I'm little and pretty. I hate to say it, but might as well. And there's no point trying for a better word than "pretty." That's what fits. You figured that out. I can tell both Seans are a little hot after me, though not all that hot and way not hot enough for anything ever to happen, even if.... Shut up!

My third friend, Terry, is a great hangout friend. He's funny and smart, not very personal, if you know what I mean. Terry hates school and his parents and the Republican Party. (He's the only kid I know who's interested in politics, not just faking it for teachers.) Terry doesn't put on hating stuff so other kids'll be impressed; he hates things with his heart, the way some people love them. Terry gets in trouble a lot, thinks I'm capable of that too. He doesn't think I'm cute; he thinks I'm a bad ass. I don't know if he likes me much, but he told me once I was smart, which nobody else ever said. He told me that when I came up with this plan to express Terry's contempt for a range of stuff.

I gave a lot of thought to a dangerous scheme, not to impress Terry but to have fun — and impress him. I wanted a plan that would fit Terry's disgust. At school Ian told us about this sports awards banquet. (Ian is Mr. Carmichael, from England, a jackass who imagines he's close to the kids, when everybody thinks he's a pederast who'd like to cane all the boys like they do in England.) Ian thought we'd be interested to know the latest news from San Marino, which Terry says is the chastity belt of the Republican crotch, whatever that means.

I cooked up this plan, just the kind Terry would love. I got help from Mr. Billard, our janitor, who everybody calls "Bill" except me, which I don't because my mom said that nobody'd call him "Bill" if he was white. That made me feel rotten. Anyhow, Mr. Billard had a cousin working as a janitor at San Marino High, hated the place, and would help with my plan, which was to substitute this really gross porn movie I happened to know about for the sports highlight film they were showing. "How'd we get in? Won't your cousin be in trouble?" I asked Mr. Billard.

"Honey; it's a rich kid school, not the Pentagon." Terry loved it, especially when it made the papers: "Vandals Pull Stunt — Not Funny!" Parents were shocked, administrators furious. Perfect!

I also have friends who are girls. Not that I'm the sort of pathetic boy who is best friends with the good-looking girls, although I sort-of am. I stand there and listen to the girls, who say, "That Wendell, he's so sensitive." All it takes is not telling them too directly the guys they like are mean or thuggish — but trying to let them know that anyhow.

Terry says these girls are only rehearsing real feelings, and maybe so; but when I'm talking with them, I do like them and feel sorry for them and want to help. I think my advice is what's cliched. And the guys they're trying to figure out and please are not always lousy either. Often they are.

Anyways, my project to find a way to have sex is not advanced by spending time with girls who regard me as a little sister. I do date a lot. I date what Sean 1 calls second-tier girls. Sean 1 can be blunt — and accurate. I aim for second-tier girls on purpose. These girls know their rank and mostly aren't interested in me at all, being so busy trying to get over the hump into first-tier. Going out with me isn't going to do that for them. It won't hurt them, maybe, and going out with me is better than staying home; but going out with me more than, say, twice, would be poison. That's just the way it is.

I think that's enough on my social activities. It's depressing me to talk about it, though I'm not a depressed person. I know a few. There's this one girl, Kelly, I got pretty worried about. Very depressed. I finally called her father, who took her to a doctor, who gave Kelly some pills, and now she's better. Not that I'm a do-gooder. I don't know what in hell was the story with Kelly's parents, though. Didn't they notice?

I don't have what Ms. Barnes-Romans would call a good connective from whatever it was I was talking about to the next thing, which is my life at home. This will be short. My dad's a mystery. He left my mom and me, just disappeared. For some reason, my mom won't put it that way, won't put it any way, doesn't want to talk about it, about him; she acts like I got found by the fairies amongst the ferns. I don't want to talk about it, either, but she's had sixteen years to come up with a story, and you'd think she'd have managed something. Nope. She's devoted to me, she is. Whether that works to my advantage is not clear. Some days I think it does; most days I'm sure it doesn't.

It makes me feel ookie when kids are embarrassed by their parents; it always seems to be a class thing. (We have scholarship students here at Cartwright Princeton, just so we can all benefit from diversity. About six blacks and seven Hispanics; Asians, of course, we got leaking up through the floorboards.) One thing I like about the Seans and Terry is that they don't give a damn about their parents. I think they have decent parents myself, though I realize most kids imagine that about their friends' parents, just because they definitely are cool compared to the parents they have themselves. Mature kids don't mind their parents. My mom embarrasses the hell out of me.

Apart from her religion, what Terry calls New Age, my mom really could be a lot worse. That's what Sean 1 tells me, Sean 2 too. You'd think that'd be very irritating, for the Seans to say that, but it isn't: they're trying to give me some perspective.

My mom was the one who set this summer all up. How Tyler got involved is another story altogether, even less probable.

* * *

I won't take long, not having such a rich repertoire of experiences and reflections as Wendell. Besides, I want to get rid of some garbage up front.

I always thought Wendell was an asshole, the prettiest boy anywhere but an asshole, not that I've changed my mind in the last week. He's the kind of girly boy who gives girls a bad name: passive, needy. He keeps getting beat up and doesn't so much as find even littler kids — there are a few — to beat up on himself. At least I don't think he does. How's he compensate for all the annoyance he generates?

But it's not "annoyance" he inspires in other boys, is it? Why do kids feel the need to kick his ass? Wendell's little and weak, so what's the point? He fights back too, so there's some slight danger of getting hurt. Related question: why do hot girls treat him like he was their best girlfriend? I've talked to him about intimate issues myself a few times; I'll admit it. He's irresistible as a confidante, which is something different from being a friend, and certainly different from being a lover. (I guess, not that I'd know. Really. I don't want to project an image of an experienced, glued-together woman. I might like to be that, but I'm not, not even close.)

Wendell gains the instant, Platonic trust of girls. With boys, he either attracts close buddies, I'd guess, or he makes them so frightened by their response they hit him. Not that Wendell's gay, I wouldn't think. I may be wrong, but I'm not wrong on why this pretty-boy (spectacularly pretty) has a fairly lousy time of it. Boo-hoo. He does better than a lot. He has money, all his teeth, no major disfigurements. True, he seems dim. Nobody objected when he wasn't chosen for the Academic Bowl team. As for being beautiful, not his fault, but he could butch up some. Right now, he keeps his hair long and wears saggers (with modest long shirts). Both are sexy, or could be. He needs help being generically boyish. The boys he hangs with won't help him there, so turned on by what he is as they are. The girls around him imagine they are close but just use him; he's unthreatening. I imagine they have him adjust their bra straps.

I shouldn't be negative. I wish I looked like Wendell. There are lots of kids worse off; he gets by with what he has. He hangs back, doesn't make noise (except when someone's beating on him). I've had classes with him and he's okay. He doesn't pretend to be a smartass subversive, probably because he doesn't have the brains. He doesn't get a lot of encouragement from the teachers, who don't see Wendell at Harvard or even UCLA in a couple of years, so they don't care.

Enough about Wendell. You want to know about me, a layered, intricate being, a challenging personality. Wendell is a character out of some after school special. No teen cliche could contain me. You don't like that, don't like me? Hey, I'm wounded.

Okay, you got me. I'm not special. Wendell, caught as he is by the bullies and his low IQ, may have more independence than super-conventional me. It makes me feel better to exaggerate, though it's not much of an exaggeration. I'm an A student, join clubs, I date boys who don't interest me because others admire them, am on the tennis team, a cheerleader. I worry about clothes, the music I listen to, and the movies I see. I abuse my parents. Worst of all, I know this, even while doing it, and I'm ashamed. Sometimes I can convince myself that I'm acting a part for a higher goal. What higher goal? Other times I tell myself that I do all this because it's easier, saves me time. But what do I need the time for, if I spend it fussing around to make my roles more complete?

Not every minute. I take voice lessons, play the piano. I read some and write. What I write isn't worth anything, but maybe someday. If not, I still enjoy it. I also volunteer in a Saturday Academy, run by USC for inner city kids. Sure, I do that to have something to put on my college applications, but I enjoy it, used to. A couple of the kids, they're ninth-graders, have become friends of mine. Or were. Long story there. If I'm going to be honest, I'd better tell it — not that honesty is my goal, more like catharsis.

They're both boys, DeShauwan and Rafael. I flirted with them and let them say remotely suggestive things to me, even encouraged it. Trivial but awful.

Have I been cruel to them? They are shy and mainly do nothing more than giggle and blush — and yes, boys of color do blush. But I think there is something worse here than flirting, something more unfair and unkind. Who would say a little fake seduction could damage these boys, these horny boys, whose SAT scores down the road I was upping every tutoring session? Anyone who thought about it — even me.

And why did I do it? I think it's because I am so bored I'd like to throw myself in front of the kiddie train at the mall. Something splashy like *Anna Karenina*. I've adapted so well it's given me a vision of emptiness so complete I found myself playing tease to these boys with so little in their lives and so little before them. Talk about "emptiness" from a teen sounds pretentious, but that's because we have a word like "pretentious" to keep kids from seeing what's there, not there. If there were a girl gang around, I'd join it. Only I wouldn't, as I'm not stupid enough to imagine alternatives are so easily found.

Can I be more pompous? Okay, like Martin Luther Jr., I've been to the mountaintop and I've seen the other side: just as barren as this side. It's more modest to call this boredom. If I were really pompous — but I'm not really pompous. Daydream Believer and a homecoming que-ee-ee-en. Oh what can it mean? Not one fucking thing.

But even if you take all that seriously, which you won't, it still is no excuse, still amounts to pure down home selfishness.

I was using these boys to make myself feel good, assuming they'd notice nothing. Insofar as I had a positive goal, I wanted to arm them against sliding into the pit that was swallowing their friends and families, throw them a life preserver, and think now maybe I did the worst thing imaginable, suggesting to them a world, a privileged world, that is not only benign but beckoning. That's a terrible lie. Maybe these kids would give me a chance to do something redemptive. That's what I thought. I needed that. I tried not to recognize that if they hooked onto my life preserver I might pull them under.

Part of the game plan, though I'd never plotted it out deliberately, depended on Rafael and DeShauwan being too dim or too scared to question my do-gooding motives or actions. Wrong for both kids, probably on both counts:

"Ty, can we talk to you about something?"

"Sure."

"You don't mind?"

I was suddenly nervous, though I wasn't yet sure why. I'm never nervous.

"No, I don't mind."

"Ty, why you doing this?" DeShauwan was the one asking, but both were speaking.

I didn't pretend to be mystified: "I like you guys, being around you."

They looked at me as if I were a standard-issue adult, a word-machine, a liar.

Made it worse that I was a kid and should know better, behave better.

"Okay. I get a kick out of being around you. That's the truth. I like helping you when I can, but I'm no fucking do-gooder."

"We homies, that it?"

"We homies? What kind of talk is that?"

They did laugh, shifted around a bit. Then Rafael picked up the ball.

"Ty, we like you. But it's sort of strange, isn't it? I mean, what do you want from us, you know?"

"Are you worried that I'd somehow hurt you?"

"God, Tyler, no. We just don't understand. I mean, why would you want to spend time with us? We're nothing special. We know that."

"You have some idea why I like being around you?"

"We don't know. You want to help people like us?"

I did the worst thing: said nothing.

"Let's just drop it. Really, Tyler. Sorry we brought it up."

"Don't drop it. You wanted to ask. You already know."

"You like improving us?" And he didn't mean it in a nice way.

"Well, buddies — "

"We're not buddies, are we? I mean, it's like we're ghetto losers." Rafael and DeShauwan both looked anguished, eager for me to take away their certainty, give them a way to feel some power in all this, some dignity. They knew what they were talking about when they called themselves such mean names.

I started making noises, without knowing what I'd say. Bad idea.

"Look, I won't lie to you." I stopped then, realizing people never say that except as a prelude to lying. These boys would know that too. "Okay, I would lie to you, if I could think how to do it. I started on all this because I was curious, wondered what it would be like to do this tutoring. I don't think I expected anything particular, just didn't know. That's why I did it, because it was like a mystery."

I paused, but they knew I was just warming up.

"I got to know you two and got to like you, not just find you interesting. Then I got to respect you too and wanted to help you if I could. That's the fucking truth."

They stared at me, expressing nothing. I had to do better. But I had nowhere to go, so I stopped and just looked, first at them and then at my feet. What light there was in the room seemed to be fading. I wasn't going to be able to find a way out of this. Better to hurt me than to hurt them. But I could find no way to do even that, leaving them feeling degraded — ghetto losers.

We keep going with the tutoring. It's petering out, more slowly than it should.

There's a moment in the great movie, "Smoke Signals," where Victor's father asks this woman he's just met, "What's the worst thing you ever did in your life?" That's the most bone-jarring question I can imagine. I don't remember the answer given in the movie; I know what the answer is for me. I hope you couldn't answer it right off for yourself. It must be nice to have to think about it.

CHAPTER 2

Mom called a Family Meeting ten days ago. (We're approaching the action part of the story.) Why she announces Family Meetings for two is beyond me. Actually, it isn't. This maniac group gives these classes in family health, that's what they're called. For good family health, it's important to "foster an atmosphere of respect." The quote is from a pamphlet my mom gave me, when I refused to go to the meeting. They tell the dupes they drag in they should "avoid giving orders" and instead "create a cooperative aura of complete honesty." This aura depends on Family Meetings, with a list ("an unalterable agenda") distributed beforehand, allowing anyone before the meeting starts, but not after, to add things, no subtractions ("sharing power means nobody has a veto").

The unalterable agenda, distributed two days before the meeting, had on it, "Summer Plans for Wendell." Since they were my plans, I didn't quite see why my mom was making an agenda item out of it. On the other hand, I was curious what she had in mind and didn't grumble. I hardly ever grumble. Maybe I never do. I am not bragging. I regard it as a weakness, one of many.

"The meeting will now come to order."

"Mom, do we really have to do this dorky stuff?"

"Well, I see your point. Does anybody have any items to add to the agenda?"

"Mom!"

"Okay, Wendy. Though Barry says...."

21

"Never mind, Mom. What's my summer plans? Do we need a motion?"

She laughed. That surprised me a little.

"No, dear heart, we just need to explore options for the summer."

"I was thinking I would train for the Olympic skeet-shooting team."

She grinned: "I'll cut right to the meat: how'd you like to drive a car to your Uncle Marshall in Atlanta? Leave it there and fly back."

"Damn. Who's Uncle Marshall? Sure!"

"You remember Uncle Marshall."

"I never even heard of Uncle Marshall."

"I suspect you wouldn't remember him."

"Is he your brother or Dad's?"

"Not exactly."

"Not like I care. So, I take Uncle Marshall this car. Drive it there and drop it off. Okay, I can do that."

"More than that. You know, dear, that, in Victorian times, in England, wealthy families sent young men out on a tour of Europe, a long tour, on their own, just to acquire experience, self-reliance. They'd study music and classical art, that sort of thing, but also, dearie, they'd learn to trust themselves."

Of course I didn't know anything of the sort. But it sounded good, so I kept my mouth shut, pretty much: "Is that right?"

"You can learn to trust your spirit — and also you could learn a lot about your inner being. You're young, but you're wise beyond your years. I know you're ready."

Even I knew I wasn't wise beyond my years, but I didn't think it was my job to enlighten Mom about that.

"How long will it take, Mom, a few days? I guess five or six days? Eight?"

"I was thinking most of the summer, honey, all of it. Pause some, explore the external and internal landscapes."

"Really? Hot damn!"

"Wendell."

"Sorry. That's a great idea." It was also an illegal idea, but I wasn't going to break that bit of news. This was the best thing ever — and it was going to get better.

"Now, dear, the scheme traditionally involved a mentor, but often, I believe, another young man. A companion not only confirms but magnifies."

Another young man? Confirming and magnifying? Honest to Jesus! I kept my mouth shut, lest I mess this up.

"I won't hide from you, that I also have in mind that it would be well to have someone to share the driving and the planning, and also, don't be annoyed with me, someone to mute the dangers that might attend a single traveler."

Why would I be annoyed? I was already about to mess myself with fear about the dangers that might attend a single traveler, until she mentioned that companion stuff.

"So, does this sound feasible, sweetie? I'm sure you have lots of questions, and maybe you'd like to consider it a while, mull it over."

"Thanks, Mom. I think it will get me in touch with my spirit, and provide lots of interesting sights, broaden my mind.'"

"Well, good!" She was beaming.

"You have this peer picked out, Mom, or do I get to try to persuade somebody?"

"Now, honey, what do you suppose?"

You think I mind these names she has for me? I don't. I mean, what's it matter? Aside from the spirit stuff, she's okay. I know I let on differently before, but I was trying to sound interesting. My mom hasn't had it easy, what with my dad leaving or something. Maybe she done him in. Got him under the cement in the basement. She's a good mom, so if she wants to call me embarrassing names, let her.

"I suppose you'll have suggestions, maybe with a discussion at a future Family Meeting? Or you have a companion for me? That's only natural."

"I don't think it's natural for me to pick the person you'd like to share all this with. One of the most interesting aspects of this experiment will turn out to be how you and your friend unfold before one another, through the flowering of a really strong human relationship. It could be tough, dearie."

She was looking at me earnestly. I think that's the word I want.

"I guess."

"Wendell, spending a whole summer in such close contact with another will teach you so much, but it'll be tougher even than being married, in some respects, since you'll have to be very inventive to manage time apart. You'll get on one another's nerves; you'll bore one another. You'll have to bend and stretch, both of you. It could be the best part of the experience, but it will be the hardest."

I said what I thought she'd expect. I didn't want to make any part of the plan wobble. This was one of those dreams granted by the genie in the lamp: "I know I'll have to be very careful choosing this companion."

"I guess you can be if you want."

Now what? If I want? "I should — I see what you mean — what do you mean?"

"You can hope to find someone who's flexible and kind. But, truly, it's impossible to know things like that in advance. There aren't any tests to determine if someone will be easygoing, inventive, generous. I want this to be all you. Trust your intuition."

Mom seemed to think I had a big stable of friends lined up and eager to spend three months with me. She figured the only problem was that I was starting a little late and might, probably not, run into previous commitments and resisting (sensible) parents. Oh, sure! It was sort of flattering, though.

Okay, Sean 1 or Sean 2 or Terry. I could hardly go up to some guy and say, "Hey, you don't know me. I'm Wendell. How'd you like to spend three months cooped up with me in a car, driving cross country and having adventures?"

Actually, there might be a few takers. If somebody proposed that to me, I might do it, so long as the proposer was a few inches this side of a psychopath. But that made no difference. I'd never propose it to anybody but these three.

Sean 1 I eliminated. Made me feel crummy to do it, but it'd make me feel crummier to spend three months with him, every minute. I didn't want to inquire too closely into why this was true, but after all, you can be good buddies with somebody and respect them and all without wanting to move in together. This is getting very uncomfortable, and anyways I am not going to ask Sean 1.

Terry was a great possibility. Only problem was he wouldn't do it. Maybe he *would* do it, probably would, but I happened to know he was set up with an intern program in Washington, D.C., to help out a lobbying group doing something to upset the Republican Party. It'd be stupid to ask, since he'd told me all about that.

Sean 2. Jesus Lord of Heaven, as Mom would say. It'd be a strain, for sure, as I never felt relaxed around Sean 2. I was always afraid he'd think I was a loser, find out that I *was* a loser. All the same, I could take that. Thing was whether I could ask him. I had no idea what he had planned. We never talked about that kind of thing.

How could I introduce the subject?

I'll spare you my "aimless dithering," a clever phrase I got from Mr. Diddle (his real name, I swear), our gym teacher and assistant football coach of some kind. Mr. Diddle used it to describe boys who were slow getting showered, a process Mr. Diddle made sure to supervise closely.

So, Sean 2 and I had this conversation, at his house. I'll give you just the ending:

"Fuck, Wendell, I wish I could."

"That's okay."

"No, it's not okay. You suppose I don't want to spend time with you, take this trip. That's terrible. Honest, Wendell, I think a lot of you. You know that."

"Sure."

"No, you don't. I know you don't. You have no idea."

"God, Sean."

"What? I like you, Wendell. You're never the same, you know what I mean? And you aren't the fucking same as everybody else."

He let it hang there. At least I didn't ask him to clarify.

"I know you're going to think there's something about you that keeps me from doing this; I just know you're going to think that. I'm not stupid, Wendell."

"I know. I believe you."

"I hope so. If I thought you'd feel bad about this, I'd just go. It'd be great. But, Wendell, like I say there's two reasons I can't. I want to make some money, as I'm sick of leeching off my parents, mostly cause it gives them some video of every fucking thing I do. Also, and here's where I worry, I don't want to be away that long, away from other kids and a few girls I have my eye on. But you think I just don't want to be with you." This went on for some time, me saying, of course, I knew it wasn't that he didn't want to be with me. But I knew it was because he didn't want to be with me. If he wanted to be with me, he'd come along.

***

I'm baaaaccccccckkkkk! Now's my chance to appear in a more favorable position. I'm lighting director, so why not. Worst foot forward, that's my motto. There's nothing about me that's lower than what I told you — I sure hope. I put it first, truth, because it might be fascinating, which is one thing I'm not. Looks like I'm more worried about seeming conventional than abominable.

The best thing in my life is my little brother, who is almost as pretty as Wendell. Only Martin is eleven, where pretty is okay. Martin is named after, you guessed it, our parents' hero, just the first name, though. They named him after two heroes, so he came out as Martin DuBois Arthur. I think that's worse than Martin Luther King Jr. Arthur. But I don't mind. When you know a person, the name fades away.

Martin is the one person who doesn't make me feel like I'm acting. I think I'll blame it on Mama and Papa. Why not? They are about as artificial as folks get. "Suburb niggers" is a phrase I thought up to describe them. It's been on the tip of my tongue and about to fly off straight at them about eight hundred times.

But I hate talk like that and I don't hate my parents. It's probably not easy being blockbusters, in their case entire-neighborhood-busters, and they have some guts. They want me and Martin to have things easier, not that they are exactly up-from-slavery sorts. But they did battle to get their scholarships and admissions to medical school. It wasn't easy, dealing with all the white assholes being enlightened, not noticing their tint, doling out public politeness and formal praise.

I know a little about that. Helps that I look like a ginger-colored pop star: small nose, straight teeth, unkinkied hair. Not all of it has been the result of science and surgery either. God made me easy for white folks to feel inner glows about. Want an escalator to the top: class president and prom queen? Be the uncomplaining black girl in a place like this. There's nobody would dare not be my friend. Some kids might bungee jump with a too-long cord, but they'd never have the guts to be anything but bosom friends with Tyler Arthur. I am very likeable — for an asshole.

Not that I'm very different from the other privileged kids here, girls anyhow. Boys are another species. Despite what I said, I think my skin color, my ethnicity, my cultural heritage are superficial things about me. They don't tell you much. What they do tell you you'd be better off ignoring. Take my word for it.

I like school okay. I like my many activities. I like my room and my hobbies. I like the car my parents let me drive with my learner's permit, sometimes without them in it. I like our swimming pool and our cleaning ladies (note the plural) and the special posture-pushing mattress on my bed. I have no right to complain and that's for sure.

But, like I said before, I am so bored I'd like to turn a trick or jump off the garage. Or something. And that's as true as it is unjustified. I don't know anything about suffering, so for me the worst thing there is, is boredom. That's a weak word for feeling that your skin is crawling with bugs, your head is too little, and you'd like to press your teeth together until they came out your skull.

* * *

It was in "Advisory" class where it all came together. You might not know what "Advisory" class was, lessen you'd gone to Cartwright Princeton, so I'll explain. It was something like "Home Room," my mom's term, but here we made a pass at discussing issues in the world around us (global warming, AIDS) and even personal matters of a pretty impersonal nature. Not sex. That was covered in a special class, taught by a couple of *bona fide* pervs. But anyways, one day about a week before the end of school, our teacher whose name doesn't matter asked us to talk about summer plans. Pretty lame: Camp Tennis, French-Speak, or Computer.

To break the monotony, a couple of scholarship kids said they were working for the city, one at Burger King. Then it came to this super-cool girl Tyler, who said, "I'm not doing a goddam thing." Advisory teacher didn't yell at her for the "goddam," as it wasn't the school style to yell at you and as Tyler almost always talked that way. She could do it because she was beautiful, not that that has anything to do with my story. Well, of course it does.

When it was my turn, I wasn't about to say I couldn't get a single person, all expenses paid, to go with me, so: "I'm taking a trip, what they used to do long — the idea was — oh yeah, The Grand Tour. Young men would do this trip and find out about the world and themselves." I couldn't think what to say next, but I knew not to stop: "I'll be driving this car to Atlanta, though I'll go anywhere I want, taking all of vacation to get there. And get back, only getting back will be fast — on a plane."

My summer plan got lots of attention. Even from the teacher.

"Have you mapped your route?"

"I want to be free to follow suggestions I get from people I meet, and whims. It's important this trip be unplanned. I'll see what comes up."

"Will you be staying in motels?"

That wasn't such a cool question, as I'd recently discovered my car was actually a camper, details not yet clear. So I said, "There and other places. Whatever comes up. I don't want to plan; that's the key thing. It's a 'Voyage of Discovery.'" I don't know how I hit on that geeky phrase.

"You taking along a girl to have sex with?" a voice said behind me.

This did bring a rebuke, mild, but not before somebody said I was taking my mom along for those purposes. Hilarious.

"Well, actually, as for company, you know...."

"Yeah?" from several people. They were curious about this point. So was I.

"I think." Pause. "Somebody might accompany me if they want. It's part of keeping everything open and not too...."

"I'll go with you."

"Huh?"

"I said, 'I'll go with you,' Wendell. Unless you've picked

another companion and three'd be a crowd. Or you want to keep things open and pick up girls along the way."

This was in front of the whole class, right out loud. Before I could think, I said the worst thing, "Why'd you want to go with me, Tyler?"

"Well, I do," was what she said.

"Okay, then," I said. And that was that.

I lied. That wasn't that.

We had a planning session. We figured we'd have to, despite what I said about not planning, said it and meant it too. I liked that part of Mom's idea so much it seemed like the door had come open for me and I was allowed for the first time to go out and see what was there. It almost made me think different about myself.

These meetings included me and Tyler and Mom. I caught Tyler looking at me sometimes. I don't mean to suggest she was looking at me with longing, with "hunger," as one of the porn stories I like a lot puts it. But I'm getting ahead of myself.

The reason we had these planning sessions was only partly to talk about the trip. Before we could get to that, we had to figure out how in the name of big lies we could get Tyler's parents to agree. Three months in a super-luxury (turns out it was) but cozy, two bed (along with a couple of pullouts or something) camper with a kid they'd never met and had no way of knowing how pathetically safe he was. From what Tyler said, they were about the last parents to agree to such a thing. It did sound wild when you said it out: drink, do drugs, mix with crazy hill people. Who would agree to that?

That was the problem. Tyler could be very blunt, which was helpful. She said her parents were "super-fucking-straight." My mom didn't even blink. She seemed to like Tyler a great deal and let her say what she wanted. Boy, I'd never get away with that. Not that I'd want to, as I'm some kind of prude.

Anyhow, Tyler said her parents were Oreos who "would wear hot dog shit on their heads if it'd make whitey respect them." She said letting their girl go off for the summer with a white boy they didn't know — which it wouldn't matter if they did — would strike them as about as reasonable as joining the KKK. The other side of their "drive to be white," Tyler said, was a fierce pride in black heritage. That sounded nice, though Tyler went on to add that it was "conventional." I make Tyler sound mean, but she was trying to get my mom to see how tough it'd be.

Session after session, Mom getting Tyler to talk. Tyler liked my mom, which was as surprising as Mom liking Tyler. More than once, I was hit with hot flashes of panic: they'd like one another so much, Mom'd come along. As it turns out, though, they were joining together just to build a strategy against Tyler's conventional, whitewashed parents. I had some ideas myself. They were listened to politely.

"How about we lie, tell your parents I'm giving you a ride to a French-language camp in Vermont. Or Arizona, in case they're worried about overnights."

Neither objected to the lying part. Mom looked at me, as if she were straining to recognize in such a dumb suggestion her own genes. Tyler punched me, kind of felt my shoulder. She did that sort of thing a lot. I would have liked it had it seemed sexual. It didn't seem sexual; it seemed like something you'd do to a little kid.

I had no idea what it'd be like with Tyler every minute for three months. Truth is, it didn't seem like it'd be peaceful. She might spend three months ridiculing me.

Still, she'd been patient, like she was twenty years older than me. I could stand that. I could stand anything better than going alone. I'm not good by myself, don't have interesting ideas. Also, I get scared of things, even the dark. Tyler would probably be okay, and absolutely better than nothing. And nothing was my backup.

It got clear that Mom would be the one persuading Tyler's parents. Tyler seemed like she'd get mad, make fun of them.

"Your parents know about the Grand Tour, I'm sure," Mom said.

"I imagine. My mom was a history major as an undergrad."

"They trust you too, want you to go to great schools."

"Do they ever!"

"You with me?"

"Make 'em think this is what all the worthy white folks do, and they'd be retarded negras if they kept me here where there's no reportable experiences."

"Other ideas, Tyler — less cynical? Don't underestimate your parents. I'm sure they're smart. We can't go at them as if they're yokels."

"That's true."

"How about material for your college application, your personal statement. You use this to show how richly creative and daring you are. 'I went off with a friend, devoted to learning all we could about the worlds outside and inside, testing ourselves against all we could experience, from museums to county fairs, art shows to bluegrass festivals.' It'd provide you with material places like Radcliffe will find irresistible. Your parents'll see that right off. It'd set you apart from the A students who starred in the school play and volunteered as candy-stripers."

"Fucking-A!"

"Tyler!" There was no force in my mother's rebuke, though, and soon they were laughing, refining the plan. They forgot to ask me my opinion.

By the time I entered the picture, Mr. and Mrs. Arthur were about ninety percent sold. I think they liked the idea of Tyler as a trendsetter. Maybe they felt bad for keeping her tied to their own fears. The reason I think it was something inside them is that this plan's not very rational, even with the blab about college applications. That made a little sense, maybe, but not a lot. Radcliffe might think it was plain stupid.

My job was to keep quiet and seem polite. Naturally, Tyler's parents wanted to check me out, make sure I was a kid they could trust their daughter with. I could understand that and didn't much mind being inspected.

Funny thing was Tyler seemed hurt for me, took me out for coffee — as if I drank coffee. She asked me what I thought. My mom would never ask me, partly because she wasn't a bullshitter, knew I was dumb. Maybe Tyler was curious about how dumb I was, but that wasn't what it seemed. I just hoped she'd tolerate me for now, so her parents would be convinced. It'd be nice if she liked me, but that wasn't going to happen. Anyhow, however the trip went, the first step was to get her on it.

Did I tell you I could sing? Not rock or anything but ballads and old things like "Annie Laurie." I suggested to Tyler that I sing a song for her parents. As soon as it was out of my mouth, I realized how idiotic it was.

"Sing a song?" Tyler said, kind of neutral.

"I know."

"I love it, Wendell. They'd never expect that. Do it!"

Hot damn!

The actual meeting wasn't so bad.

"We're very happy to meet you, Wendell."

"Me too." Not the best start, but at least I didn't make it worse with an apology.

"I'm sure you know why we're meeting."

"Yes, I do. You want to examine me, see if I'm responsible." I kept myself from adding more (God knows what more, but I could feel it coming).

They both laughed.

"Well, are you?"

"I've not thought a lot about that; I didn't know you'd ask my opinion. As my mom knows and Tyler too, I'm not extremely intelligent. I try to make up for it by thinking a lot, which is not exactly true — not really a lot, but more than not thinking at all."

I was on a roll and wouldn't have stopped if somebody poured boiling milk on my balls. Sorry for the vulgarity.

"I think some parts of being responsible are not doing things and some are doing things. Mostly not doing things, with people my age. Kids doing nothing seem responsible, but that's not much. I think it means not wanting anybody to get hurt, being careful not to hurt anybody. That's the negative part, and I think I have that."

They both stared at me blankly. I couldn't tell if they were impressed, revolted, or angry. They didn't applaud. Wish they'd smiled. I had no clue, so I went on.

"The other part means doing things for others, starting businesses, helping hospitals and old people. I do a little of that, but less than most, to be honest. But the negative I've got covered. I don't do dangerous things or crazy things. I'd be even less likely to do them with Tyler around."

They were still silent. I should have been too.

"You probably want to know other stuff. I don't do drugs, that what you meant?"

They smiled at this.

"Really, Wendell, we didn't mean to grill you. I can imagine how awful this is for you. We just wanted to meet you. Our notion of being responsible, you see. I don't know if either of us has the slightest idea what we were looking for. It just seemed the thing to do. I expect we should apologize. Your mother has us on the edge of being convinced, and Tyler wants to do it. It's just that it seems a little — I don't know...."

"Crazy," I offered, like an idiot.

"Unusual. Perhaps extreme."

"That's what I like about it," Tyler put in.

"Me too," I said, though that sure wasn't what I liked about it.

Right then I dropped my glass of Coke. I'm not usually clumsy. That's one benefit of being small, not having elbows reaching across the room. But just at the worst time I dropped my glass of Coke right on their white expensive rug. I felt like crying, but maybe it wasn't so bad. It gave the parents something to say: "Oh, it's nothing." It allowed my mom to take a hanky out of her purse and make a pass at cleaning. I could stand there. Tyler could laugh. After that, there was nothing to do but leave.

I never did sing. I would have, but there was no place to slip it in. You can't just interrupt a conversation and say, "Hold that thought while I sing 'I Heard It Through the Grapevine.'"

Things went pretty fast after that. Mrs. Arthur called me two days later.

"Hello, Mrs. Arthur, nice to be talking with you."

"Hello, Wendell. It's nice to be talking to you, too. You're a very polite boy. Do you mind if I ask whether you're always this polite?"

That sort of annoyed me, though I didn't want to get annoyed with her, so I swallowed my anger, which wasn't too hard, as I do that a lot.

"Not always, Mrs. Arthur. Always with adults. It gives me something to say."

She laughed. "That's extremely candid, Wendell, and not a bad insight into why we have manners. I can see how kids would be forced into that with adults."

"Yeah."

"And you don't seem the Eddie Haskell type."

Now I laughed. I knew what she was talking about from *Leave It to Beaver* reruns. I love Eddie Haskell and kinda wish I could be like him. Sure, he was a terrible phony, but he had a plan with his phoniness. I especially liked it that he overdid it and kept at it. Made you think most adults were suckered in, which is believable. Maybe Wally and Beaver's parents saw through him, but Eddie was too cagey to use it if it weren't working most everywhere. He could turn it on and off, too. I liked the way he was a real prick with Beaver, a very irritating character in my opinion, and then be all sweety with the parents. What an artist.

"Ronald and I have decided to allow Tyler to embark on this adventure, Wendell. You can imagine that this wasn't an easy decision for us, but your Mother convinced us it was a risk worth taking, worth taking because it was a risk, if you follow me."

Not really. "Oh, yes ma'am."

"Of course. I imagine you and your mom arrived at this mutually, talked it out. I must say it's a very original, very artistic idea, actually quite profound. Very unique."

Even I knew you don't say "very unique," so I wondered how much Mrs. Arthur might know about profound, but I answered with a friendly chuckle. I'm really bad at making these sorts of noises, "conversational grease," Sean 1 calls it.

"In any case, all we added was a requirement that you two check in every day or two and let us know if there is even a hint of trouble, trouble of any kind. What I mean is we require Tyler to do that. Naturally, we wouldn't presume to require that of you."

"Sure you would. That way you'll know where we are and what we're doing. It's fine by me. Is it fine by Tyler?"

"It had better be, or she's simply not going!"

Brother! I was sorry I'd brought that up.

She was silent, probably fuming, so I had to say something.

"I'm sure Tyler will think it's fine."

"How would you know that?"

Lord Jesus. Could I hang up? Every word I said seemed to get her madder. A few more minutes and she'd head over and beat me up.

"I'm really sorry, Mrs. Arthur, gee I...."

"I haven't heard anybody say 'gee' since I was a kid, Wendell. You sure you're not Eddie Haskell?"

This was going way past annoying. "I am sure of that."

"I apologize, Wendell. For all I know, you're what you seem, a perfectly nice boy. Tyler refuses to tell me anything about you. But that's not your fault. I have no right to screech at you because I have a lousy relationship with my daughter. To tell you the truth, I don't see how you'll be able to stand her for three months."

"Uh-huh."

"I feel terrible that I said that. I love Tyler, Wendell, and even admire her. It's just that sixteen is a lousy time for kids and parents."

"I'm sure it is."

That was such an idiot remark that we both laughed, which helped.

"I think I know why you decided, the turning point, when you decided Tyler was going to have a rich and fulfilling time, which is what my mom calls it, when I spilled the Coke all over your best rug."

At last something worked. She laughed again. Finally I got off the phone. One thing Mrs. Arthur brought up I've been thinking about too: why Tyler would go. I didn't think real hard about it because I knew I wouldn't get anywhere.

* * *

I won't repeat the 3000 conversations I had with my parents about this trip. The only one that counted was orchestrated by Skye, which gave me the following script: say nothing, without seeming sullen. (I do sullen real good.) I was also to be committed to the trip but without reasons I was able to articulate. That left it open for Skye to come in with her stuff about college applications, the development of the full authority of curiosity, the importance of risk, the flowering of creative confidence.

All this time, Wendell hardly said a thing. Sat there like one of those Downs Syndrome honeys that set my parents off into predictable baby talk. Wendell's eyes do follow stuff;

it's just that his body is unnaturally still, almost as if he had his hands folded, frozen, like kids in early photos: boys dressed in sailor suits. Wendell's a little bit of a mystery. I hope. His mother's so smart, I wonder if there's more to Wendell than I thought. His sitting there like an immobile idiot didn't give promise of a quick wit.

Just found out about the camper. I'd been worried, irritated more like it, imagining motel nights with Wendell. I was to the point of picturing dressing him as a girl, to get past desk clerks. Only then he'd look better than me. But the camper solves that. Twin beds, of course. Not that he'd be a single bed worry — or attraction.

There's only one week of school left. I'm not sure when we're leaving. I assume there isn't much room to store stuff, so we'll take only a little. Books and music. What's Wendell bringing? His ukulele? Guess we have to have a meeting, me and him. We haven't seen one another to talk since this has been settled. He casts his big-saucer, long-lashed, eyes down when we pass in the hall. Maybe he is genuinely shy. I hate shy.

* * *

Tyler called. Ordered me to attend a meeting, less a meeting than an interrogation. We met at the Denny's. She smiled when she saw me and, as that poet in English class says, "my heart leapt up." That was the last nice thing that happened.

"You ordered fries, Wendell?"

"Want some?" One thing I noticed about Tyler is that she uses your name a lot. I did it too, when I wanted someone to like me. With her, it didn't seem to be a strategy.

"I also don't like arsenic gravy. Fries exude fatty grease into the atmosphere, worse than secondhand smoke. I'll get clogged arteries just sitting here."

"Sorry."

"Lord, Wendell, I wasn't being serious. Try and sit in the same stadium, okay?"

I stared at her. Didn't seem like anything I'd say would keep her from clawing. She was just sitting there frowning, so finally I said it.

"Tyler, is there anything I can say would keep you from clawing at me?"

Her face, which is very expressive, changed, got softer. But the softness didn't last all that long.

"You have a point. I guess I'm nervous."

"Me too."

"Well, aren't we perfectly matched! Like in a romance! So much in common we might as well just drive this camper to the chapel, get married, move into a RV park."

"You sure you want to go, Tyler?"

"Huh?"

"I really want you to go, but it doesn't seems like you want to."

"Look, Wendell, I am what I am. Obviously, you're pretty good at making people feel guilty, but I hope we're not going to have a summer of you being wounded and me apologizing. Try to be less fucking helpless."

I figured I couldn't be worse off saying nothing than something, so I shut up. Tyler had dainty features, so sweet looking maybe she acted like a bitchy person to compensate. I know all about "compensate" from peer adjustment classes at school.

"Okay, Wendell. I have some specific questions. Money?"

I knew better than to say, "What about money?" so I said, "My mom is so anxious for us to have this experience, she'll cover everything, without asking us to report. She thinks part of this experience will be making mistakes with money and learning from them, something like that. She'd be hurt if we didn't spend a lot. We'll have to call a couple of times saying we're out of cash, maxed out our credit cards."

"That's pretty good, Wendell."

Something about the way she said that. "Gee, thanks, Tyler."

She looked at me more friendly than any time since we started.

"What about clothes?"

This time I couldn't help the dumb thing: "I guess we should take some."

"For a second there, Wendell, I thought you might have some wit. I mean, does our luxury gas-eater have a washer/dryer?"

"No."

"You sure?"

"No."

"Then why do you say no?"

"I know some things, Tyler, damn you."

I kept myself from apologizing. One problem was that I said it kind of soft, not like you should say, "damn you."

"Okay, Wendell. Don't get your panties in a wad. How do you know that?"

"Cause washers and dryers take space. We don't have an exercise room either."

She didn't laugh — I hadn't said anything funny.

"We got a half day Thursday, last day of school, Wendell. When do we get to leave? Right after class?"

"If that's okay with you."

"Pack the night before then. Right, Wendell? Your mom picks up this million dollar rolling mansion Wednesday morning? So we get together that night. We get food as we go? You suppose we can avoid a two-family meatloaf feast that night, a *bon voyage* nightmare piece of shit?"

"I hope so. No."

"You're right. We need fake IDs, Wendell. Give me your school thing and I'll take care of it."

"Great! They'll think we're twenty-one?"

"They'll think you're twelve no matter what. The card'll say we're eighteen. That's enough of a stretch."

I kept myself from looking hurt: "Not like you look thirty, Tyler."

She did laugh at that, and it also wasn't funny.

"This is going to be an adventure, sweet cheeks. I wonder if I can keep from wringing your neck. I guess you'll have the same trouble."

I was all set to say, "No I won't." But I forced myself to say, "I guess."

* * *

Sho nuff, Wednesday night I haul my stuff over to Wendell's, telling my parents we need a couple of hours to pack. I didn't bring much. With all the spending money we have, plus food and gas money, emergency money, entertainment money, "margin" money, I figure this'll be a summer shopping spree. We had, according to reports, computers, two TVs of some sort. Brought jeans and some shirts, shorts and a bathing suit. A jacket. I don't wear makeup, so I didn't need much more than a toothbrush in that line.

I expected Wendell to have a load of shit, cosmetics kit and an electronic leg hair remover; but he didn't have any more than me, maybe less, but that included board games and a lot of maps and travel books, some of which looked fun — wacky attractions and festivals, country's stupidest museums, worst places to eat. Things were looking up.

The RV wasn't a teen dream, more suited for Fred and Velma people you see with the Good Sam stickers on the back. All the same, it was terrific. I asked Skye how much it cost. She didn't blink. "Three hundred ninety-three thousand dollars." Didn't apologize or pretend not to know. Seems to have the whole family's supply of cool. Wonder where the daddy is?

I took the tour through the RV with Wendell, who was seeing the inside for the first time, too, having waited to share the experience. That's sweet, but more annoying. I don't want to think of Wendell as sweet. A summer of sweet would suck big time.

Wendell and I put our stuff away. Amazing how many cubbyholes and hidden crannies, hooks and sliding things. It was a custom model, with all the extras Skye had the dealer add on. Had a slide out extension in back. The whole thing was dizzying, so I'm going to describe it a bit. I hated how I was edging around the inside, mouth breathing and oohing. Wendell was much more relaxed about it, the fucker.

The back end slid out on rollers, extending the twin bed area into an entertainment pit, with another home theater and the second TV. The forward seats were loungers, "captain's chairs," swivelly and padded, heated too, which would come in handy when we were motoring cross Alabama in July. (Wendell came out with that hilarity.) All the seats were massaging. After a hard day of touring, some magic fingers in the neck and ass might be just the thing. You could use the front seats as beds too, I forgot to mention, which we could do if we got in a spat and needed to separate about eight feet.

Even the eating table was leathery. There was another table in the extension, came out of the wall somehow. There was a computer workstation too, with two laptops stored away. There was what they called a "power slider sofa," which was what you'd suppose. Solar panel. Cooker and a microwave. Nice bathroom but crampy, no way Wendell and I could get in there together — gag. And, get this, a washer/dryer.

The brochure said we had heated holding tanks, a two thousand watt inverter, a central vacuum system, solar panel charger, and a 6.0 turbo diesel engine. Good.

Wendell's mom was good at making herself scarce, not over-explaining nor issuing cautions. Wish I could say the same for my parents. They seemed worried about everything.

At least they didn't heave obvious sighs of relief over the twin beds. I knew, of course, that their main concerns were alcohol, drugs, and sex — in reverse order. They wouldn't say anything, probably thought they'd best not put such ideas in my head. You'd think one look at Wendell would have reassured them, but they worried that I was easy prey for pretty white boys, any white boys, any boys.

My parents brought along wine for the three genteel adult alkies, bubbly apple juice for the kiddies, two pies, and some god-awful pumpkin bread. Also Martin. Martin took to Wendell right away. Wendell just talked to him, answered his questions, was nice. If I were Martin, I'd have liked him too. But I'm not Martin.

The big folk went inside to cook something, leaving the three of us plotting. I was planning to lay down some rules for Wendell, but they were pretty strong stuff in the bossy line, and I couldn't do it with Martin there. So I kept things, for the moment, soft:

"Well, Wendell, where we going first? I expect you have maps all highlighted."

"You think we should, Tyler, plan ahead I mean? I don't care. Maybe we could just do it one day at a time."

"Take me with you." Martin's pipsqueak lilt was not even close to a whine.

Wendell smiled as if he'd like to do it. I'd like to do it too, though there'd be problems, starting with my mom and dad never ever even coming close to allowing it.

"You won't, will you?"

"We can't, honey. So might as well shut your piehole."

He giggled. What a great kid.

I was afraid Wendell might suggest some compromise. He didn't though, just looked at Martin in a commiserating sort of way.

"So, we pick up some burgers after school and then take off, right Tyler?"

"Take off where?"

"Yeah, where you two going?"

Key question, but before we could engage that issue, Martin switched subjects: "You got a nickname, Wendell? I mean, Wendell's a nice name, but...."

"It sucks, doesn't it? But no, I don't. I've tried giving myself nicknames, but nobody ever picked them up. A few kids call me Boy-Boy but that's not so much a nickname as abuse."

"I could make up a good one for you."

"Okay. What is it?"

"God, Wendell, give me some time."

"So, what's your nickname, Martin? Hotshot like you gotta have a good one."

I was just standing there, annoyed, but also intrigued.

"Mine is 'Penis.'" Wendell didn't blink. I'll give him that.

"'Penis,' huh. That's a good one. Wish I had a fine nickname like that. Kids must like you a lot, call you 'Penis.' That's cool. You're cool."

Martin glowed.

"Wanta know my sister's?"

"Martin, no! You tell mine, 'Penis,' and you'll be without yours!" I knew he was going to say it, the little shit.

Wendell grinned, didn't say he wanted to know. Didn't have to.

"It's 'Titty.'"

"Goddamn you, Martin!"

Wendell was using his full allotment of aplomb; it was a surprise, pleasant, to see he had any to draw on: "Those are great names, funny and nice. They show how close you are, how much you like each other."

No, they didn't show that, mush head asshole, but I let it pass. He was being so nice he made me want to de-nut him, but it was also pleasant. Best to change the subject.

"So, where we going first day? Surprise me and pass: you don't know, it's up to me, anywhere I want, don't want to be boss...."

"Big Bear."

"By Lake Arrowhead?"

"That's pretty yuppie, Tyler. Let's go to Big Bear, expand our minds."

Would wonders never cease? Here's Wendell taking charge. Fine with me.

"Big Bear it is, Boy-Boy." Sorry I added the last part. Snotty. Wendell didn't say anything, didn't flinch exactly; but he blinked.

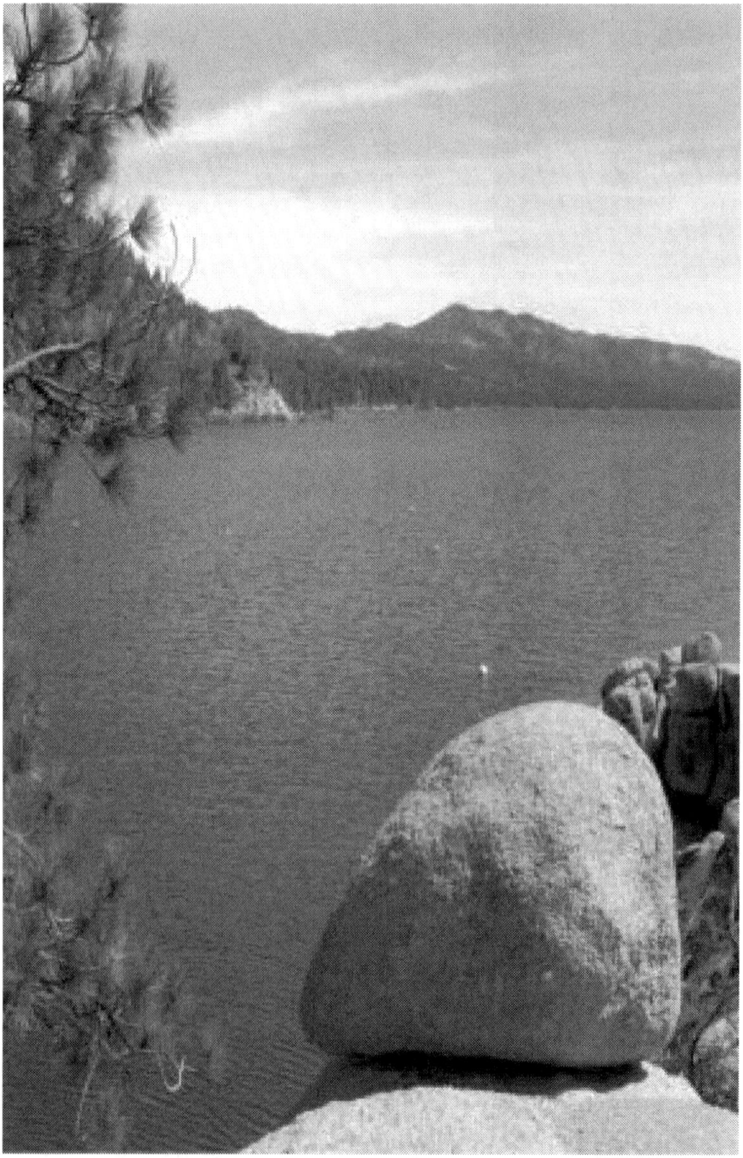

CHAPTER 3

Thursday — Los Angeles to Big Bear

Day 1

I was going to pick Tyler up, but there she was at my house, talking to my mom, looking pretty, wearing jeans and a light blue shirt that left bare below: her belly and upper hips.

"Okay, honeys. Get out of here. Let me know where you are from time to time."

That was it? "That's all you gonna say?"

Mom laughed. So did Tyler.

I got in my captain's chair, turned on the massage. It felt great at first, but soon became annoying. Maybe you had to be sore. Tyler took a while adjusting hers, playing with mirrors, fiddling switches, changing air vents. I sat quietly by. I had the feeling I'd be sitting quietly by a lot this summer. Tyler was driving. We'd decided we'd share. Tyler had got us both fake IDs, useful for cops and bartenders. I'd never had any alcohol, apart from beer sips, but I had no principled objection.

Tyler had a principled objection to McDonalds. I know that because I suggested we stop there for burgers on our way.

"Tyler, where'd you want to get food?"

"I don't care, Wendell. You know a place?"

"I eat anything, even sushi. There's a McDonald's up here next exit."

"Did I hear you right? McDonald's? McDonald's? Motherfucking McDonald's? *McDonald's?*"

"Anyplace is okay with me, Tyler. You don't like McDonald's?"

"Wendell, what's your view of Heinrich Himmler? You like him?'"

"I guess you're right. They're real unhealthy."

"Unhealthy! They drive out legitimate businesses, pay low wages, exploit old people and kids. They've destroyed the working class — worse than crack dealers."

"I didn't know that. Don't get mad. Fine by me if we never eat there."

She looked at me, still kind of mad, you could tell. But she didn't say anything.

"If you want, Tyler, I'll help you bomb a couple, set rats loose in 'em, paint big dongs on Ronald McDonald."

She didn't laugh, but she looked softer, I think; not so much like she held me responsible for the stuff McDonald's was doing to the rain forests.

"So, where you wanta eat, Tyler? You a vegetarian?"

"No, Wendell. Just McDonald's. I know an In-N-Out off the Santa Anita exit out in Arcadia, maybe a half hour away."

Fine with me, though it was more than a half hour, traffic being terrible. It was almost an hour before we got in the line at In-N-Out: long, moving slow, since they made every order from scratch, for some reason.

The burgers were good and the fries were terrible. I didn't say that, since Tyler'll probably tell me I was used to McDonald's fries, which were greased up with dolphin fat.

We crawled up to Big Bear not saying much. I let Tyler pick the music, since I knew she'd hate what I liked.

Big Bear was filled with fudge stores, video arcades, and shops selling souvenirs I admired and knew Tyler wouldn't. Not that I bought any, since they weren't aiming their carved bears at the teen market (me) exactly. There was a skiing store and a hardware, plus a quilt shop, devoted to the world's least interesting activity, not that I know anything about it. There was also a year-round Christmas store, tree ornaments mostly, but also lawn and window decorations. Tyler dragged me in, meaning I followed her.

I was prepared to ridicule it, but I found myself picking up sparkly glass and metallic ornaments, looking at prices, admiring for a long time a light set, called 'retro candles': skinny tubes with fake flames on top where a waxy liquid bubbled inside. I was wondering if it'd be a good gift for Mom, mailing it, not carting it across country. Here's the part I'm ashamed of, I didn't buy them because I figured Tyler would make fun of me. This was going to be a great summer. I wasn't going to please her anyways, so why try? I knew I would try, though, try and fail and try again. I'm like that.

We ate at a place that had karaoke. Here was my chance to demonstrate independence from Tyler's mean opinions. She had been nice since we got to the town and found our trailer park. We walked into town — it was close — and she was chatty. I wondered what kind of couple we made, whether people would think we were a couple. She was so pretty they'd probably think I was her strange cousin from Dallas.

She looked older than me, even I could see that. What these people thought about what we were didn't matter, but it was interesting. I imagine it'll come up some this summer. Wonder if anybody, anywhere will take us for boyfriend and girlfriend? As we get away from California, people might notice we looked different, white and black to be blunt. Maybe people saw that here, but I doubt it. It's not what's important these days.

This was a fine place, I thought. It was a German restaurant, in my opinion, with red cabbage and great meat that tasted like vinegar. During dinner, Tyler talked a lot, mostly about school and Martin.

The school talk had nothing about me in it, but she wasn't being mean. I finally worked up nerve to say I thought it was a good restaurant.

"You do?"

"Yeah. I've never had food like this. Probably you have. You don't like it?"

"I do, pretty much. What do you like about it?"

Oh hell! "The meat tastes like vinegar. I guess it surprises me that I enjoy it."

"You're proud of yourself, Wendy?"

"No. Well, yeah, sort of. But I also like it, not just being proud. It's good."

"So you mentioned."

At least I didn't break into tears. "Do you really like it, Tyler?" She'd had the same thing as me, and I ordered first, impolitely, I guess.

"I do, Wendell. I've had this before, sauerbraten, and hated it. But this was good. What do you think of that guy's singing?"

Some guy, Japanese I'd say, was trying, "Rock and Roll Is Here to Stay," making it sound like "Lock and Loll Is Hewe to Stay." It was funny, in a lousy sort of way. He was also off-key, off the beat too. I started giggling.

Tyler stared at me as if she was going to get mad and say something snotty, but then she started to giggle too: "Oh Rendy, rick my rips and prease stop raffing!" The singing guy heard us laughing and waved, grinning real wide. I guess he was drunk, or maybe just a nice guy.

"You going to sing, Wendell?"

I love singing so much. "I will if you will, Tyler." She looked shocked.

"A duet?"

"Why not? We couldn't be much worse than that guy. Looked like he was having a good time."

"You're serious, aren't you, Wendell? I'll be damned. I'm much too chicken. You go ahead. Will you?"

Sure I would. I got up there, second in line behind a woman who was pretty, kind of, though sort of old, fat too. They gave me this list of songs to pick from. I knew most of them, the ones catching my eye in "Old Favorites." The woman ahead of me started in on "Lucille," a country song that wasn't too suited for her. She should have been singing "God Bless America." She had a big voice, if a little wobbly.

I picked out one my mom liked, me too, "Shine On Harvest Moon." The main part of the song was nothing special, but the verse was terrific, a solid minor key, strange thing setting up the lyrics of the main part. That verse was beautiful: "Oh the night was mighty dark so you could hardly see, for the moon refused to shine."

The "shine" note was great to quiver on, make louder as it extended with the bass throbbing beneath it. The song should have ended there. You could swoop up to "shine" with style, even if you didn't have much style, which I didn't. My mom liked me to sing "The Lost Chord," which was about 300 somethings beyond me. Besides, I could never understand that song: chords were chords, and how could one disappear? It was as if God had thrown in the number eight without anybody having noticed. Pure silly, if it weren't for the music, which kicks butt.

Before I knew it, the woman was on the last phrase, which she did great. She smiled, said words to me I couldn't catch apart from "something, honey, something."

The music started as soon as I got to the mike. Straight off were a couple of bars to clue me to the key, lyrics on a screen. Then my part, with the keyboard playing chords behind me pretty solid but not much of the melody line, which was fine by me. Anybody could've made this sound good.

Oh the night was mighty dark, so you could hardly see;
  for the moon refused to shine (shy-yi-yi-ine).
Couple sittin' underneath the willow tree;
  for love they pined.
Little maid was kinda 'fraid of darkness, so she said —
  I guess I'll goooo.
Boy began to sigh, looked up at the sky.

From then on, not much. But that verse!

Wasn't like I had an audience. Most people were talking, and I was singing soft. I always sing soft, even with boomers like "The Lost Chord," since soft seems natural to me and since I sound less good loud. I didn't dare look over at Tyler. A couple of people clapped. They were old people. I don't think Tyler clapped.

She glanced up, though, with what might have been a tiny smile and didn't spit on me. "So what's up now, Wendell? You plan on making an evening of it here?"

"You like video games, Tyler? There's a couple of places I saw here."

"Not much."

"Me either. We must be the only ones our age. So?"

"Bingo."

"Okay." Was she serious? She was. She'd seen a sign at a great big auditorium, turned out to be the American Legion Hall on the main road.

It was a world of beehives and potbellies. They checked our IDs and didn't believe them, winked a lot and called us "kiddos." Never been called a "kiddo" before.

We sat at a long table with people on both sides, about thirty in our section. They were all playing five or six cards at once. I played two and that wasn't easy, as the caller didn't go slow. The games were complicated, though the people around us were good at explaining. Once they told me I had a Bingo and I hadn't seen it. I won eighteen bucks: two other people had Bingos at the same time.

Only thing was, they weren't so nice to Tyler, not mean, just spoke mostly only to me. She didn't say anything, Tyler, but I'm sure she noticed.

After about an hour, they passed around chocolate sundaes. Free. During the break, people talked some around us, not really to us. It was one of those times when all of a sudden the noise shuts down and you can hear a word you otherwise wouldn't. And the word you could hear now was "nigger."

I started to get up and leave, but Tyler grabbed my jeans under the table and pulled me down.

After the sundaes, they had something like a meeting of the American Legion Club, only they didn't kick us out. First they all said this oath, the Preamble to the Something of the American Legion: "We associate ourselves together...." I remember that because it was such an odd way to put it. They included lots about freedom and justice, along with news from the national headquarters in Indianapolis, Indiana.

The other funny thing was a bit about the importance of upholding "one hundred percent Americanism." Tyler did snort when they said that, but she was naturally a little edgy after that "nigger" stuff. Maybe we got the word wrong, only we didn't. And Tyler was the only person in the room even close to not white.

The guy in charge kept saying we'd get right back to the games, kind of sputtering and laughing when nothing was funny. Maybe he was in the bag. A couple of times he pointed to the flag and choked out, "God bless 'er." Then he said he wanted to explain a paper he was sending around, asking us to sign and support The Boy Scouts of America. I was never in Scouts myself, but I knew some kids, including Sean 2, who were and hated it. Sean 2 had quit for some reason — because he hated it.

The fat guy running things told somebody in the crowd

who must have objected to something that he was the one in charge and didn't think this was a bad time for one hundred percent Christian Americanism. "What's wrong with that?" he'd like to know! Then he started in on The Boy Scouts again.

"This flag is drooping today. Why? Because of what's happening in three states, where we have chapters but where they also got Communist Courts and the ACLU. The Boy Scouts of America is protected by the flag as to their right to Christian morals. Am I wrong? The ACLU atheists would love to see homos getting even more positions as scoutmasters, for reasons I won't sully our mouths with saying.

This is a threat to America as big as Muslim terrorism, with respect to anyone here of that faith, but we will stand proud against. So let's rise now in silent tribute to our boys in — abroad, fighting against all those people who envy our freedom."

Everybody stood but me, until Tyler grabbed my jeans again and yanked me up. It wasn't clear to me why we were standing, but I wasn't going to do what Tyler didn't.

We stayed to the final complicated Bingo game, which, I swear to heaven, Tyler won: $150 dollars! They called her up to the front, because, in addition to the money, she was awarded a stuffed bear (Big Bear, get it?) and a T-shirt saying, "One Hundred Percent American!"

The emcee made a big deal about the presentation and was corny-nice to Tyler. Maybe he had heard "nigger" from a fellow loyal American and was embarrassed.

Clearly, he expected Tyler to smile and go away, but she slipped between bald chubbo and the mike and said, very polite and slow, "I want to thank you all for being so nice to me and my brother tonight. I'd like to donate the winnings to your fund to support the Boy Scouts and win the battle against homos and niggers. Thanks again."

I couldn't believe she'd said that, but she did, all smiley and sweet. The place was so quiet you wanted somebody to break the tension. But they stayed quiet where they were, nobody moving a muscle. Tyler had got the money in an envelope, and she made a big show of taking it out, handing it back to the emcee.

Were he any smarter or less drunk, he'd have kept his mouth shut, but no: "You and your little friend or any other friend or family members are always welcome here, and I'd like you to know, Miss, that we have many African members, you know, and honor them for their service to the flag and this great country."

Tyler stood there grinning, making no move to leave.

"So let's give this young lady a great big hand, in honor of all our black men who have died to serve their country — and our country too, 'tis of thee."

I kept myself from laughing until everybody started clapping.

By this time, I'd lost being uncomfortable and hoped Tyler would keep it up, which she did: "I think we should all honor our great flag and all the dead brothers with a big chorus of 'God Bless America.'" And she started singing. Tyler had a really good voice, but it seemed like nobody else in the room did and they sang very loud.

Instead of leaving after the song was done, they stood around, probably wondering if there were more observances Tyler had in mind for the fallen black soldiers. But she let them off the hook, came over to me, called me "bro," hooked her arm in mine. Lots of people said, "Come back, now!" Seemed to me they'd rather chop off their fingers than have us come back, but they tried hard to sound like they meant it.

We'd walked from the RV park to the Hall, about a mile, so we had to plod back.

"That took a lot of guts, Tyler."

"Thanks, Wendell." I tried to see her face, check if she was being nasty, but I couldn't see too well in the dark. Didn't sound nasty, but she always was, so probably.

This was our first night sleeping together, and I was worried how to handle two things: getting the beds unhooked and slid out, and getting our clothes off and all that. The first didn't figure to be a big problem, maybe, though the instruction book went on for about ten pages, which was nerve-wracking. As for the second, I figured Tyler would have a plan about undressing, and I'd just do what she did.

The bed was easier than I'd supposed, electric and automatic — just push a button and get out of the way. The old folks big chairs against the wall opened out into beds, five-inch mattresses with heavy foam stuff on top for added comfort.

I never wore pajamas, just took off my pants and got under the covers. But I'd packed pajamas, for safety. Now that we were at pajama point, I didn't know how to be safe, and it occurred to me that maybe it'd be better to get into bed and take stuff off under the covers. In the morning, I could dress before getting up. Thing was I changed all my clothes every day. And by now I had my pajamas in my hand, standing there, trying not to look like I was waiting for Tyler to give me instructions.

"You waiting for me to tell you how to undress, Wendell?"

I tried to laugh, but couldn't.

"Well?"

"No."

"Okay, then, do it."

"Where?"

Tyler put her hands on her hips, being sassy, like in old movies, staring at me like I was a fool, which I was.

"Maybe I should — okay." I took off my shirt and sat down to take off my shoes and socks. She stood there looking. I put my tops on then, and they were pretty long. Glad of that. Then I unzipped my jeans and pulled them down, only too fast, so I tripped, almost right into Tyler, but I didn't quite hit her. Wasn't too cool, though.

"You wear whitey-tighties, Wendy. Do they have Spiderman on the butt?"

I don't know why, but I felt like crying. That was the last thing I wanted to do, but I almost did it and then I did. I couldn't help it. I felt like my stomach was all of a sudden empty and my legs were shaky. I didn't care, then, about Tyler seeing my underwear, and anyhow she already had, and I did care. I turned away, but she knew I was crying. I put my hands up to my eyes, shoving against them, trying to block the tears. But I was making noise, and shaking. I'm not sure why I was crying.

"Oh Jesus Christ, Almighty!" she said, all disgusted.

Friday — Big Bear City

Day 2

I slept late. We'd turned the lights out right after what I mentioned. Hope we didn't every night go to bed so early. I loved staying up late, though I almost never did it. My mom didn't lay down policies, but I had it in my head that I needed lots of sleep during school. That's what makes a nerd: following your own rules for no reason. This summer, I was thinking we'd stay up all night if we wanted. I'd mentioned that to Tyler, and she'd said, "Yeah," meaning that she agreed or disagreed or didn't care or thought it was unspeakably geeky to mention it.

I don't usually sleep late, partly because I like mornings, and not just because of the fake business Sean 1 and I have. Even before that I hardly ever slept late.

I woke up because Tyler was cooking, about six inches from my head, it seemed. She was doing fried potatoes and crepes and ham with some kind of fruit. She had her back to me, her butt. I stared at it. Wasn't like she was wiggling it, but she was moving around naturally. She also had the table set. Whooie.

I didn't want to be stupid and pretend to be asleep, so I looked up and said, "Hi."

I wasn't sure how she'd act after last night, but she didn't. She said "Hi," just said it. The food smelled great. Much better than my mom's, and my mom wasn't bad. I had no idea why Tyler was doing this. Maybe she cooked all the time. I didn't think it was an apology or had anything to do with me, for that matter.

A problem. Here I was in bed, Tyler on top of me, about a foot away. After the "Hi," I had to get up. I could ask her to turn around. That'd be so geeky, even I didn't consider it, only I did, decided it'd be worse than being embarrassed.

So I got up and put on my pants, trying hard not trip again. It wasn't smooth, but at least I didn't burst into tears. I made it into our terrific bathroom and washed up good, my hair too, and then went to the back and changed all my clothes. There was a curtain, but did I draw it?

Not old cool Wendell. I don't think I've ever been so embarrassed. Was Tyler looking? I don't know. Not like I was looking at her.

"This is great food, Tyler. You could get a job as a chef or something."

"Thanks, Wendell. Good to know I have a talent." I didn't register that she was being sarcastic, so maybe not. She wasn't smiling especially, but she hardly ever did, I'd noticed, and not just around me. I smiled all the time, so it was kind of odd with somebody who never did, but I'd get used to it. Maybe.

Anyways, we were back to where we were, wherever that was.

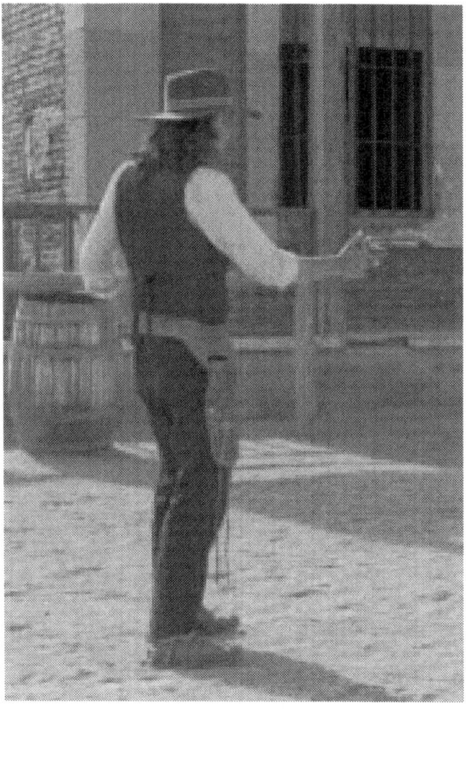

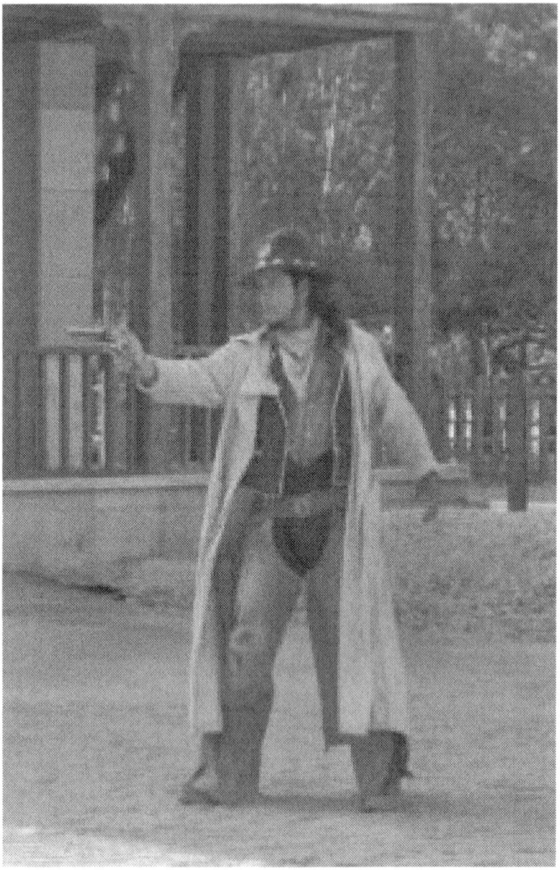

Chapter 4

Wendell has a cute ass; he should enter it in a contest. It's chubbier than you'd think, but firm, to all appearances, and — truth! — dimpled. I know this because he put it on display before breakfast. Isn't that just what a diddledum would do, after last night's ridiculous performance. I'm on a trip with a freak. True, he is compliant and possessed of one of the genuine fine asses in the region. Would that make up for three months with *The Littlest Mermaid?* Not likely, but too early to bail — just yet.

He didn't eat prudishly. Glommed it right down. I watched him, not so he could notice, trying to see a little better what he was like. Some things I knew: he was gorgeous. Eyelashes drooping down to his chest, huge blue-sparkler eyes, skin all flushy, no facial hair and only fuzz on his arms, small nose and ears, tiny mouth but a strong chin, long bright blond hair that was always flying around but never messy, slim and wasp-waisted. It's a wonder the boys weren't all over him. Maybe some were.

He ate fast but didn't spray things around or make noises. He looked over at me now and then, smiling demurely. To be fair (and why should I be?) he wasn't trying to win me over, just grinned his loser way through life. Maybe I'd do that too, if I looked like Shirley Temple, only pretty. No I wouldn't. Wendell has the temperament of a cheerleader, one who would progress to sorority doll, later to one of those hard women who sell real estate, attend the Lutheran Church, vote Republican, give outdoor parties, and contract breast cancer when they're fifty-five.

"So, Wendell, what do you think?"

"Thanks for the great breakfast, Tyler. I know you didn't mean was I thinking about that when you said what do I think. You meant, 'what are we going to do now? Where are we going?' And you expect me to smile and say something sweet, then squirm and blush and leave it all to you."

Damn! Wonder if he could keep it up? Almost. When I stared, he seemed flustered, but then: "I say we take a hike on the Pacific Crest Trail, at the point where we can drive up to it. Then we have lunch. Then we go bowling in town. Then we go on that alpine slide. Then we go on the water slide right next to it. Then we have dinner someplace. Then a stroll in town. Then we come back and watch a DVD."

Stop there, Wendell. No apologies. Give me a heart attack. Stop yapping. Of course he didn't.

"Unless you don't wanta."

"Okay."

"Okay, what?"

"What you said, lover." I shouldn't have said that. He looked a little nonplused, but he often did. (I know "nonplused" is a show-offy word, but how else is a girl to build her vocabulary?)

Pretty much did it all. The trail was my idea of a pussy hike. Wendell got a map at the ranger station, talked all knowingly to the guy in charge, who looked to be about Wendell's age though more manly of course, then drove to the ridge and found a place to park our monster. We walked along this level trail a couple of miles, turned around and came back. Yeah, it was gorgeous up there: views of the lake, some little blue flowers, some little yellow flowers, some sick-looking cactus, great old pine trees, rocky cliffs, cool breezes. The trail was packed pine needles, soft and sweet smelling. But it was as much of an outdoor adventure as a Disneyland ride.

We ate lunch at "Country Cupboard." Wonder if we can fit in a cool hundred of Country (or "Kontry") Somethings this summer? The only excitement in the afternoon was when Wendell went over the edge of the Alpine slide. Didn't think that was possible, but it is. He got going so fast he couldn't slow for a curve and went right the fuck over. I was behind him, sensibly braking but close enough to see every scary thing.

He was accelerating like mad on the steep and rocky hill, when the heavy cart soared up over the edge of the track, flipped upside down with Wendell in it, and came down on him hard, sliding him down the hill all the way to the next bend in the track, right into the pole holding things up. I managed to stop just above and was still trying to figure how to get out of my damned cart, when Wendell emerged from under his.

He was laughing, rubbing his thigh but laughing. I laughed too, why I don't know. He'd zanged and torn and barged at least fifty yards down the hill at high speed and didn't look too messed up: his jeans were ripped, and his shoulder or something up there was bleeding.

Most of the people working at the slide were about our age, but the guy who came running up was some middle-aged sack of pathetic. Imagine having a career wrapped up in maintaining order in lines and showing people how to use the brakes, a lesson lost on my companion. Anyways, here comes this guy in a uniform, at least the shirt from a uniform: white with a red horizontal line, "You Must Be Taller Than This to Ride Alone."

"What's goin' on here anyways? You read the board up there? There's boards at the top and bottom. What I wanta know is, did you read 'em?"

Wendell, whose instinct was to cringe before anybody,

stared and, Jesus wept, laughed, loud and right at this guy.

"Oh, you think it's funny. Funny. You think it's so very funny."

"Sorry. It's just that I about tore my butt off, and you yell at me about reading the boards. Sorry. I can see how you'd be mad."

The guy was mollified, probably ready to be nice to anybody who wasn't mean to him, in that way a lot like Wendell.

"That's okay. How can I help you, kid?"

This golden opportunity was collapsing into loser sting, so I helped out:

"You can help, assistant trainee, by checking with your lawyers about how to handle a seven figure lawsuit for criminal negligence."

"Huh?"

"This boy has suffered permanent disability, a lifetime of earnings lost. Your carelessness has landed him in a personal, expensive hell. And you're paying. My Daddy's a lawyer. He's a big time lawyer, and he specializes in — this kind of thing."

This guy acted as if I'd taken a shit in his bunk bed, didn't say a word. He stood there a minute fumbling at his belt. I at first thought he was going for a weapon, but it was only one of those useless first-aid kits.

Wendell, as emotionally pained as the attendant, mumbled something and presented to him his skinned thigh. It looked like raw meat, flesh two layers down. He'd opened his pants some, or rather they were ripped and he held back the corners; but he was making it tough on the guy by keeping so much hidden.

"Wendell, just take your fucking pants off. He won't look at your pecker. I'll make him promise."

Wendell and the other guy both shot me these "how could you?" looks. Like I'd just goosed the Pope.

Neither said anything. Wendell started opening his pants, and old guy mumbled, "That's okay," respecting Wendell's delicacy. I gave up. Wendell winced as Nursey Nelly tended to him, but he didn't fuss. Must not have hurt as much as it looked. Nice body Wendell had, not that I was dying to see it all chopped up like it was.

That night we watched *Freeway*, a cool movie I figured Wendell'd dislike — violent and witty. It's a slick parody of "Little Red Riding Hood," Reese Witherspoon tarting it up with her homicidal maniac act. It's done like a cartoon, sophisticated and way beyond Wendell. He said he liked it, though, made a couple of un-imbecilic comments. Wasn't as if we had a stimulating discussion.

Next stop, we agreed: the high desert. All our books and maps and advice from friends and Wendell's Internet researches yielded — dah, dah — a meander to the east and north, not very far either way, lest we miss something especially lame.

I changed the bandages on Wendell's leg — thigh, butt. I thought he'd object, but he didn't. Tell the truth, I was the one self-conscious. It was like undressing my pretty little distant cousin, had I a cousin so pretty — very, very pretty.

* * *

Saturday — Victorville

Day 3

I figured I'd better get used to being undressed around Tyler. Wasn't like it was easy or right. It was hard and wrong. Last night and also this morning, she changed the bandages on my leg, which meant pulling my underwear up to get to my thigh and a part of my butt side. It was Tyler took us to Sav-On to get bandages. Of course she was snotty with the pharmacy helper there, told him it was a wonder anybody in town was upright, if they depended on him. She was gentle with me, asking once if it hurt. "You sure?" Maybe I should jump off slides every so often. It improves the atmosphere.

We had breakfast made by me. I did eggs beat up with chunks of ham, cut real tiny, and green salsa mixed in. Also pieces of green pepper, green onions, and garlic. And some great cheese, feta, which I'd never had before.

I burned the toast, but Tyler pretended not to notice, which of course she did, since it smoked up the inside of the camper. Set off the alarm. I didn't know how to make coffee, so I tried. Big mistake. It tasted like chocolate milk mixed with old dirt. Tyler mentioned that.

This eating was fun, though all the cooking we'd done so far was breakfast. I thought about suggesting we get cookbooks and try other stuff. Maybe another time. Actually, I did know a few dinner things, not many but impressive.

"Where exactly should we go? We decided on northeast, the desert, but where?"

"What's close? We don't want to make it all the way to Atlanta today, right? Spread it out some? You're the boss, Wendell."

"Close? We can dip over to Victorville. There's other stuff we might do, but kinda back toward L.A. That'd be bad, like retreating."

"Tough asses like us? I've always wanted to go to Victorville."

"Really?"

"Fuck no."

"Oh."

"Don't look like I just insulted your peeny, Wendell. It's not places that matter."

"It's me, isn't it? You just gotta be with me."

She looked at me funny, then softened. "Sometimes you're not so bad, Wendy. I meant I think any place we'll go is okay.

Who knows what we'll find? Not like we're driving through Paris and Rome. But that's okay. Don't you think?"

"Yeah, I do, but...."

"You didn't think I was sophisticated enough for the existential life? Open to the moment, enemy of the predictable. Not what you thought of me?"

"No." She looked a little pissed.

"Wendell, tell the truth, you know what 'existential' means?"

"Not too well, Tyler. Really not too well. I did hear it this term when we were reading *The Stranger* and *No Exit*. I went in to talk to Mr. Clancy. I like all that about emptying oneself of hope, being free, knowing there's not anything out there, nothing at all. If we have to die, then life has no meaning. Sartre said that, right? I really got interested, but it's not as if I know much. I like that about free, unprotected, alone. I don't want to pretend — not like I can even read French like you, Tyler." I couldn't tell what she was thinking, but she didn't look like she was dying to have me go on.

"Victorville or Bust! How far is it?"

"From here to here." I pointed on the map.

She snorted, adjusted her seat, drove us there. On the way, I figured out two attractions, Roy Rogers and Dale Evans Museum and something called Exotic World. The Roy Rogers place was right on the highway, but Exotic World, the book said, was "17 miles east of D Street; for directions, call Dixie, 800-555-5261."

Roy first.

"What's that?"

"A stuffed horse, I think, Tyler."

"Why'd anybody do that? There's another. Holy shit!"

There they were, two stuffed horses you wouldn't want to touch. "Trigger" and "Buttermilk" were their names, and the sign said they were famous in movies: "the world's most famous horse, 'Trigger!'"

Maybe so; I couldn't think of any competitors.

"There's a fucking stuffed dog!" Tyler said, kinda loud.

This woman who looked like that famous evangelist's wife with the hair piled all the way up to the ceiling, heard her and walked over. I thought she was going to yell at Tyler for saying that word so loud, but she didn't:

"We're so pleased you youngsters have stopped by. Now, I know you are far too young to know about Roy Rogers and the lovely Dale Evans, but your grandparents, old folks like me, you might say, probably knew their faces and loved them better than the people next door. That's how important they were. And kind! They were so kind. I'm not saying big stars are not kind now, but it'd be hard to be any kinder than Roy and Dale. You know who did my job before me, greeting people and showing them around?"

We said we didn't.

"You maybe won't believe this, not that you'd call me a liar. You're too well mannered, I can tell. You might say I'm a blabby. Oh, I know I'm a big fat blabby. Perfect job for me. But I really try to say not one word that isn't the truth."

Tyler was staring at her like she was a Martian, so I said, "I'm sure you don't."

"What a dearie you are, and how lucky somebody is — nudge-nudge." She said the "nudge-nudge" part, which I guess was better than doing it, but I figured Tyler was about to say something with "fuck" in it, so I cut in fast:

"How old was the horse when they stuffed it?"

"What a fine question. Trigger passed away at the age of — some say twenty-nine, some thirty-three. Or did you mean Buttermilk? She lived to be thirty-one, and that's verified. Advanced ages for horses, but then they were taken better care of than a good many children. Doesn't it make your heart sick the way some children are treated? I never had children myself, you know, since it takes a husband for that."

"But when Trigger died in 1965, it hit Roy hard. He even

said, and I can quote this to you accurate, 'When my time comes, just skin me and put me right up there on Trigger as if nothing had ever changed.'"

She paused a second. "Of course we didn't do that."

I was stuck back at where she said nobody'd want to marry her. That was so sad, but she was laughing as she said it. She wasn't the last person you'd want to marry, but you could see what she meant, not that I'd agree with her. That'd be beyond rude.

Our guide was running on.

"Did you know Dale was married four times? It takes a while for some women to stick, I guess. Dale's first marriage was when she was fourteen, and she soon had a baby. Her husband left her two years later, a single mom, depending on herself. I think she's very admirable for that, don't you? I am not aware of anything interesting about her next two marriages, but she met and married Roy in 1947 and they had forty-one happy years together, before he died in 1988. Dale died three years later, of a broken heart. I suppose that's a little romantic, since she was eighty-eight years old then."

She laughed, but she was also sniffing.

Turns out the dog's name was "Bullet." I didn't ask its age. We didn't ask anything. She just kept going, showed us the photo albums, the cars, and personal stuff that wouldn't sound interesting, but she made it so. Still, there was so much stuff I thought we'd never get away. Plus I worried that Tyler would say something. Roy Rogers wasn't exactly her type.

"All those other things stuffed...."

"I know, young lady, I know. I was hoping you wouldn't notice. There are 347 hunting trophies here, almost all of them, all but two, shot by Roy himself. I can guess what you're thinking, and I agree. I wish he hadn't. I don't understand it myself. Deer, too, and bear — it's all so sad. It was a another time, I guess — another time."

We didn't say anything.

"I hope you don't think less of Roy Rogers and Dale for this, young dearies. You know, it was different then. They did so much good in the world, for sick children, too. I don't understand it myself, but there's lots I don't. Still, I wish he hadn't done it. I never mention them unless people ask. Lots of people do."

I couldn't believe what Tyler said: "You know, ma'am, lots of wonderful people have these things about them we have trouble understanding. Thomas Jefferson, for instance, owned slaves."

"He did? I didn't know that. Oh my goodness, Thomas Jefferson. The one did The Declaration, wasn't he?"

"That's the one.'

"Oh, he owned slaves. Oh my."

"It was a different time, like you say."

"Yes, it was. But...."

You got the feeling she didn't see the connection to Roy Rogers, or if she did, wasn't comforted. One more great person she didn't understand.

Just then a flock of people came in past the stuffed horses, thank Jesus, and she perked up — or tried to.

"You two honeys please take your time and make yourself at home. I really must greet our new guests, you understand. But don't leave if you have questions or just want to visit a bit."

She started toward the mob of gawkers and then spun around, graceful in the way real heavy women often are: "I never did tell you who had my job before me: it was Roy Rogers himself, yes it was."

She smiled even bigger than usual, then turned again and went toward her new people.

We headed toward the exit just as soon as our guide was out of sight. I should have kept my mouth shut, but I didn't:

"She really seemed upset about Jefferson."
"Just shut up, Wendell."
That was clear enough.
Next, Exotic World.

I called Dixie, who gave us directions, though she sounded like she'd been drinking whisky for the last three hundred years. It was actually nice hearing her voice, all raspy and curdled.

Exotic World wasn't. That's a good sentence. But I will say that Exotic World was fun. For one thing, Dixie didn't treat us like we were cuties or honeys. Maybe she didn't notice. That's a possibility, as she seemed at first to think we knew all about what she was telling us, which was the world of strippers, the history of burlesque shows. It took me a minute to realize the subject of her gargly talk, since she kept talking about "artists" and "dancers," but I finally caught on from the pictures. About the same time, it dawned on Dixie that we were a little under the age of ninety-seven.

"You two seem very smart, but you're young. That's not your fault, I'm not saying it is, but you can't know what it was like. It was a different idea of style then, of elegance. I'm not saying every entertainer today is cheap, don't get me wrong. Too many girls today, though, don't understand the art. For one thing, it's a striptease, or used to be, as in T-E-A-S-E. Me and Gypsy and Tempest, lots of class acts, we spent a lot of time thinking about wardrobe, not just taking it off. Today, it's flip, strip, and that's it. We knew how to dance, tantalize. Only at the very end of the act was there a shake number, usually, and that was, I don't mind saying it, art."

"We never had a chance to see that." Tyler seemed to like Dixie a lot.

"Yeah, we never had the chance."

"Well, things do change. Iron skillets aren't going to come

back and replace microwaves, so we live with what we have. I'm not saying we shouldn't. But I'm glad young people like you come and see what it used to be."

We seemed to be the only ones there, but it was an interesting place, big too. It was kind of funny seeing old G-strings on plastic models, like in department stores, but I liked the posters and stuff. It wasn't dirty at all; it also wasn't sexy.

Dixie seemed to me a really intelligent woman. I say that because she was talking about how burlesque was a form of entertainment for the working class, and that's the reason it lost ground.

"When blue collar jobs disappeared, so did blue collar art." I'd never thought of it, but it sounded right. I'm going to find out more about burlesque.

"Are there lots of books on burlesque, you know, histories?"

She looked at me like Mom would if I told her I'd accepted Jesus Christ as my personal Lord and Savior. "Are you interested? I'll give you a couple, glad to, but there isn't much, honey. It's swept under the rug, like most of the lives of workers." I kept my mouth shut and let Tyler move to the front with Dixie. Truth is, I was getting a little restless, since the place had a lot of the same stuff in it; and also I was hungry. I knew Tyler wouldn't ask any questions. Wrong.

"Was this always a museum?"

Any hope I had of getting out soon ran right down the drain.

"You know what it once was? It was a goat farm. Really, it was. My good friend Jenny Lee, you heard of her?"

"I think so," Tyler lied.

"Sure. She ran the Sassy Lassie down in San Pedro, moved up here with her own collection, when her health went bad. Jenny was always real good to me, a friend for years, you know?"

"Yes, we do," Tyler lied again. All this time we were moving, like crippled snails, from room to room to room, no end in sight.

"Well, I came to live with her, help her out. There was this write up said I came to 'nurse' her, but that makes it seem like some Florence Nightingale, which I ain't. She was a good friend and you'd a done the same thing, right? I mean, for a friend."

"I would," Tyler lied yet again.

"Someone you loved and who loved you," Dixie added, to nobody in particular.

When we left, she gave me three books, just drop them off next time we were by.

We stayed in Victorville at a hook up campground place. It was well appointed, I think you'd say, not that we needed the extras, having everything we wanted here inside. We cooked for ourselves again, Tyler did. I washed dishes, which I enjoy doing.

After dinner, we played Rack-O. There was this real old couple in the site next to us I ran into hooking up the hose thing. I suggested to Tyler we invite them over later. I knew she'd say something rude, but she didn't. So they came over and played Rack-O with us. Nothing special happened, but it was a lot of fun. I can't figure out Tyler at all. She was nice to these old people, but then, later on, after they'd left, she made fun of me again, me and my panties and that kind of thing.

Sunday — Barstow

Day 4

I drove over to Barstow. Not very far, an hour or so. Tyler edged into the other seat, reclined it, got the vibrator going, hooked up her earphones, and said not one thing all the way. Not that I wanted an intellectual discussion. We watched this movie night before last I liked, Little Red

Riding Hood made modern and feminist. Reese Witherspoon was hot, as usual, though in this film she's like in a Mafia movie, ready to shoot somebody's jaw off. I should have mentioned the movie earlier. I forget the title.

We got to Barstow and went to The Chamber of Commerce. Tyler noticed the sign on Main Street. The lady there was so nice, I was afraid all the time that Tyler would do her snotty act with her, make fun of her. But she didn't.

This Chamber lady was chatty, a little like the Roy Rogers woman, only less bubbly. She did go on, but you could tell she wanted us to have a good time, and she was proud of her town. We'd come here as a joke, and she was telling us all these neat things to do. She didn't seem curious about how Tyler and I were connected and kept putting her hands on our shoulders. I didn't mind, but knew Tyler would, only she didn't seem to. Maybe I should start relaxing about Tyler. Maybe it was only me she lit into.

If you're not used to them, these desert towns look like the moon after a tornado and then a fire. No grass or trees, and lots of dirt. Not really sand, like in the movies, but more like scrabby soil that nothing much grows in that you'd ever want to grow on purpose. It's not flat here, exactly, but there's not much breaking the view except dirt hills. I used to think it was ugly as hell, and maybe it is, but it isn't messed up.

I say that, and then here's Barstow. Fast foods and Wal-Marts, but there's also hidden great stuff, which we found out from this woman at the Chamber. She told us it was once a big railroad town, and you could still take a walk along the old Santa Fe Railroad tracks. Before the trains, there were big silver mines here, in the Calico Mountains. Maybe that's why they built the railroad, because of the silver mines. The lady probably covered that. When the silver played out, that's the way she put it, the miners vacated, but the town stayed prosperous because of the railroad. Why a town would do well because there was a railroad there was lost on me, I'll admit.

She gave us brochures: many attractions, plus an outlet mall with 119 stores. I love those places, but I wouldn't suggest going unless Tyler wanted to, which she wouldn't. Besides there were other great things: The Solar Generator Plant, The Calico Ghost Town, The Mojave Valley River Museum, The Route 66 Museum, The Western American Railroad Museum, several Canyons, Rainbow Basin, an archaeological site called Calico Early Man. I waited to see what Tyler would say.

* * *

"So, Wendell, what next?" I could see he was getting all excited over Fat Sally's recital of the shit here, things like factory tours.

"I really don't care, Tyler. What sounds good to you?"

"Some other town?"

Pathetic Wendell was now trying to hide his deflation. I didn't mind deflating him, but I also didn't have another town in mind, so I let him wriggle off the hook.

"Nah, hun-bun, this town is loaded with thrills. Tell you the truth, I could resist the canyons, since it's 300 degrees and all you can do in a canyon is walk into it. I don't know what Rainbow Basin is, but it sounds like more heatstroke activity."

Wendell interrupted: "It's just a place, fifteen miles north. Used to be lakes."

"No more lakes, right?"

"Not for maybe millions of years."

"Damn, we missed them!"

"Bet they were something, though. Now, this paper says that even without the lakes the dry stuff makes 'a rainbow of scenic beauty.'"

"Thus the name. That'd be okay in the morning or evening. I kinda like stuff like that, Wendell." I almost added some kind of apology about being negative, but I'm happy to say I restrained myself.

"Yeah, okay. What else?"

"All the rest sounds happy, except for the power plant. I don't know how solar power is generated, and I don't give a shit."

"Me either. So how about the archaeological site?"

I hated to admit it, but that was my choice too.

On the way out — it was twenty miles away — we passed the Ghost Town, which looked more like a seedy carnival attraction. I felt sure we'd end up there, since the fat lady had recommended it.

The Early Man site was run by two women whose combined ages reached four figures. One of them took us around, pretty surly at first but she perked up when I asked some questions. Wendell, thank God, kept his mouth shut.

She took us into this little declivity and started scraping at the ground.

"Look at this! What is it?"

It looked like a rock sliver to me, but I knew this was a test, so I focused on it. To be nice — why? — I showed it to Wendell, which meant him getting close to me. That made me realize he never did that. He did smell good. Very neat, Wendell, and clean too — and — oh my!

Turning the rock over and over, anyone would have noticed the complicated pattern of cuts and edges. It was also pointed at one end, pretty sharp.

"I'm about as ignorant of archaeology as one can get, but I'd say this was a tool, a cutting or scraping tool, maybe used on hides?"

I was about to go on and make matters worse, when this old woman, who looked more male than any male I'd seen, hopped up from her hunkered-over position, like she was six years old, and yipped.

"Yes! Yes! Of course it is. It's a tool, almost certainly for scraping hides, not a weapon and not a digger, but a tool. You're a smart girl, not that it takes all that much smart to see that, no insult. But you know what?"

All of a sudden she switched from glee to fierce: "You know what, honey? Those goddamned fools, those big league assholes, those masters of incompetence at Davis say .... You know what they say?"

"No. What?"

"You know what they say?"

Was this ever going to end? "No I don't."

"Those double-dyed fools up there at Davis say...."

I thought she was going to ask me again if I knew what those testicles at Davis said, but she was just building up steam for the explosion:

"Dromedaries!"

"No!" I tried to match her indignation. Wendell did too: "Not dromedaries!"

"They say these ancient hoofed animals tromped these stones into what we women are mistaking as tools and, in other cases, weapons."

"Why do they say that?" I asked.

She wasn't ready for that. "Do you know who was here? Said it was by far the earliest man site in North America, revised all previous ideas. You know who?"

"No, we don't. Who?" I had a feeling we were in for another round.

"You know who? Who these Davis pissants are ignoring?"

"No we don't"

"Only Louis Leakey, Dr. Louis S. B. Leakey!"

I was terrified Wendell would say, "Who's he?" So I real loud let out, "No! How could they?" Wendell chimed in, "What dummies."

"Yes, Dr. Louis S. B. Leakey!"

I knew what I should say. Since this was fun, I said it.

"They're jealous, don't want their fixed notions upset. It's because you're not in their club."

"Goddamn right. You're goddam right, that's what you are."

I could sense Wendell breathing deep to say something and moved to stop him. Too late: "It's because those Davis idiots are men and you are women."

The old crone looked sharply at Wendell. I figured she was going to spit on him, but instead she smiled: "You're goddamn right it's because we are women. What a sweet boy you are to see that. Some girl is going to be very lucky." Then she looked at me and winked. Jesus Christ.

This doesn't sound like it took long, but it did, talking to this scientist and her partner. Wasn't so much "talking to" as playing the role of impartial-guys-they-wanted-to-convince. Duck soup. What did we know?

They enjoyed themselves, these two women, and it was easy to admire them, lunatic as they may have been. They'd devoted their life to this work, which even we could see was important. My guess was they'd badgered old Leakey until he caved in and not only visited but agreed with them. Why hadn't his word carried more weight with the archaeological establishment? Whatever that blind bunch was, it apparently found its center in The University of California, Davis, up near Sacramento.

They kept saying they had to let us go, but for hours, it seemed, they didn't. They wanted to present their case, no matter that they might as well have been arguing before a council of parakeets. It was interesting, though technical, beyond our grasp. When we finally wrestled ourselves loose — "Helen, we must set these sweet youngsters free!" — I was hungry as hell. Nothing to eat since breakfast. It was four o'clock, and we were twenty-five miles from what passed as the town, where all the fine dining was located.

As good fortune and alert Wendell would have it, we

didn't have to go all the way back, hollow-eyed and big-bellied starving.

"You know that Ghost Town we passed? I'll bet they have restaurants."

"And great ones too!" I said, intending to convey a sneer, which I did, judging by Wendell's flinch. Still, it was a good idea. Wouldn't be too crowded on a Sunday.

But it was, with people watching kids pretend to engage in honest to Olde West gun battles and fights filled with flips and ugh-ow noises. It was so campy I enjoyed it. These kids were throwing themselves off buildings, crashing through fake glass windows, rolling in the dirt. It was the lowest sort of schlock, but easy on the cynical-index.

Wendell didn't have to give himself permission to enjoy it. Being simpleminded, Wendell had an easy time of it in this festival of low-culture shit. This is the sort of fun people call "adolescent," but you never see adolescents enjoying it. Yeah, but Wendell did. I did even more — for a time.

"Wendell, let's get to a beanery here before they pick you for a role." That was a real danger, and he'd a done it, too. I know that because — you'll see.

The food was okay, or we were just so hungry anything would have gone down well. After lunch, as I warned before and you guessed, we failed to make a getaway.

"Here's our newly-elected deputy sheriff!" Oh Jesus. We no sooner slunk out of the restaurant than one of these fake Wild West doofuses recognized one of his own kind and glommed onto Wendell.

Wendell was reluctant — no he wasn't. He aw-shucksed his way out into the middle of the dirt street — the dirt at least wasn't fake — and put on the outfit they gave him, Barney Fife.

You know what I was worried about? Wendell's skinned-up ass. Here I am bandaging him every night, and my First-Aid skills, considerable, are being squandered by this reckless dimwit.

Turns out Wendell went into a huddle with the paid nerds to learn his part. I thought about leaving, can't imagine what possessed me to stay. Even when I saw them peeking at me, I remained rooted. I can't bear to tell you what happened. It involved a bank robbery, a *mano a mano* shoot-out, some tumbling out of windows — all of which was okay. What wasn't okay was Wendell with a bandana over his lower face, sidling up to a hostage, and setting in motion three minutes of the deepest embarrassment I've experienced since I peed myself on stage in the kindergarten spring festival in front of a full house.

I guess you've figured out who got to play "the hostage."

"So, Tyler, that was fun. Not for you, I guess. How about a museum — there's the river one and the Route 66 one and a railroad one."

"Wendell?"

"Yes, Tyler?"

"Fuck yourself."

"That'll work too." He'd like to bust a gut, just as if he'd said something funny.

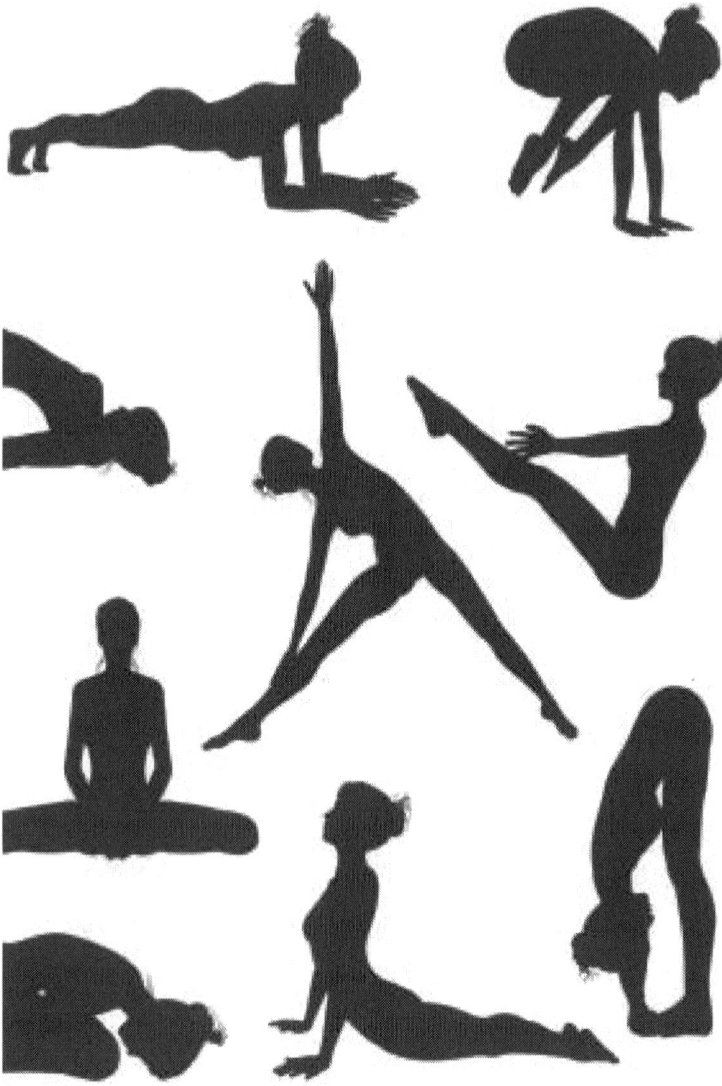

CHAPTER 5

Monday — Barstow to Tecate

Day 5

"Whose turn to drive?"

"Where?"

"One thing at a time, Wendell. That's the thing with you, demanding too much. I'm a simple girl, can't hold much in my mind. I try, things spill."

"Okay. Tyler, you like to drive? Reason I ask is I enjoy it and figured you did too, so we could divide the driving. But if you don't like driving...."

"I like driving."

"Okay, so whose turn?"

"Mine, I guess. Don't you remember? You okay? It was just yesterday you drove — very safely too, a model for all youth. You don't remember?"

"Just making conversation."

"I'll drive. Should I take off and flip a coin at intersections?"

"Sure, Tyler. See what happens and if we end up in Atlanta somehow."

"That's about as — Wendell, do you have any — look, you know what'd likely happen, just by the odds?

"No."

"A random heads-tails would keep us going in circles, never get out of Barstow."

"Why do you keep setting me up, Tyler? I know you're smarter than me. You gonna spend all summer demonstrating that?"

"Guilt-tripping me, Wendell?" Yeah he was, and it was working.

"I don't mean to, Tyler. I just wish you'd stop tearing at me."

"So, we've settled I'm driving. Where to?"

"How about we look at the map and books together?"

"That's a plan."

"You care if we don't go east, Tyler, I mean all the time? One thing we could do is swing up and down and just generally creep east. No hurry."

That was pretty good. Gave voice to what had been in the back of my mind, though I hadn't realized it until he said it.

"That's good, Wendell. We can float up and down, like you say, even slantways and backwards, if we want, just make sure we're a little bit more east one week than we were the one before, right?"

I expected he'd be ecstatic, but he just nodded. Wendell chose the oddest times to be cool. Wish he were consistent.

We played with the maps and guides for a while. I noticed last night Wendell was reading the instruction book on the snazzy Italian coffee maker. He'd also stopped at the Barstow gourmet shop — the Target — and got some Brazilian beans. The result was some awful coffee—just kidding, good once you got used to it. I thought of mentioning it, but figured one nice comment was enough, per week.

"The book here talks about Tecate."

"The beer? Limes in it?"

"Yeah, but the town too; it says it's a good border town, clean and interesting."

"They say what's interesting in it?"

"They mention souvenir shops and *cantinas.*"

"Whooie! I'm up for it. At least we can drink beer. You drink beer, right?"

"I have."

"Just as I thought. So, we head south? Only a guess."

He shot me his pretty look, all his looks being pretty.

Long drive. Took us back west and down. To save time, we used the I-15, uninteresting road, but I could do 75 on it and still have cars passing me. Down by San Diego we cut southeast, through a couple of shitty, dump towns and then to Tecate, California, a slop-over from our destination, the authentic Tecate.

"The book says we should park here and walk across the border, Tyler. It says we should do that for insurance reasons."

"Glad you read that, Wendell. There's a chance we may end up in a Mexican prison, and if the car's on this side they can't impound it. That's the truth. Also, leave your valuables here in that safe under the sofa there."

"Leave me valu-a-buls hee-yur, under the so-wo-ohh-fa they-ur." Wendell sang all husky and slow, almost sexy, were that possible for him.

"Wendell, your underpants are sticking out."

He turned red and checked, trying to be casual.

"Gotcha!"

He looked more angry than hurt. That's an improvement.

"You wanta hear what we've got ahead of us here in this adventure, Tyler?" He was being chirpy now — better than wounded.

"Can't wait. That what you been reading there, a guidebook? I thought you were reading one on music. I saw staffs and bars. Is this town a center for advanced symphonic composition?"

He seemed embarrassed, but it was a book with musical notations in it. "God, Tyler. What you talking 'bout? You been sniffing'?"

"Smoking? What do you mean, 'sniffing?'"

"Ha! You know very well, even you do. Anyways, the town's Tecate, like the beer, as I mentioned earlier and you'd have caught, if you'd been listening, which you should be. I was looking at two different books, one being a guide book, really stuff I collected off the net, and put in this binder, so not really a book."

"Not a book, but giving us the inside dope the way a book would, right, ace?"

"Well, since you ask, Tyler, here's a short list of Tecate-don't-miss-es, staring with a KOA campground, if we decide to cross over, a fine one where they have horseback riding, which I've never done, and volleyball, which I've done, and a club house, goody, hiking, which is you and me's favorite leisure time activity, horseshoes, which I am very good at and you aren't, nearby golf, of interest to a country-club girl like you and I'm ready to learn, a playground, where we can go when we're drunk from the brewery, and many shade trees, under which we can put our folding chairs and stare off into space, $35 dollars for two people, full hookup."

"Irresistible. That's all that's there, the KOA?"

"Run by Herman and Zelda Ibanez Bracamontes, always has been."

"Herman and Zelda know how to supervise the septics. In addition to the KOA?"

"You want more? 'A pleasant Mexican community less like a border town than a small central village. Here, life centers around a tranquil, tree shaded plaza.'"

"Whee!"

"'Tecate has long been,' I'm continuing my flow of information, 'a farm market for a productive region that harvests grapes, olives and grain. Industries include beer, instant coffee, and *maquiladoras*.'"

"What?"

"It says right here. And now we get to the attractions aimed at active young people like us: we got a festival next month; we got several shops; we got a gallery, we got tree-lined streets and a gazebo in the center of town; we got a museum featuring some of the finest rupestrian paintings in the world, but you knew that; we got hot springs out in Guadalupe Canyon, which feature sizzling hot water straight from the earth, lush native fan palms, cascading waterfalls, ancient Indian caves, and hot tubs filled with geothermal mineral water; and if that isn't enough, and it isn't, we got the brewery."

Wasn't like I was thinking this trip would be okay, but that it might not be as bad as I thought. I mean Wendell, not this town.

"The brewery?"

"You're wondering about the tours, the free beer, the — what do you call it?"

"*Frauleins* in short dresses and lotsa petticoats?"

"That's it — *rathskellers.*"

"That's German, Wendy, though maybe they do that in old Mehico too."

"Beer garden! That's what you're wondering about. Here's what they say, wanta hear? I know you do. They say, 'Brewery Beer Garden may or may *not* be open; tour operations many or may *not* be operating. Hey, tuff...that's Mexico.'"

"What hilarious guide books you have, Wendell. Books written by the intoxicated for those who hope to be. As for the brewery tours, we take our chances. Anyhow, this town's packed with fun opportunities. You just gotta reach out and grab em."

"Like peaches on a tree. Wait, though. I haven't mentioned the best thing of all."

"Mention it."

"I will. Right here in town is — you ready for this?"

"Give me a minute. Not a *cantina;* don't tell me there's a *cantina.*"

"Not one. But there's something even better. You sure you're prepared?"

"No, but go ahead."

"A spa, a spa for the jet set, says the guidebook."

"A spa? Mineral baths, you mean, hot tubs? I guess I'm not too sure what a spa is. Don't hate me, Wendell."

"All those years you spent in the convent, how could you know about spas?"

"Is it some sort of whorehouse?"

"Exactly — for the jet-set."

"So, tell me."

"It's called Rancho La Rancho. I guess that's not a joke. I don't know Spanish. It's a complete spa. There's no phones, no television, no computers."

"So far, so good."

"This week is couples week."

"We're in luck. Couples week for what?"

"Living in our own special villa, no two alike. Food guaranteed low fat. Everything low fat, especially you and me. Here's an average day schedule:

7 a.m. Your low-fat breakfast
8 a.m. Workout with fitness machines
9:30 a.m. Hike
12:00 p.m. Low-fat lunch
1:00 p.m. Pilates
2:30 p.m. Tennis
4:00 p.m. Swim
5:00 p.m. Lecture
6:45 p.m. Low-fat dinner
8:45 p.m. Evening program—varies
10:30 p.m. Lights out

"And this only costs us $3,200 bucks for a week, Tyler. I think our parents would regard this as mind-expanding."

"Wendell, are you serious? And what's Pilates?"

"I'll tell you when you're older. Why don't we sign up? I want to experience evening programs and lectures. You play tennis?"

"Yeah, do you?"

"No, but I'm an old Pilates shooter, so we're even."

We take a walk through town, go to an authentic cantina, one of three we saw, lying asshole Wendell, and have the best food. The food seemed so fine, I expect, largely because we waited until four o'clock to have lunch. I don't know why, but the last couple of days we've been screwing up any kind of sane schedule. I mention it over lunch.

"Why are we eating so late, Wendell?"

"Isn't this food great? I love salt, and Mexican food is perfect for salt."

"You got hearing problems, cutie? You a deafie?"

"Sorry. I heard you, but I wanted to get that out about the food first."

"I agree about the food, not about the salt. Why don't you just eat green apples?"

"I do. Granny Smith, also tomatoes and popcorn. I read salt's not really bad for you, doesn't cause high blood pressure even. That's a myth."

"You know odd things, Wendy. Why in the name of fisting would you care about blood pressure?"

"I don't know. You're right. I get interested in this and that, find out things. Not many, not generally the things that do you good."

"Like how to dress, the art of picking up girls, *Kama Sutra* techniques?"

"Huh?"

"Never mind. Wendell, you remember what I asked you an hour or so back?"

"You were curious about the latest news on salt. No, you asked why we were eating at such funny times. Lunch at 5, dinner at 6."

"Strike you as odd?"

"Yeah."

"Want to change it?"

"No. Do you?"

"Guess not. It's sorta nice eating when you get so hungry you have to."

"We don't stay up late, Tyler."

"I know what you're saying. We can do any goddamned thing we want, on our own like we are. We could sleep all day, get drunk, shoot up, practice unsafe sex, even go so far as neglect tooth brushing. We're about as wild as two nuns off on a Greyhound Bus trip looking at the autumn leaves."

"This is only our fifth day. Maybe we'll drift into disgusting things slowly."

I admit I smiled at him.

We decided that the town didn't offer much except little boys selling Chiclets and their own sisters, I imagine. I suggested to Wendell he could pick up some cash joining them. Easy to joke with him, since, thank God, he had no interest in me.

Anyways, off we went to the spa of the stars. It looked like the sort of place where birds were forbidden to shit on the walks and the bushes had to grow evenly or move the fuck out. Manicured paths. It made you want to talk in low tones about how this was the life and how it put things in perspective. That was what my parents would say on visits to places they took me to, up at Big Sur and suchlike New Age gathering spots for people who wanted to imagine they had an inner life. There were pigeons with an inner life richer than my parents', though no pigeons were here, as I mentioned.

The reception place was tasteful. They'd spent a lot of money making it so you'd feel like a loser if you weren't relaxed. But the reception man was a baggy-faced fatty with a big smile and a Hawaiian shirt that would've fit better at a KOA than here at the spa for the stars.

We'd walked in not having the slightest idea what we were getting into: what humiliations, what dangers, what pedophile priests with designs on innocents like us, what boredom. But Wendell moved forward with his calm, mastering self-assurance:

"Hi. Sorry to bother you, but — ah — we...."

"Hello, young people, and welcome to the most rejuvenating place on earth."

"Thanks a lot," Wendell explained.

"How can I help you?"

"Well, my friend and I, Tyler, are taking a trip across the country, expanding our minds, you know, like they used to do in the old days in Europe."

This was not much less humiliating than watching my parents try to make themselves liked by white people, but for some reason I kept mum. The fat guy, used to the drunk and demented, didn't lose his smile.

"Of course, of course," he hummed.

"We saw about you," Wendell kept going, "and wondered if we might stay a couple of nights."

"Well, we only rent by the week, you see. Only by the week. That's our policy, unfortunately."

Wendell, obviously primed for a different sort of difficulty, said, with a mad glint in his eye, "But we are eighteen. We have ID."

The smile quivered a little but held: "I see. Well, that's good. You're so young and glamorous."

He paused, as if taking us in for the first time. When he started up again, he seemed a little sad: "You see, our policy is that we only rent by the week. And only by advanced reservation."

Wendell looked so disappointed, you'd have thought this was something we'd wanted to do.

"Thank you anyhow. You're a very nice man."

"I wish I could — wait just a moment, please, young friends. Just a moment, please." He seemed upset at raising his voice, though only a meter would have detected it. He picked up a phone and started talking to somebody. Wendell and I were about six inches away and could barely hear his mutters. The conversation went on about an hour.

* * *

This guy was spooky, whispering at us like we were locked inside a never-ending funeral. But he felt sorry for us, not that we deserved it, like we'd flunked the SATs which ended our last hope of escaping the ghetto, lost, like the campers in "Friday the 13th": "You're dooooooomed!" that old maniac says. Interracials like us couldn't last a minute in the cold world. And maybe I was wrong about him; maybe he was just a nice guy wanting to be nice because it was his nature to be nice.

I shouldn't have called him spooky. He was different, that's all. As the king of being different, I should be the last one — shut up.

He got off the phone, smiling and nodding, trying to keep himself from giggling or something, maybe running round the desk and kissing us.

"Here's good news, at least I hope it's good news. First off, though, could you stay three days? Would that fit in with your plans?"

Tyler looked at me and then answered, "Well, sure. We are pretty free, actually." Then, as if she were worried we might be trapped for months: "But we need to get moving in three days — on east, you see, as I may have mentioned."

It seemed to me funny, what Tyler said; so lame, as if she were me. But if I laughed she'd think I was mocking her, so I didn't.

"No, three days is exactly the length of the plan. Naturally, you're curious about the plan. Not to keep you in suspense, how would you like an Adventure in Fitness?"

I found my tongue, as they say: "Fitness? I don't know."

"Of course you don't. I apologize. Not being privileged to spend time around young people, I'm not — you might say — well, not usually so much at a loss for words."

I couldn't believe it, but Tyler cut in: "We're nothing special, don't know what the hell we're doing. But we can recognize a nice man when we see one."

He said super-soft, "Thank you."

I started to squirm. Everybody was looking at the floor. Were we going to sit here in silence, erupt in sobs? Finally, Hawaiian-shirt guy pulled himself together:

"Well, I shouldn't assume you'll be interested; but Rancho La Rancho will gladly provide you room and meals and all the amenities you might find amusing, such as tennis, golf, and massage programs. What we'd like you to do is help us work out a balance between three exercise models we've been developing."

"I see," I said, not seeing anything.

He smiled, probably realizing I was dumber than average. "For several years now we've been featuring a program known as Pilates. It's worked out well, and we have an amazing staff of certified teachers. What we're been pondering is diversifying this program by adding others that would supplement our emphasis on Pilates. Of course, Pilates will still form the center; that goes without saying. With that in mind, here's where you come in."

He paused for some reason. I had no idea what he was talking about. I understood better before he started clarifying.

Thank God he continued: "We'd like you to spend three days testing these fitness models and give us reports. We think young and fit people will be able to tell us more directly things than our standard clients who tend to be older," here he laughed softly, "might not notice, or might have difficulty fully comprehending while they're in the midst of the programs, adjusting to them."

Tyler seemed interested. You could never predict what might interest her:

"Or finding themselves so winded and beat up, confused and dizzy, they wouldn't know a damned thing. I can see why we'd be better, and we'd have no reason not to be objective. Also, since we're young and supple, we aren't likely to be injured."

"Yes, we wouldn't want that."

"Neither would your lawyers," she said.

He looked hurt, but Tyler moved in fast: "Just kidding. We appreciate the way you're taking us in. I know a little about Pilates, as my mom and dad do it, my mom faithfully. What are the other programs you've been trying?"

"Nia and yoga. We can explain those as we go, I expect."

"Sure," Tyler said. What was she getting us into?

"Are these programs where we keep our clothes on?" It was one of those times I found something coming out of my mouth I'd have given anything to stuff back in.

Tyler and fat man reacted like they were in a movie and had some script. At the same time, in unison, as if attached with wires, they stared, then looked puzzled, then looked startled, and then busted out laughing.

"Yes indeed, young man, these are programs that are absolutely — ah — decent."

Tyler started sputtering: "It'd be a hot idea to have nude Pilates." She tried to keep talking but just choked out random words: "those old — blubby — wrinkled...."

The soft-spoken guy wasn't so soft-spoken now. He was howling with Tyler, helping her along. He was the first to notice me, naturally.

"We're not laughing at you. It's just such a funny idea. All those people...," and he started cackling again.

We ended up moving stuff into this fancy cabin that only a really expensive place would ever call a cabin and being handed papers explaining — I don't know what.

Tuesday, Wednesday, and Thursda — Tecate

Days 6 to 8

At the end of three days, we turned in our reports, me and Tyler, not as different as you might suppose. We agreed on things like, "cut down on the explaining and promoting." I mean, the customers were there already, so we couldn't see why there was so much talk. Letting you know what to do was one thing, but telling you how great it was, was strange. Maybe I should illustrate this point. We took our jobs seriously, especially at first, carried along tape recorders. Anyways, we got a record of the sales pitch the general instructor gave at the start of each session. I say "general instructor" because there was a troop of officials, one in charge and other bosses who were coaches.

No wonder this place was so expensive. The point is that we got a complete record. But don't faint; I'm not going to copy down the whole thing.

Pilates was best. First, though, we had to sit through a lot of blab. I usually don't mind, like in class, but this was pretty bad.

They started off with the life of Joseph Pilates, a crippled kid with lots of handicaps, which he overcame all on his own, using exercises to make his body better and also, in a way I couldn't understand, his mind. Later on, Joseph found himself in England as a boxer and some kind of performer, maybe in a freak show, they didn't say. He was a German, and so when the war broke out he was put in a camp. Joseph used his time there, which I imagine was actually a prison, working on these exercises and also teaching fellow Germans how to develop their bodies and minds on mats, the system he used being called "matwork" which he developed machines for, primitive machines, though, like straps for the feet so you won't slide around, and spring tension things.

In 1926 Joseph was let out of prison in England and came to New York to open the New York Pilates Studio. His wife was named Clara and she worked along with him, doing important things; I don't know what they were.

It kind of disappeared, Pilates did, until about twenty years ago, when some movie stars started doing it again. Tyler says it appeals to rich morons, but actually she liked the exercises, even more than I did.

I copied down what Joseph said: "I must be right. Never an aspirin. Never injured a day in my life. The whole country, the whole world, should be doing my exercises. They'd be happier." Tyler found that hilarious. I think it's nice, being so enthusiastic, but it does seem lunatic. Imagine thinking that stretching on mats — he called it "Controlology" — would keep you from being *injured*, like doing "the elephant" or "the swan" daily would help a lot if a tree fell on you.

Along with all this talk about Joseph, there were dozens of testimonials, the best from the injured and the sick, people who went into detail about disabilities that Pilates had cured. What got me was how some of them spoke of changing their insides. Here's one example I copied down. It's not too long:

"The Pilates Method has transformed my body but that's only the outside part. I've changed from inside out and brought about a whole new personality. I remember walking one day and having to stop and look at my legs, which didn't feel like they were mine. They were longer, thinner, lighter, as if I was walking on air. The Pilates Method changed the smells of flowers and the songs of birds; it even changed the sound of my voice making it more dynamic. The system truly works from the inside out."

Some others talked about what the instructor said was "deep therapy triggering repressed memories and making healing possible." One said, "The sequential breathing clears my head but also and more important it clears my soul."

Tyler liked ones that said things like, "My whole body has physically changed!" or "My arms used to be bigger than my stomach is now!" or "After one year on Pilates I received three marriage proposals inside of a single month!"

The general instructor went into his own sermon:

"But what can this technique do for *You?* That's the question. What can it do for *You?* And in seven days? Not much, right? Wrong! I'll promise you this. I say I'll *promise* you this. This is no fat farm; no starve yourself for a week, lose three pounds, then right back to what you were. Nothing here is empty promises, temporary and frustrating results. We'll provide you not only a roadmap but a new car, a new self. You'll never be the same. Once cleansed, from the inside out, you wouldn't be able to go back to where you were even if you tried."

I looked over at Tyler, who was messing with her mat. Wondered how she was taking this, but didn't have to wonder long. She caught my eye and made this face like she was loony, crossing her eyes and letting her tongue loll out of the side of her mouth. Made me laugh, though I covered the laugh with a cough pretty well.

We wrote up the exercises positively. They did make you feel good, didn't seem hard, like I say. I'd never thought about my bones before, and it was pretty interesting connecting with them. I liked trying to make my navel touch my spine. They kept talking about a new awareness of my powerhouse. After a while, I realized what my powerhouse was, though it took me a while. I had to ask, not Tyler, but this nice-looking old lady, about forty, who looked like she'd be nice, not that she was good-looking.

"Excuse me, ma'am."

"Yes, beautiful?"

"It's embarrassing to ask this, but I think I'm the only one who doesn't know what my powerhouse is. What's a powerhouse?"

"Want me to show you?"

This wasn't going where I felt comfy, as they say on one of the soap operas I used to watch with Sean 2. But I'd asked her, so I didn't know what to say back except "sure."

She backed me against the wall, reached around and started kneading my lower back. Then she turned to rubbing my stomach. Then she reached back around and started digging her fingers into my butt. I won't say it didn't feel good, but it was very embarrassing. She looked a little like Mom, this lady, and there she was treating my butt like two of those balls you squeeze to build up your muscles. She was also kind of panting away there, leaning against me and going at my butt like she was being paid by the grab.

I didn't want to be rude, but I didn't want to get caught either. They weren't paying me and Tyler to be handling toys for the guests, after all, or seduce them, though that sure wasn't what I was doing.

"I see. That's what my powerhouse is, all that part. Thanks." I realized I didn't know her name for sure. It was, I think, "Cloud" or "Clear." Odd name. Meanwhile, she showed no signs of letting up, so I said something exceptionally lame: "Well, thanks a lot. I have to be getting to Nia class now for my job, you know."

"Oh fuck your job," she said.

"I see what you mean," I said, very stupid.

"Fuck your job'" she said much louder, "fuck your job, sunshine. Fuck me!"

I forgot to tell you we were in the hallway right outside the Pilates room, not exactly private.

"You know," I said, "I'd really like to, but I...."

Then I made this high-pitched squealing sound, and the reason I did was that she had moved one hand off my butt and around to the front where she was groping and rubbing. It kind of hurt, but mostly it was like getting your toe stepped on or something unexpected that you didn't know how to react to except by yelling.

"Oh lover," she said, humming in a wet, sloshy way. And she kept going.

Squeaking wasn't going to stop her, so I grabbed her

hand and at the same time twisted away. Trouble was she wasn't set for this and went banging into the wall where I had been, straight into it, leading with her nose, which started to bleed. Even the blood didn't stop her from trying to get to my private parts, so I kept edging backwards. She trudged after me, not fast but steady, as I retreated, trying to think of something to say.

"You're bleeding real bad," I tried.

"Want to lick it, lover, lick up my blood, all my juices?"

"No, I don't," I said, before I thought. That was pretty rude, but she was stalking me like some monster in a horror movie and I was getting scared.

It was hard making her realize that I didn't want to lick anything. Finally, she got the point and seemed to notice that she was bleeding all over her exercise outfit.

"Fucking Christ, kid, did you punch me, you crummy little bastard?"

So much for being her lover.

I beat it over to the next building for the Nia part of my job. I wasn't lying to her about that.

I might as well keep going, since all three days were pretty much the same in the classes, and otherwise too, except for one thing, which I'll get to.

The Nia chief officer, whose name was Kee, also went into the history, but apparently there wasn't any, really, except for this husband and wife team, named Debbie and Carlos Rosas, who thought up the name. It means "with purpose" in Swahili, but it also means "neuromuscular integrative action," if you go by the initials.

She talked a lot, did Kee, but it was similar to the Pilates pitch, this time about how Nia brings people inside themselves. The one big difference I could see was that we were barefoot. Kee said, "Just being barefoot you become more sensitive to your deep energy and your own spiritual space." Tyler made a vomiting motion, pretending to stick her finger down her throat. I agreed with her.

Kee went on: "The body doesn't operate in isolation from the rest of our being, which means that cooperation leads to liberation. All our natural ordering energies get liberated when Nia takes over completely, freely. If the emotions that come bubbling up aren't happy, then that's just what happens. Nia is a place for anger as well as joy, things you simply *do not find* in other fitness programs."

The exercises were okay. Like Pilates, they weren't hard, though this time there was nothing about bones. I liked Pilates better, but I've never been fond of being barefoot. I think it's because my grandmother's sister — what relation's that to me? — lived on a farm and made a big deal out of kids going barefoot because — something about being in the country.

She had chickens everywhere, in the yard, on the porch. You do the equation. Plus she kept bees. But it was chickens put me off for life from enjoying barefoot. True, there were no chickens here in the Nia room, but the principle was the same.

It was complicated, actually, for all the talk about relaxing. They played music real loud; Kee said we'd "work and dance" to the "driving sounds of African and Indian beats." She kept yelling at us to find what was locked inside and let it out. "Beautiful! Beautiful!" she screamed. I doubt that it was beautiful. For sure, I wasn't. First off, there were fifty-two moves, each taking inspiration from any of the nine basic movement forms. Not very relaxing, as I didn't even know what a "basic movement form" was.

The third group was yoga. I thought it was painful, only for the double-jointed; and it was also the most "inward" of all three. Two strikes against it. The meditation seemed softer than my mom's version. Still, it was gooey. You know how Tyler would react: "KFC spirituality." The leader talked about how ancient it was. "So's astrology," Tyler hissed; "so is fucking camels under a full moon to cure warts." The leader was nice, spoke in a whisper, quite unlike the Nia cheerleader.

After a day of this and healthy low-fat food, the place got pretty boring. Our cabin was luxurious, but there wasn't much to do in it. We hadn't brought any games from the camper, so Tyler begged a deck of cards from our friend, who snuck them to her as if it'd been smack. I guess you were supposed to spend free time doing push-ups, exploring your insides. There was a swimming pool, and Tyler and I went a few times. It was crowded, though, and the spiritual guests kept talking to us, friendly but making us uncomfortable, as I, at least, had no idea what they were talking about. I don't really have much of a spiritual life, to tell the truth.

We also played tennis twice, but Tyler was so much better than me it wasn't a lot of fun. For no reason I could think of, she was nice about it, saying things like, "Wendell, you aren't bad, just stroke the ball instead of whacking at it." Or "You're doing better keeping your wrist stiff, only don't forget." Or "Don't get so close to the ball, Wendell; you get bound up with your racket and elbows." Maybe she was just anxious to have somebody to play with and didn't want to go at it with one of the other guests, who'd be sure to ask her about the progress of her meditations.

When we weren't in classes, we were mostly reading or playing cards. Our front-office friend bent the rules, went out and bought us Cokes and microwave double-butter popcorn the second day. We invited him to come play cards with us, and he looked pleased; but he said he wasn't supposed to fraternize with the guests. Anyhow, the set he gave us had rules for different games, which allowed us to discover cribbage. It required a board with pegs on it, but we didn't have one, so we kept track on paper. When we're released from this place, I'm going to find one of those boards to buy. We were pretty evenly matched too. I won about a third of the games and am getting better.

Just as we were having a real good time, Tyler started in on me again.

"Wendell, are you gay?"

"Why?"

"No need to be ashamed."

"I didn't say I was ashamed. Why do you want to know? Are you?"

"Thought about it. Not. Are you?"

I should have said I wasn't or I was and maybe she'd have shut up, but I didn't: "That's pretty personal, Tyler. Anyhow, you know, it's not like I...."

"What the hell are you saying, stumble-butt? Gotcha, didn't I? Confusion about own sexuality. Covered that in Sex Ed. Were you absent that day? Watching gay porn?"

"Tyler, I...."

"Maybe you should meditate on it, Wendell. Ask your inner spirit. Ammmmm Ayyyyeeee Gayyyyyeeeeee? Commune, you know, like they say. Burrow inwards." She was laughing and having a good time. I wasn't.

"Yes, I'm gay, Tyler, okay?"

"Really? Who you fucking?"

"I didn't say that."

"That's true. I didn't mean to be personal and prying, Wendell. After all, it's your own business. It's private. I hope I didn't hurt you."

"Nah, you didn't hurt me."

"Good. So who you fucking?"

That went on for a while, her winning and me losing. Then a lapse. Then she started in on my underwear.

"Fifteen-twelve, fifteen-fourteen, and two is sixteen. So, Wendell, do you even own boxers? I notice you wear whitey-tighties every day."

"How do you know?"

"I peek."

"Really?"

"God, Wendell, we live in the same ten-foot-square place. Of course I know."

"I don't know about yours."

"My what?"

"Yours."

"You can't even say the name?"

"Tyler, what's it matter?"

"It's very important, Wendell. Do you think you can ever amount to anything in this world wearing briefs like a preschooler?"

"Very funny."

"Besides, it squeezes your sperm-makers, means you can't have babies."

"Very funny." Actually, I'd heard that about sperm. Wonder if it was true.

"You know what you should wear for maximum health, Wendell? This isn't a matter of fashion but an issue vital for your future and that of the woman you marry, if you decide you can stand women."

"Can we talk about something else?"

"You mean you want to talk about *MY* panties? You like mine better than yours? I saw you handling them."

I was trying not to cry. I know it was ridiculous, worse than that. I hated myself for it. I knew she'd stop if I'd joke about it, but I couldn't.

"Here's the secret to long-lasting health, Wendell. Go commando!"

I tried to say something like "I will if you will," but I didn't. I know that sounds sexy, but it's not sexy when you've just found out you're a stupid fucking pig.

* * *

This three-day stay was fast-paced fun, from morning granola (soy milk too) to a good night cup of Sleepy Time herb tea. Wendell and I were reduced to playing cribbage and conversing. Conversing with Wendell wasn't quite like talking to a hamster. Hamsters don't have such micro-sensitive feelings. But it passed, the three days, and we wrote our reports and filled in the astonishingly detailed evaluation forms.

We worked on them separately and came out with almost the same scores. If you can imagine anything more dispiriting than discovering that your views, tastes, spiritual capacities match up with Wendell's, tell me. I won't explain the numbers, since I didn't understand them. Here's our totals, higher is better:

Pilates —
My total was 1,427; Wendell's was 1,336

Nia —
My total was 631; Wendell's was 580

Yoga —
My total was 404; Wendell's was 146

The worst part was that Wendell had an even lower tolerance for spiritual flowering and psychic rumination than I. We both liked the yoga instructor, but Wendell hated the meditation.

True, he also said the yoga exercises "hurt," but he detests what one of these instructors called "the noumenal world." It's the one bit of claptrap that doesn't capture Wendell, makes him very nearly impolite.

They were kind to us at Rancho La Rancho, though my own view, Wendell's too, is that they're none too bright. Why else would they want our opinion? We sure didn't represent their usual clients.

As we talked about it, me and Wendell, it struck us — to be fair, it struck Wendell — that they didn't want our opinion at all, that Orville Overeater at the front desk had got us this cushy job cause he liked us. That's pretty touching, unless he was a pedophile, Wendell being an ideal target. But it wasn't like he was hanging around us. Apart from hitting him up for junk food and cards, we didn't see him. Poor guy. We could have made him some hot porno movies. All he had to do was ask.

So, bye-bye Rancho la Rancho!

Friday — Jacumba

Day 9

It was Wendell's turn to drive. Whose turn it was didn't matter, but I figured his manhood needed a boost after all that about undies and sperm — my usual meanness. I don't know what it was about Wendell made me want to vivisect him. Maybe he was a fake. I don't really think so, but so what anyhow? As we learned in Mr. Glendon's class, another name for faking is surviving. I liked that, what he said about there being no genuine self, just a lot of roles. He said an "authentic" person was one with many scripts, good at switching among them. Wendell didn't have but the one script. And it's pretty much the same with me, as you were about to remark.

Driving east a little ways brought us to Jacumba. I was occupying myself not paying attention. Wendell drove sensibly, irritating if you noticed.

Just a little ways past Jacumba — we'd looked it up on the Internet — was a casino they wouldn't let us into, not believing our IDs. It was an Indian casino too, and we were ready to lose big money just because it *was*. Make up for Sand Creek. So we went a ways beyond to a place called Desert View Tower.

The Tower itself is not what you'd call magnificent, but it's cheap to climb, two bucks, and it does what it says, lets you view the desert. They had a museum, something for everybody, especially if you could work up interest in how the tower was built, step-by-step. I couldn't myself, but it was impossible to be here and not to find out just how this wonder was created sometime in the 1920s: photos of every stage.

The Tower was made out of local rocks and stands as a testament to one man's stick-to-it-iveness in service of a truly dumb idea. No helpers. Didn't want 'em, though he probably didn't have to beat away volunteers. Lonely old loony, following his dream. Like the ads thrown at inner-city kids: don't let anybody rob you of your dreams! What a bunch of pacifying shit. Like Jesus for slaves.

Where was I? I hate people who lose the thread of their monologues. Teachers do that; it's one of the requirements for the job. Which brings us back to Desert View Tower, brought into being by one human all by himself. Bert Vaughan, a man of means, according to the placard, who outright owned the town of Jacumba. Jacumba may not be much, but owning a town is not in the cards for everybody. Mr. Vaughan deserved a lasting monument, even if he did put it up himself. Speaking for posterity, I'm glad he did.

As I say, the museum wasn't quite as impressive as the view, which was drab. There were things stuck on walls you couldn't help but look at as you climbed, designed to keep you distracted from the grunting work: pictures of pioneer days and astronauts. Overall, I can't remember being so interested since the time my dad got it in his head I was mechanical — "She's very handy, Taneesha; she really is!" — and forced me to endure an explanation of how a toilet worked, wherein he overflowed the tank, broke the stem holding the floating ball, drenched his good shoes, and said "Fuck." It was the first time I'd heard it, but I knew not to ask what it meant, just took my word of the day to kindergarten, with predictable results and lies from my parents: "I don't know where she would hear such things!" I was easily cowed then, let them get away with it.

Our Desert View Tower tickets also included admission to "Boulder Park," where you encounter giant rocks, some of them carved into human faces, the shapes of lizards, and other desert creatures. Here you can frolic and get sand up your nose. Best, there was a maze made from these rocks, not tricky, just dusty paths winding round and making you stoop, fall, bang yourself pretty good, once you started running. Wendell loved it. You could tell. I could tell, since I did too. There were about ten little kids there with their parents. The parents stood around yelling at them not to get hurt or rip their clothes.

They paid no attention, of course, and were ripping clothes like mad on the rocks and tackling each other on the paths, shrieking like kids do. Wendell joined in with the kids, who started chasing and clinging to him. I started jogging along, when these two little girls, maybe six years old, dropped down real quiet from one of the boulders, jumped me from above. Scared hell out of me, and I was ready to shake them off and yell at them, when I saw their faces and couldn't. So I jiggled them around and rolled them on the ground and soon found myself in this mass of small squirmers.

I caught a glimpse of Wendell and about the same number of kids through an opening. Naturally — naturally for 6-year-olds — my group developed a plan to attack Wendell and his gang by circling round. I think they knew we were coming — we weren't exactly silent — but they pretended not to until we were on them. It was one wild scramble of arms and legs and bellies and bums.

As we writhed there on the ground, ripping more clothes and skinning more knees, I realized I had under me the pieces of some small bodies and the bulk of a slightly bigger one, Wendell's. To be fair, I had no suspicion he had engineered anything of the kind. These kids were little but many and they managed to throw us around pretty good, by way of tripping and clinging.

They'd got Wendell down and me on top of him, face-to-face. Just as I realized where I was and where he was, three or four kids lit on my back, forcing my body whamming into his, chest to chest. My nose was mashing right into his until I gathered leverage to scrunch my face to the side a tad. Neither of us could move, so there we were, intimate, faces not a half-inch apart. Being pressed closer by the squirmers, my upper lip slid down over his lower, caught on it. I couldn't see a thing, was aware only of the closeness, his lips and his breath. Seems like we were there forever. I couldn't move; I don't know if I tried. Like being hypnotized. Finally, Wendell started giggling and said, right straight into my gums and teeth, "Tyler, I had no idea!"

I should have spit into him, just letting a little saliva transfer, but I giggled too. Maybe it was the kids: "Oh, Wendell, my angel; I couldn't help myself!"

How we got out of the human snake pile I don't know. We played there in the Boulder Park maze for maybe two hours, honest to Christ. I figured the parents would get mad, but they didn't seem to, even stopped yelling at their kids. It was a good time.

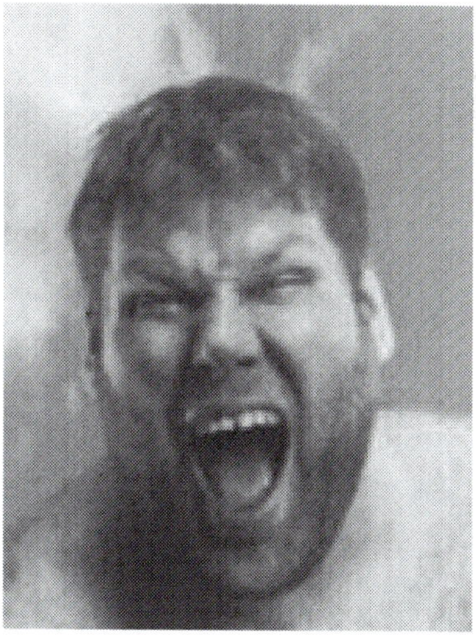

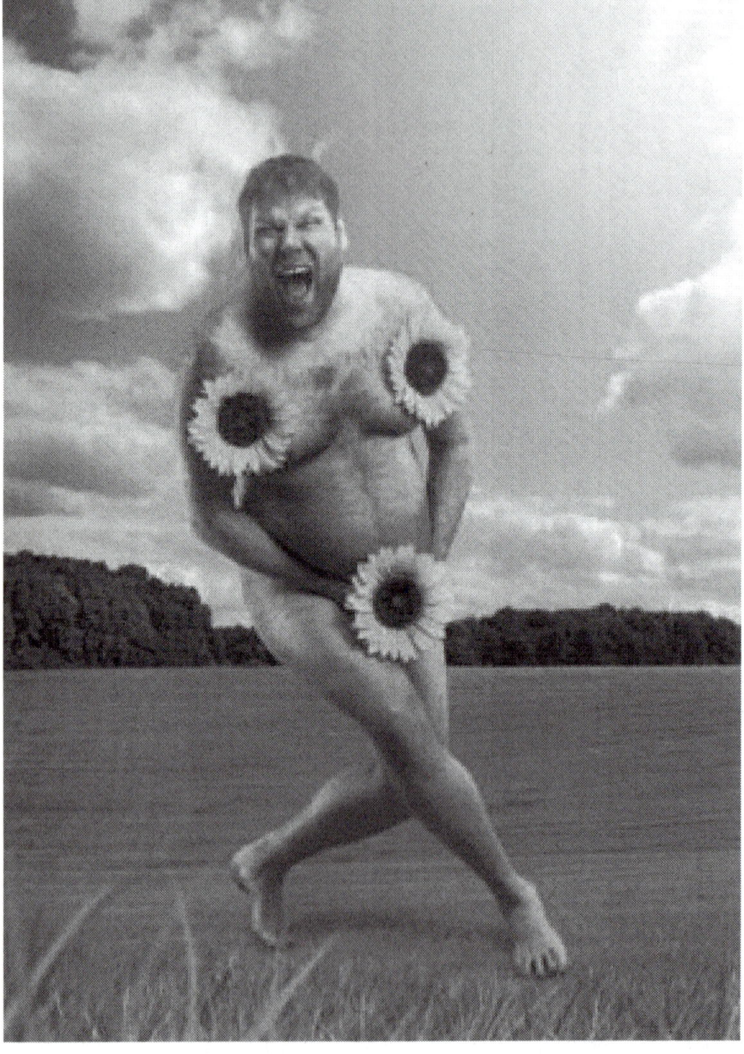

CHAPTER 6

That was as much fun as I've had in I don't know how long. Having Tyler on top of me wasn't bad either, but best of all was the way she made a joke out of it. I even got the idea that she was getting to tolerate me or even like me. Ha! Just as soon as she could, she let me know she didn't.

We were having dinner there in Jacumba, at a place called The China Doll Steak House (I'm not making this up). We were talking about what we were going to do the next day and joking about this place I'll tell you about in a minute. She was all easy, I thought, and I made this mistake of going with that:

"That was really fun back there at Boulder Park."

"I guess." She said it cold, like she didn't want to talk about it. I should have detected that, left it alone.

"Yeah, me too." What a dumb thing to say.

"Look, Wendy, let's move on, okay?"

"Okay."

Now it was her not leaving it alone: "I'm real happy you had fun, Wendell."

"Yeah."

"Found your level, rolling on the ground with Lolitas. Cute little cub scouts too."

"Rolling on the ground with you on top of me, licking on my lip."

"I also stepped in dog shit once. That was about as welcome."

"I was kidding, Tyler."

"Well, don't. You're about as funny as you are appealing."

We were quiet a little bit. What could I say?

"Hey, Wendell, you know what?"

Here we go again. "I'm about as funny as appealing?"

"Don't be hard, pecker. I thought we'd moved on. Live in the present, like those existentialists you love. Here's a close-by institution we can invade. I got us free guest passes too. Free! You hearin' me?"

"I'm up for it. Where is it we get in free?"

"De Anza Springs Resort, not far away, which is only one of its attractions."

"Not far from here, huh? You said that before, Tyler. You're repeating yourself a lot lately. I'm having this effect on you. You're getting to be just like me."

Another time I wanted to swallow words I'd just spit out. Tyler looked like she might smile, which was so unlikely I hurried on:

"Danza Springs, huh? Sounds like another spa. Pilates and yoga? Meditating?"

"De Anza Springs Resort, altogether different from Le Rancho Rancho. Here's their slogan: 'You'll Love the Way You Feel! We Guarantee It!' That give you a clue?"

"Massage parlor? Sports camp?"

"That's a small part, massage with a certified massage therapist. But more."

"Horses?"

"No, I don't think so. Just humans, very special humans."

"Freaks? Acrobats? Circus people? The winter camp of a circus!"

"It's June, Wendell. Let's try a different line of inquiry: over 500 acres; elevation 2600 feet; RV hookups including one for us; a clubhouse with dancing and a game room; volleyball; Ping Pong; tennis courts, brand new; exercise room but no Pilates; swimming pool; horseshoes; children's play area; and clothing optional."

"Uh-huh," I said.

"I must confess, Wendell, you're cool about it. Okay. Here's your coupon, which counts for me too, good for four people. Anybody you want to invite along?"

"Clothing optional?"

"Meaning you have a choice in that department."

"A nudist camp?"

"Optionally. What'll your choice be, Wendell?"

"Oh."

Saturday — Jacumba to De Anza Springs Resort

Day 10

The first thing we saw was some hairy guy's testicles, an old guy. I thought they'd have an office in the front, keep the naked people behind a hedge. We climbed these steps, looked up, and there they were, right between his spread legs. Hard not to fix on them. He was sitting beside this desk, so that we advanced upwards right into — you get the idea.

Tyler was a little behind me, but she saw. Nobody could miss it, and besides I heard her smirk.

"Welcome, young friends!" He had one of the kindliest voices I'd ever heard. The building was sort of a hut, but everything behind it in the camp looked nice.

"Hi, sir," I answered, after waiting for Tyler to say something, which she didn't.

"Are you here to see our resort? Well, isn't that a dumb question! Sorry. I lost my job at the Ritz-Carleton for asking such questions."

Tyler laughed, so I did too. Lame joke, but talking-testicles seemed friendly. I was very nervous, naturally — get it — "naturally"?

"I guess we'd like to, yeah, see your resort, maybe rent a place for our camper, a hook-up? Can we do that?"

"We'd be so happy if you did, young beauty-contest winners. No offense. We tend to be chummy here, but we mean nothing by it. I think it goes with nudism."

He chuckled, but looked closely at us. I think he wanted to be sure we got the point about nudism. Like his own balls didn't announce that pretty clear.

"We have this pass from the internet," Tyler said, "but I'm not sure you honor them. We don't mind paying."

"I don't know nothing about no passes. Just by entering the grounds, you owe me $300 dollars. Volleyball is $200 dollars extra."

"What?" I said. Tyler laughed, though; and the guy laughed too, bending over in the process, thereby hiding his privates and giving us some relief.

"Coupons are fine: Dominos Pizza, Dr. Scholl's. Don't worry about admission. I just hope you enjoy yourself and I think you will. We don't have a lot of guests right now just at your age. Several families, but their kids are mostly young, not old grizzled veterans like you." He really amused himself, this guy.

I was dying to find out whether we could hang out in our clothes, but that's not the sort of thing you ask. I wasn't going to take much off, no matter what. If I got kicked off the shuffleboard court, hooted at and ridiculed, so be it.

"I imagine you'd like to look around on your own, but I can get a guide if you'd prefer," he said, handing Tyler a map of the grounds. Tyler just cuddled in with him over the map, asking questions and laughing, like they were in on something together, old friends sharing a yogurt.

"Where'll we go, Tyler?" I waited until we were a little away from the hut.

"Maybe we should go back, hook-up our rig and dress, Wendy. How about that?"

We did just that. Tyler was inside while I puttered with the hoses, wondering whether she'd come out naked. Wish there were some way she could and I wouldn't have to. But that'd be almost as embarrassing as me doing it.

She emerged with old clothes on, jeans, and a loose shirt.

"We going swimming, Tyler?"

Before she could ridicule me, I said, "I figured you put your suit on underneath."

She stared at me.

"How about horseshoes, Tyler? I'll bet you're an expert, a fucking champeen."

I wanted to ask about the clothes and whether they had rules. I should have asked hairy balls, since he'd have been nice about it, which Tyler wouldn't. What she said was, "I don't mind horseshoes, Wendell. You know, though, I wish you wouldn't use the 'F' word. I do, I know; but I wish you wouldn't. I don't know why. Okay?"

"Okay."

There were five horseshoe courts. One was open. The others had naked people worming around them, flopping and wobbling. Most of the people were as old as the camp guide. No kids our age. I noticed that because I looked. There were four or five kids younger than us, maybe twelve or thirteen, I would say. Not like I examined them closely or anything, yes I did, but not in an intrusive way.

"You know how to play, Tyler?"

"No, but you do."

I did, but I thought a second before admitting it.

"Can we play with you guys?"

This from two young kids, blond kids, naked kids, boy and girl — came up easy, like they weren't aware they'd put no clothes on.

"Sure. You can teach us how to throw these things, at what and why. I'm Tyler. This is my traveling companion, who goes by the name of Wendell, not his real name."

The kids seemed to think that was funny and shook hands with me. So we split up to play, me and the girl against Tyler and the boy. The boy looked like a younger version of Sean 2, and the girl was just as pretty.

"Are you and Mike brother and sister, Jennifer?"

"Cousins, Wendell. We've been coming here since we were little. It's fun. They have volleyball and two pools and good video games in the clubhouse. Do you like it?"

"Well, sure. We've only been here maybe an hour."

"There's hiking too."

"That's nice. Do you—?" I stumbled, gargled, and got all red.

She laughed but it wasn't mean. "You mean nudism. I know. It seems weird."

"No, no. I don't mean that it's weird."

She looked at me like she knew I was lying but wasn't going to say so. "You can keep your clothes on, if you want. You just be comfortable. It doesn't matter. Really."

Then we had to throw, she pretty well and me not so very, but better than Tyler, nyah nyah.

After a minute, I said the dumbest thing yet. "Jennifer, don't all these people walking around — you know — nude and all, don't they..."

"Have sex?"

"No, no. Not that."

"Want to have sex?"

"I'm sorry, Jennifer. That's a terrible thing to ask."

"No it's not, Wendell, but I don't know the answer. You should ask Mike. He thinks everybody being nude all the time isn't sexy, messes people up. He thinks nobody'd want to have sex if they stayed here long enough."

I was fascinated but should have kept quiet. I didn't: "Do you think that?"

"No."

She smiled and I found myself having to pretend to be as sophisticated as she was.

I sort of saw what Mike meant. Maybe after years you might lose interest. Maybe Mike meant sex between people like hairy balls and some of the ladies, all sinky and saggy. I played this game in my head of pretending these women had clothes on. When I worked at it, I could see them in dresses and gowns and they looked much better. They didn't look sexy, but maybe if I kept at imagining they would.

When we switched partners and I had Mike with me, I asked him and found out what he meant, which was what I thought. Mike had a foul mouth, demonstrating that all nudists are not pure spiritual beings: "Fuck, Wendell, those baggy-asses could never do it after they expose their secrets day after day. The only way they can get it on is to pretend like hell, go at it in the dark with their eyes closed. They got to imagine there's something worth getting to. There isn't. And now they see it, right there — garbage."

"But...."

"Yeah, but it's different with others, some others." He winked at me.

"You mean like Tyler."

"Shhh. Yeah, like Tyler, your hot girlfriend. Don't be pissed, man. I'm just saying, man; don't be pissed." He talked like we were equals, which was flattering, though he was about two years younger.

"I'm not upset, Mike. She's not my girlfriend." He was looking at me with concern, his face wrinkled up in anxiety, worried that he'd offended me.

Mike was good at horseshoes and we started to win. Finally a break, so Mike and I could go get Cokes, which seemed to be free of charge. Tyler waved to me, in a way a stranger would think was friendly. She let me know with her eyes and shoulders she was going to stay with Jennifer. They were having a good time, I could tell, and that surprised me. Jennifer was a great kid, but Tyler was a mean bitch. Still, there they were.

"Next week is National Nude Dude Ranch Rodeo Week here, Wendell. You don't want to miss that."

"They have a rodeo? That's hard to imagine."

"I never seen it, but they do. I'm thinking what you're thinking. Riding a bucking bronco, roping calves in the nude. All those mashed balls."

"You're right — just what I was thinking."

"You and I are fucking a lot alike, Wendell. You play tennis?"

"Not as well as you."

"It's called 'Tennis Naturally' here. Ain't that cute?"

"It's adorable, Mike."

"Like me."

"You're about as adorable as that hairy guy at the front desk."

"You know, Wendell, the reason people aren't pawing one another, not even me — or you or even Tyler — isn't just because they see too much. We four ain't blubby or hairy. There's others. I think it's more that people turn off being like that here, like a switch. They stop being horny in that sneaky way. Not just because nobody wants to fuck either. I think there's nicer people here. You know what I mean? I think it's more that they just wouldn't hurt anybody, you know?"

"I think so."

"It's like people who run around naked have more respect."

"That's what they say on their brochure."

"But it's true, lame as it is. Funny thing, these wackos without clothes are not as messed-up as people all covered up. Don't tell anybody I said that!"

"Nature's way."

"That's just what it fucking ain't, Wendell. They want you to think taking off your clothes makes you natural, but I think it's just the opposite."

"Really?"

"Here's what I mean. They talk in the brochures like people were getting back to nature here, like waving your pecker and bobbing your tits would let you get rid of the social shit and let you be what God intended, down inside. But it seems to me there's nothing very natural about humans running around naked. Just think about it. In nature, you'd freeze and burn and not last very long if you was naked, except maybe in California. So how the fuck's that natural? Sorry."

"Talk the way you like."

"What I think is that these people who take off their clothes are doing what goes against nature and that makes them more kind, not more real but thoughtful about other people, respectful. It's like they were walking through a hospital filled with little kids, without any defenses, and would die if you did the wrong thing. That about the hospital I didn't just think up. I thought about it before. Loud assholes get quiet when they get nude. People seem more careful, or try to be. Not everybody. I guess some people are screwed up and some are pervs, like you and Taylor."

"Tyler. She's not a perv, just me."

"Oh you, yeah!"

We stayed with our friends all day. We played tennis, me and Tyler on the same side, not dressed "naturally," took a hike, played putt-putt; in between, we had lunch, less organic than at the spa. About five, Jennifer said it was time for swimming. Nobody seemed to care that Tyler and I were non-nude, but somehow swimming brought the issue up again. Swimming is different from tennis. It's not so unusual to skinny-dip. I hadn't ever done it, of course, but lots of people did. I don't know how to explain it, but wearing a bathing suit seemed insulting to this place that had been so nice to us. I wish I could ask Tyler her view, but instead I asked Jennifer.

"Do anything you want. You don't seem to want to be nude? That's fine."

"Yeah, sure; but what will people think?"

"They'll think you decided to be comfortable."

"Nah, people'll be so anxious to see my butt, they'd pull my bathing suit down."

"Nobody wants to see your butt, Wendell."

"You wouldn't say that if you knew what you were missing. I won third prize at the county fair, butt competition, eighteen-and-under."

"So, you're gonna swim nude?"

"I don't think so."

Back at our super-camper, Tyler and I got into our suits. I liked seeing Tyler in her suit, and really wanted to, even more than I was scared to show that I wanted to. I was so curious I turned around too fast. She still had the suit around her ankles, getting it on, facing me, looking me in the eyes. She pulled the suit up, not super-fast, just like I hadn't been there. Then she grabbed two towels, threw one to me, and went out the door.

* * *

Fucking pervert, scoptophilic pervert! Almost worth having Wendell gawk at me so I could recall that word. I was surprised I didn't much care. Having Wendell see you naked was a little like having the family cat watch you take a shower.

As we were walking along to meet our friends, I wondered why I had a suit on at all. Or Wendell either, despite his pathology. It was making a prudish display, us being the only ones hiding our treasures. We were being geeks together. Also, if I didn't mind Wendell staring at me, why was I worried about Mike and Jenny, much less some very friendly, if half-witted other nudists here at the camp? Maybe I wasn't worried. Maybe it was Wendell taking charge. Jesus!

"Tyler!"

It was Mike, looking so much like his cousin that one generally had to check lower down to see which was which. Odd thing now was he had a suit on, probably in deference to me and Wendell. Wasn't much of a suit, though, and he wore it extremely low.

Before long, we were in the pool, separated by genders,

with Mike and Wendell playing together like 4-year-olds, splashing around and forcing me and Jenny (also in a bathing suit) to play kiddie games against our will — and have a great time.

At a break in the jollies, Wendell sidled up to me — I thought he might be going to make physical contact, but he didn't, just said, "Anyhow, Tyler, what do you think of inviting Mike and Jenny over for supper? It'd be a break for them from the usual stuff. But maybe you don't want to, which would be okay. Not important."

"Good idea. Let's do it. You want me to go ask their parents or aunts or however they're being chaperoned?"

"First the kids."

"No need. They'll come."

And they did. Wendell made chicken piccata, chicken breasts he pounded flat, along with capers and lemons and about six pounds of butter, with pasta and broiled tomatoes with Parmesan cheese on top. We had strawberry soup to start and these meringue things with ice cream in them after. The meringues we had bought before, though Wendell knew how to make them from scratch. We just didn't have time to do that.

The strawberry soup had sour cream and toasted almonds on it, and a sprig of mint. Prissy? Truth, I found it pretty and it tasted fantastic. We'd bought this wine too. I guess it was okay, though the single thing hun-bun and I had in common was complete ignorance about wine. We'd taken the word of the liquor store guy, who didn't question our IDs and therefore probably knew about as much as we did.

Both Jenny and Mike had dressed up. We'd shoved dinner right at them, since we didn't have any *hors d'oeuvres* what would go with our fancy-assed meal. Wendell and I had been trying out cocktails in the evening. They tasted like shit, actually. I guess going alphabetically through the bartender's guide wasn't the best way: amaretto, anisette, apple brandy. Maybe things would pick up when we got to bourbon.

Back to the dinner. Jenny and Mike came bustling in all excited. We had our table fancied up with our good dishes. The kids didn't faint before our grandeur, went after the soup ravenously, making great yummy noises.

"What's in this fucking soup? Jesus, I never tasted soup like this."

"Mike!" Jenny said, only half-shocked.

"Oh, sorry. Tyler, I'm sorry."

"You ain't apologizing to me, peanut-penis? I'm the cook here!" I was surprised to hear Wendell use the 'P' word. This kid Mike was a good influence, not that I wanted Wendell potty-mouthed.

After that, it was all downhill, great fun. The squirts loved the food and didn't drink much wine, sipped it a little. I don't know if they didn't like it, were worried about the reaction of the grown-ups they were with, or liked it fine and didn't want to get silly.

It was getting pretty late for them, past eleven. We were telling cornball jokes, in between playing charades, probably the way kids entertained themselves in the eighteenth century. Not bad, if you didn't worry about it being dorky.

"Twister anybody?"

Dickwad Wendell with another game, just when we should be herding these kids to their nest. Were we responsible adults or not? Should have objected but didn't, thrown off course by Jenny's, "You wanta get nude for Twister?"

"Jenny, Wendell and Tyler don't like that. Don't be mean."

"Oh yeah, Mike, you're right. Sorry."

Wendell and I stood there, jaws agape. Nude Twister! Wendell the unlikely saved us and ruined our harmless innocent fun.

"I'd love to play Twister and I'd love to do it nude, but I sort of think you're both too cool for that, if you know what I mean."

What could he possibly mean? I'm sure Wendell didn't know.

"I know what you mean, Wendell, I really do," Jenny chirped right up. "We don't care about nude, Mike and me. Twister is fun, and it's not like we were going to sex each other or anything."

"Sex each other, Jenny?" Mike laughed, "I think we won't ever get to do it and we'll have to live our whole lives as poor deprived kids who never got themselves sexed, even when they played Twister in the raw and hung around nudist camps."

So we played Twister with our clothes, all of them, on.

* * *

It was great. Mike had mumbled to me and Tyler something about playing in our "undies," which made me a little scared, partly because I thought Tyler might want to do it and partly because I thought Tyler might start in on me right in front of these kids. But she didn't and the threat passed. Finally, Tyler said the obvious, that it was really late:

"We'd better get Mike and Jen back, Wendell."

I was ready to protest — what **was** Tyler, their Mom or something? — but the kids didn't object to the idea, so maybe I was the only irresponsible one here.

"Fucking, fucking shit!" Mike said. "Yeah, I guess we should."

"Fucking, fucking shit!" Jenny said, giggling.

"If we don't get you back and show how responsible we are, your adults will never let you hang out with us again." I said it before I thought.

Mike and Jenny lit up. Tyler, who I was looking at, frowned even harder.

Nobody said anything for a minute, standing where they were, frozen. Then Mike whispered, still without moving, "Can we come with you?"

"Just for a while?" Jenny added, right on top of him.

"We could help out. We won't fuck things up. We can be okay": a chorus of this stuff from both of them. Damn!

I see why Tyler had frowned. Here I'd set up little kids to be disappointed, either say yeah and make things worse when Tyler said no, or say no and hurt them myself.

"It really wouldn't work," I said weakly.

"You'd never be allowed," Tyler said, very firmly. "You know that."

"Maybe we would," Jenny said.

"Yeah, maybe," Mike said. "It's Jenny's parents; they're a lot nicer than mine."

"Mike, look at it this way. I'm sure they're nice. They bring you to this super-cool place and let you stay up till — what is it? — past midnight. But Wendell and I are only sixteen — don't tell anybody — and doing all this illegally. You see?"

"No," Mike said.

"Kinda," Jen said.

I was on Mike's side, though I saw what Tyler was saying.

"Also, they don't know us."

She hadn't said a word about how we wanted them to go, but the kids seemed to know it anyhow. They both looked like they might cry, only they wouldn't. But looking at them now made me see what little kids they were.

"I have an idea!" I popped up, just because an idea had sprung up inside me.

Tyler looked as if she'd like to suck my eyeballs out, but she didn't say anything. The kids changed to sunshine immediately.

"Where you kids going from here? I mean, we're leaving tomorrow, but why couldn't we meet up someplace and hang?" It struck me that I had no idea where they might be from or heading. Maybe they flew in from Australia.

"Tucson. We're here two more days, and then to Tucson. Our other aunt and uncle live there, and Brandon and Blake. You'll like Brandon. I don't know about Blake."

"They don't know Brandon or Blake, Jen." Mike wasn't mocking her: too busy watching us, watching Tyler. Pretty good instincts for where the power was located.

Tyler looked skeptical, was figuring things out. Finally, she smiled.

"Tucson's not all that far, right Wendell?"

"It's close."

"Okay, then, Wendell's plan is a good one — or might be. It'll be up to Jen's parents and Mike's — and Billy and Blooper's."

The kids kept saying everybody'd approve, we'd get together in Tucson, and we'd like Brandon, though Blake, who shortly became "Blooper," might be another matter.

It seemed cruel to deny the kids one last game of Twister. A couple of minutes in, there's a knock on our double-steeled, combo-locked door. In came what we figured were Jen's parents, clothed, both of whom seemed about seven feet tall, with huge muscular bodies. Jen's Mom smiled and grabbed a foot, extricating her from the knot and then holding her upside down, wiggling. Jen's Dad did the same with Mike, who was bigger but nothing more than a squirmy minnow upended in the hands of this huge guy.

These hulks soon made it clear they weren't mad about the hour, about the Twister, about the wine (which Jen spilled the beans on). As for the Tucson plans, they immediately vouched for Brandon and Blooper's parents: they'd love to have us! Spend the summer! Move right in! I'd sure never seen anything like them for being loose, and all along I had thought my mom was careless and hippie.

* * *

Wendell and I talked some after the giants left. It had all been a little dazzling, like Alice down the rabbit-hole. These goons had invited us to come and play in Tucson. Wasn't clear when we were going, when they were going to be there themselves, how long we'd stay, even if these particular overgrowns would be there. The next-to-last point was clearest: Wendell had said "two-three days," the figure emerging from his babble reservoir.

Accidentally, it did seem like a sensible duration, so it came to be accepted. We exchanged phone numbers and said we'd set up the exact meeting time "right away," whatever that meant.

As the seven-footers left, crouching low to get out of what we'd thought was our high doorway, Mrs. Giant turned round and told us to be sure and wear our BVDs there in Tucson since "Mary and Lou" didn't go in for the "naturist style."

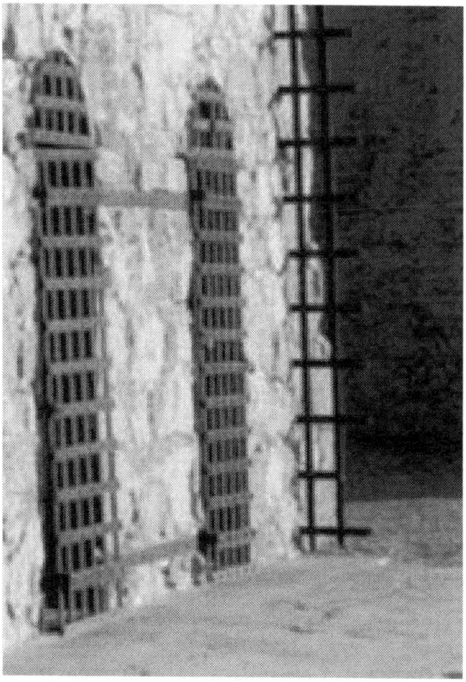

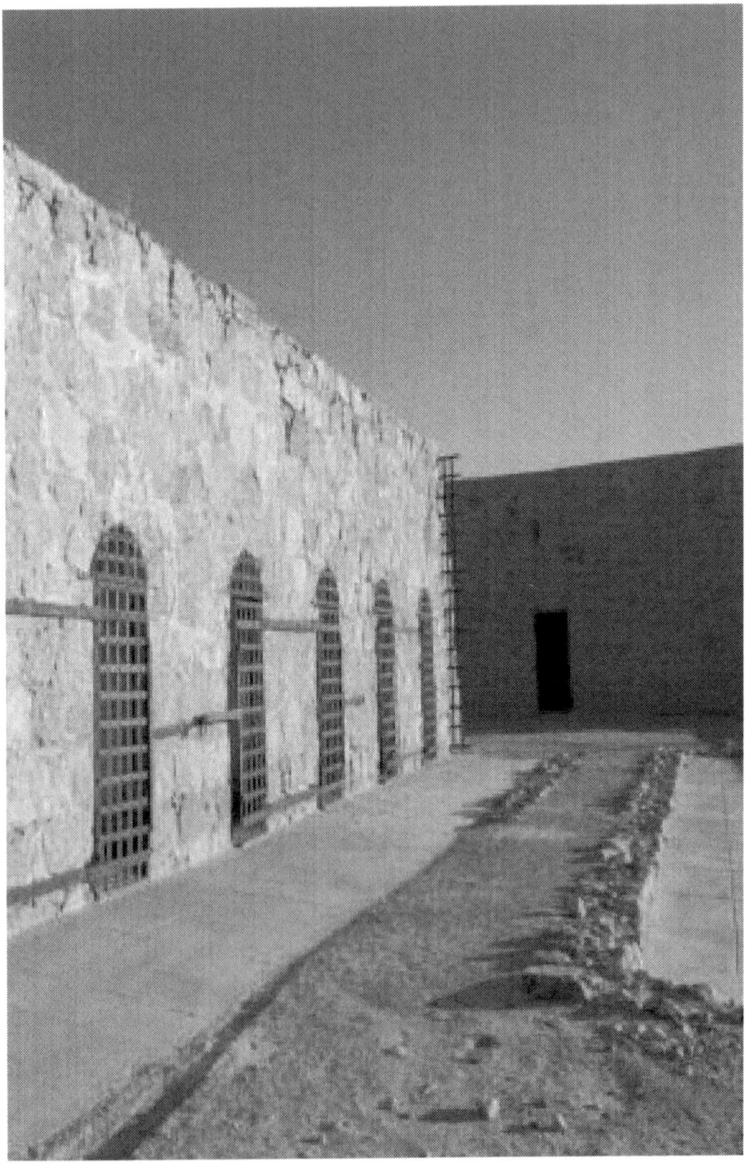

CHAPTER 7

Sunday — El Centro/Felicity

Day 11

Next morning we waved good-bye to the friendly naked folk and drove a few miles to El Centro, whose web site declared it to be "one of Southern California's most promising new commercial and industrial regions." And I am "one of the world's most promising pianists." Who's to argue? Turns out the place existed only because water from someplace let them grow dates. We stopped for breakfast at Millie's, which the guidebook, one of forty-odd we had, recommended as "a popular truck stop cafe," which it sure was. Always trust them guidebooks.

While we were drinking our fourth glass of juice — Millie's, unlike any place I'd ever been, gave us free juice refills — the waitress suggested we hop on over to Felicity and catch the late morning services at "The Church on the Hill."

That was loony enough to be in our line and it was eastward, our general direction, so to Felicity we went. Felicity had escaped urban sprawl, so it was easy to find the hill in question and the church on it. Before we ascended, we tarried below, examining a structure, which the sign said, and Wendell verified, was a section of the original Eiffel Tower. It was a staircase to the sky, ending at nothing. Up twenty-five feet, according to the placard, soared this iron monster, weighing in at over three tons and moved here at great expense over the oceans in 1989, only three years after the town was founded. Truth is I have no idea (which means Wendell doesn't) why anybody gathered the staircase and other similar shit here, but I do know who did it, or can at least pass on the misinformation: Jacques-Andre Istel, who came from, you see, France, in Europe.

We had read that the official population of the town was "Two," though that census was taken a decade ago, and the figure may have edged slightly in one direction or the other.

The gift shop, which provided the center for much (all) of the town's activity and employed half its inhabitants, offered many things you couldn't find elsewhere. For instance, they made it possible for you to engrave a name on a handsome "Wall for the Ages," a low pyramid, with a good many names already emblazoned, dedicated to forever and lasting that long.

As it cost $50 bucks (covering engraving and a certificate), we passed. Part of our seasoning involves learning the value of money. Wendell said we should engrave Martin's name for the ages, which was nice of Wendell, a guy who never ran short of nice. I figured Martin would rather have a cd or a visit from Wendell.

The Gift Shoppe also sold even more certificates, bumper stickers, pins, and T-shirts saying, "I Stood At The Official Center of the World." That's what this was, Felicity, the verified (self-proclaimed) center of the world. Some T-shirts had the latitude and longitude printed, just to win over skeptics: 114 degrees, 45 feet, 55.35 inches and 32 degrees, 45 feet and 1.38 inches. That's the Center, established by God.

There were letters of congratulations from several Frog dignitaries, President Reagan the subnormal prickster, House Speaker Tip O'Neil, and some US Army thugs. Also some tongue-in-cheek telegrams. A guy at Princeton's Institute for Advanced Study wrote, "You have beaten us all to the ultimate idea." The Chairman of the Federal Reserve System: "I thought I was at the center of the world, now you have disillusioned me." Fine, though the Federal Reserve Chairman ought to learn how to use semi-colons. The best was Ed Koch, mayor of New York City: "Nothing to rival Felicity's truly breathtaking ascension to the Center of the World." Only one of these telegrams was moronic, and it was from, you guessed it, a religious nitwit, Cardinal O'Connor, Archbishop of New York, who got his hands out from under the robes of the choirboys long enough to write, "Be assured of my prayerful best wishes that Felicity may continue to prosper." As the prosperity of the town depended on bilking the public, offering nothing in return, I guess the Archbishop recognized an ally.

One thing more at the gift shop, available only here at The Core, was Felicity perfume, named, said the clerk, for the mayor's wife. The mayor, already identified, had named the town for this wife, Felicity, said the confident woman hawking the perfume, perhaps the very Felicity in question. We hadn't asked, feeling we had a mystery on our hands that needed sustaining. You see, this woman, perhaps, as I say, the Felicity in question, or the wife of another man, or the true founder's wife with a different name, *if there was a wife*, told us a naming story completely at odds with the information that Wendell had gathered and for which he had solid Wikipedia evidence.

According to this source, this town was named for a fictional city that Jacques-Andre Istel, the founder, had concocted for a children's book he had written long ago, *Coe the Good Dragon.* All was wonky confusion. We had contrasting origin stories, just like Evolution v. Creationism. Which was it? Wise people ask no questions. Wendell isn't wise, but I silenced him.

Turns out The Church on the Hill wasn't saving souls that morning, maybe because the population of Felicity (both) converted to a different superstition. I thought at first these apostates had been directed toward a new spot by another artifact on the site imported straight from Europe, a bronze reproduction of Michelangelo's "Finger of God," a finger which does indeed point, insistently, only not anywhere in particular.

Maybe it *should* direct one toward the Church, but it doesn't. Wendell and I tried to follow where the finger was urging us, but we ended up in empty space, which Felicity has a lot of. I told Wendell to sit on the finger, let it penetrate him, and I'd commemorate the moment on film. Didn't get a rise out of him. (I'm aware of the pun.) This Church on the Hill was erected in 1996 on the highest point in town, three feet above the lowest, named then "The Hill of Prayer."

We didn't see anybody around, but there was so much here it was hard to believe that but two people called it home. The internet it was gave us the figure of two, but that was in December 1987, when the Post Office opened, an occasion highlighted by a speech from the Consul of The People's Republic of China, whose name, we found out, was Zhou. Probably still is Zhou. But why would he travel to Felicity? Was the mystery wife perhaps a Chinese Empress? Was Zhou the world's leading expert on the planet's center, brought here expressly to authenticate?

"Let's go see this church, even if it has shut its doors to us!" exclaimed Wendell.

The church was a replica of a house of God in France, said the sign, a French church which must have been a lumpy cement thing, judging by its faithful copy.

"Do you boys seek to worship the Lord?"

We both jumped. Somehow, a lanky desert dweller had crept close behind us.

"Jesus Christ almighty, prickface! How'd you sneak up on us? Damn you!"

He smiled beatifically: "Come with me, boys, oh yes!"

"You putrid asshole! Who you calling boys?"

"God tells me you are looking for a place to worship."

"Sorry to yell at you but you scared the living hell out of me."

"Are you looking for a place to worship?"

Was it a man or a recording?

"Maybe," Wendell said.

"Yes," I said.

Long and short of it, we ended up backtracking about eight or nine miles to a place where we could worship. Our seeker of lost souls followed us in a pickup.

Neither of us saw a thing resembling a church, but the truck behind started honking, the toothless yokel accompanying the honks with waving arms and screams: "Right up thayur, on yer lift, turn lift!"

So we did. Into a dirt road leading nowhere we could see. Wendell slowed down a bit, only to activate more yelling: "Jist keep on, right up ahid, boys!"

The road ran out before the oddest house I've ever seen. It had what looked like six sides, for one thing, not additions like most places but some kind of hexagon. Painted, not too recently, a very shiny black without any relief, no trim or anything. There were wooden animals, also shiny black, stuck all over the lawn, in place of grass. Also, the obligatory seventeen dogs, a mule or something of the sort that I first thought was stuffed but then moved a little, three or four small, wide-eyed, scared-looking kids, no trees or shrubs, and no sign of a place of worship.

"Let's get out of here!" I realized I was hissing, not because there was some need for quiet but because a need to be scared was clamping in on my vocal chords.

"His truck's right up against us, Tyler. Sorry. Leave it to me."

That scared me even more, putting myself in the hands of Wendell.

We sat there, maybe thinking we'd lock ourselves in the camper and steam to death. But we didn't. The Texas

Chainsaw dick knocked on the window, smiled what actually wasn't a toothless grin, and we got out.

"Welcome, Children of God!"

"Thanks," chirped Wendell. "But we thought you were taking us to Church."

"Oh yes, praise the Lord, oh yes. Right into the lap of the Lord."

"That where we are?"

"Oh yes, children, please come in."

"Where?" I choked out.

"Into the hall of worship. You lead the way."

As there was only one door, painted white at some ancient time but now mostly black peels, we didn't have much choice. I thought of yelling for help, but the forlorn kids, the stick figures, the dog pack, and the mule-thing didn't offer much hope. Our guide stayed close behind us, too close. I could tell Wendell was with me on this, knew something was wrong. We both wondered later, but only later, why we didn't run.

This sure as fuck was no church.

We stepped through the door and into an unfurnished room. The door shut behind us, too fast and too loud.

"You just go through there and down them steps." The voice wasn't loud or threatening, which seemed to make it more frightening.

Wendell stepped aside so I could go first. I didn't understand for a second, but then realized he wanted to put himself between me and this guy. For some reason, I let my mind go blank, which was damned easy, scared as I was. Never been so scared, just slid into this blankness, letting Wendell think for both of us.

The guy herding us was smiling in a way one might at first mistake as kindly. We had. It now looked demented, especially when it was attached to such a big body. I hadn't noticed that before.

There was a terrible smell to the place, and it got worse as we got to the stairs.

"Look, Mister, I know you mean well, but we're leaving. I'm sorry, but we're not going down there."

Before he quite got the "there" out, Wendell was hit with the hardest slap I've ever seen or imagined. Right across the cheek.

"You boys are going to sit in the lap of the Lord whether you want to or not. Now please do get down there, please. God is waiting."

Wendell was about twenty feet away on the floor, scrambling to get up. My friend was tiny and he'd got hit by a sixteen-wheeler truck, but he wasn't backing off. He got up and rushed at the guy, flailing, trying to engage him.

"Run, Tyler!"

I had no chance, and I don't think I would have left Wendell there anyhow. That's what went through my head. I wasn't helping; that also went through my head. Meanwhile, Wendell's attack didn't even throw the giant off balance. He grabbed Wendell by the throat with one hand, held him at arm's length, and made a threatening gesture toward me.

Then he laughed. That was worst of all, worse than the slap. Of course I wasn't the one slapped.

Wendell didn't give up writhing, trying to cause some damage, distract him, find a way to get us out, to get me out. I did nothing, didn't even say anything.

Goon-man pushed me down the steps, handling Wendell like a grocery bag, cackling and carrying on about prostrating and a lot of stuff about laps. The basement had carpeting and chairs, a stage too. The chairs were arranged in rows, enough seating for maybe fifty. I realized soon that it wasn't a stage but some kind of altar.

He set Wendell down, then smacked him again.

"Approach the altar, boys. Prepare to cast your sins into the lap of the Lord. Retribution is mine, saith the Lamb."

"Go to hell," said Wendell, getting himself hit again, really hard.

Finally I got so ashamed I yelled at the lunatic. I tried to yell, that is, but only croaked, "Stop that, mister. You're hurting him." Lame and cowardly, but a step up.

"I am the instrument of the Lamb, preparing sinners for their new life in the Lord. You must undergo divine pain; ready yourself for the Lap."

He was gazing upward, looking for guidance or maybe in a fit.

"Remove your vestments, sinners."

"No! Run Tyler!" said Wendell, raising his fists to this guy. I didn't run; I started to take off my shoes. I don't know what I was thinking — nothing.

Just as this lunatic was moving toward Wendell, his own fists clenched, a lot of noise came from upstairs and somebody started banging like hell on the door. I was so scared then I lost control of my bladder, peed myself and started sobbing. Wendell, all bleeding and red-faced, looked over and tried to signal something. I have no idea what. He took a couple of deliberate steps towards the big guy.

Whatever wild plan he had, we didn't need it, nor did we find our way into the lap of retribution. The hammering on the door and yelling turned our tormentor into a passive, shamefaced whiner.

"I weren't doin' nothing, really, Sondra, nothing."

"You let me down there this moment, Donald, this moment."

He did. It was a middle-aged woman, decent looking. She sent the big guy upstairs; he was now whimpering, promising all sorts of things, suggesting it was Wendell and me who'd drawn him downstairs: "They done it, Sondra. They made me."

"I'm more than sorry. He's harmless, really." Looking at Wendell's face, she seemed to realize that wasn't going to work.

"He's very ill, obviously, and I am afraid he might have been about to hurt you — even more than he did. I am so sorry. I'm his sister, been taking care of him. He's really sick. I didn't see how sick, didn't see this coming."

She looked very frightened. I could see why.

"You have every right to go to the police."

I still hadn't gotten above the paralyzed mode. I suppose I was all for going to the cops, but I really just wanted to get out of there and stop crying and yell at Wendell.

"What else can we do?" Wendell seemed to be opening some door for her.

"I don't have any money to give you." She hurried on, realizing she was insulting us, "I know that's not what you are after. I can promise you, promise you, that I'll get Donald treatment, real treatment, place him where he can get well."

"And?" Wendell wasn't being mean, but he wasn't going to settle, either.

"Get him where he can't hurt anyone."

And that's where we left it.

* * *

It was a long time before either of us spoke. We got back to the highway and started east, Tyler driving. She looked over at me pretty often with an expression I couldn't read. I didn't want Tyler to be uneasy, but I didn't know what to say.

We drove back through Felicity, kept on going east. Neither of us turned on our seat massagers, the first time we'd driven without them. No music. We got to signs for an Indian reservation, "Home of the Quechan Community." The guidebook told us it was really a spillover of a deadly Army fort that used to be at Fort Yuma. They'd rounded up the friendly natives and penned them here, shooting and having sex with them whenever they felt like it. Maybe that was an exaggeration, only it wasn't.

Tyler looked at me, into my eyes, a long time, almost like in the movies, where the fake driver of the fake car looks away from the fake road so long you want to yell at them to watch what they're doing. They just keep looking away and wiggling the wheel back and forth the way nobody driving a real car ever did. Tyler at least didn't wiggle the wheel, but she kept her eyes on me. I looked back but we didn't say anything.

"Hungry?"

That's all she said; then she pulled into this place on the reservation, a gas station.

Then she started crying, while I sat there like a dork. My body was leaning toward her, wanting to hug, but Tyler would have killed me if I'd done that, I think. Anyhow, I didn't. I sat there, until I knew I had to say something:

"That's okay, Tyler. You're okay now."

She kept crying and I kept saying it was okay. Finally —

"I let him hit you, let him, just stood there."

"Fucking hell, Tyler, he was the size of our whole football team put together."

"You went after him," she choked out.

"Yeah, but I'm used to getting beat up."

She sort of laughed, I think.

"I guess I must enjoy it."

Now she did laugh. I couldn't think of anything to say, so I didn't.

"Those kids outside, Wendell. Do you suppose...?"

"God, Tyler. Donald and Sondra.... Whoo!"

"You got a tissue, Wendell?" I produced it and she blew her nose.

"I guess you're my hero."

"You be a better girl, you have a better hero, but you stuck with the very bottom."

"It's because I'm black, isn't it?"

"Yep."

We went into the building, which had a beat-up old counter where I imagine they sold stuff, hard to know what. There were three kids there, a little younger than us, and Indians, I guess.

"Can we help you?" The girl smiled really pretty. The two boys didn't smile.

"Do you serve lunch?" Tyler asked. "We were just driving through on this trip, me and my friend, and wondered if you served lunch or anything like that."

Tyler was starting to talk like me.

"You guys are taking a trip? Cool!" One of the boys, now smiling, moved over behind the counter beside the girl. "Where you going?"

"We're on our way cross country," I said; "but really we're just looking around."

"God! How you pay for it? Your parents gotta be rich."

"Yeah."

"Must be nice."

"Yeah."

The girl started talking then. "You're nosey, Trent." (An Indian named Trent?) Then to us: "We can make you lunch."

I think it struck Tyler and me together that this wasn't a restaurant, that they were going to make us lunch because we had stopped and asked. It was like Bill Gates looking for a handout in Compton, but how were we going to get out of it? I knew not to offer to pay, and I'm sure Tyler was way ahead of me in terms of ethnic sensitivity.

She spoke first, thank God. "That's really nice of you. We feel like assholes coming in like tramps off the road and asking you to feed us." They all giggled.

"We'd like it," said the boy, who seemed to have a keen appreciation of Tyler's knockdown prettiness, judging by how he looked at her.

"Yeah," said the other boy, "and after lunch we can do you a rain dance and show you some visions."

"And scalp our asses," said Tyler, just in the right way: they laughed and shuffled around easily, the boy hot on Tyler actually giving her a shove on the shoulder. I should have told him it'd be like jostling a cobra, but Tyler turned to him, gave him a kind of love pat. For such a little kid, maybe thirteen or something, he was cool, threw up his hands, doing a pretend Indian dance right there.

They let us help cook. We made beans — heated them up — and microwaved fry bread, which I'd never had before and which tasted terrible, but that's okay. They produced some ham too, which was leftover and wonderful, all coated with mustard and spices. I went out to the camper and got some sweet rolls, which we all had for dessert.

After lunch and some horsing around, which took about two hours, things started to wind down. I asked if we could take their picture.

"Wait'll I get my loincloth," said the kid not named Trent.

"Damn you, Willy," said Mary (the girl's name), who really was pissed.

"That's okay," Tyler said. "You get your loincloth and I'll eat some watermelon, and Wendell can do some European imperialist thing, maybe shoot us all."

We got an iPod out of the camper and pressed it on them. Tyler was really good at it, joking about making a presentation "from our people to your people," and the kids were glad to get it, you could tell. It was out of proportion to what a gift might be in this case, but what was right, considering? These kids were living still in a kind of prison, a real prison. I'd read some about this, as much as I could stand, last year, about how Indians live in poverty and are depressed, drunk, and hopeless. It'd be better to be in jail.

Tyler and I were quiet again, driving over the bridge to Yuma and our second state. The quiet now was for the opposite reason from before. Too much had happened and we were drained.

We found a campground in Yuma, pretty close to town, walked in and went to a movie, I can't remember what one, some teen comedy, and then got groceries and went back to eat and play cards. We didn't say much. Tyler didn't even make fun of me getting undressed in such a half-assed way, and for the first time she said, "Good night."

Monday — Yuma, Arizona

Day 12

Yuma was a slightly larger version of many of these pissant towns we'd been touring through: fast food joints and minimum wage retail dumps. Here's what the Chamber of Commerce says:

> *Did you know that more people are moving to Yuma than almost anywhere in the country. [Sic] In fact, Yuma is the third fastest growing area in the United States! Now all of these people can't be wrong — so why, out of all the great cities in the U. S., does Yuma stand out? What makes Yuma a great place to live, to raise a family, or start a business?*

Ain't that the fuckin' ticket? My papa loves that expression, without the "fuckin'" part. I asked him what it meant. "It means something's real good, honey."

"Gee, Dad, I figured that; but where's the phrase come from?"

"It comes from somebody reaching in their pocket, just as they got to the river boat landing, and finding a ticket, without knowing they had it, and thereby able, they are, to go to Louisiana and find fame and fortune, instead of being stuck in Cairo shining shoes for the rest of their days."

"Sounds like Booker T. to me, how the smart darkies forsook the North and headed down south, where everything was free and sweet."

"Now, Tyler, don't be nasty. Not everything's about race."
"Is anything about race?"

"Tyler, why do you have to be so mean?"

"It's my nigra blood, Papa. It's a battlin' with my white blood and it's a winnin', just like in that Faulkner novel you love so."

"That's about enough out of you, Tyler."

"You gonna whop me, Papa? Oh please, Massah, don't whop me!"

"Tyler, you have no call to be so vicious. Stop it."

"Or?"

"Or I'll make sure you do."

"That'll be jes the ticket, Massah."

Sorry. I think I'm so mad at that freak or at myself or at Wendell for handling it so heroically that I can't stick to the subject. Besides, Wendell got the bright idea of putting "Air Freshener" in our otherwise nice rolling digs. It smells like a KOA toilet now.

After breakfast, Wendell making that egg scramble of his where the eggs are no more than glue for thirty other ingredients. One hell of a lot of garlic, too, which goes well with the air freshener. I see I just dropped a fragment up there in the first sentence, which is either careless or arty, let's say careless. But it does roll us right into what Wendell and I did, after breakfast: attack the paragraph from the Yuma Chamber of Commerce, just like we would in old Cartwright Princeton's rhetoric class: expose the logical fallacies, the cheap tricks, the obvious flattery, the use of stale commonplaces, the slippery slopes of fake connections. It was so much fun I came within an inch of touching Wendell in a chummy way. But I didn't.

I won't reproduce our analysis, just point out that, in the paragraph in question, we detect a transparent fakery: "more people are moving to Yuma." Falls flat when the "more" gets exposed, when they have to admit that two other spots are faster growing, thus trying to make hay out of "We're Number Three!" when any asshole eager to join the thundering herds would pick the top spots.

Then there's the slick understatement, "All of those people can't be wrong," asking us to think they are by damn "right." How so? Well, these proper-thinking folk are trampling one another on the way to this blank inferno, not only because Yuma "stands out" from "all of the great cities in the U.S." [Why move to San Francisco when Yuma beckons?] but because it is "a great place to live, raise a family, start a business." No coloreds need apply and certainly no Mexicans, as those folk don't "raise" families but go on welfare and pop out babies; they don't "start businesses" but leach on the business community through welfare and child support.

Realizing they couldn't altogether avoid specifics, the Chamber goes on to tell us what is so "great" about Yuma. Boldly putting its clubfoot forward:

> *Probably the most obvious reason for Yuma's outstanding growth is, of course, our wonderful climate.*

These guys should work for the Humbert Humbert Cheerleading Camp, or the Richard Nixon Institute for Ethical Government. They sell 120 degree wind-blown sand air as "probably" — "of course" the top attraction. The sheer stupidity of "probably of course" may appeal to the minds they seek to attract. The terrifying thought, entertained by Wendell but too bone-chilling for me, is that the Chamber is not writing tongue-in-cheek, not even cannily. *Maybe they believe it*!

True, they do have a river here, keeping the decent white population safely segregated from the savages in the reservation on the other side. "Thousands flock" to the river, mostly to cross it:

> *Since prehistoric times, Yuma has been the best site for crossing the Colorado River.*

There's the ticket! Come to Yuma, where cave men crossed the river — back and forth, back and forth. And don't bother to ask why you'd be drawn to a place just to cross the river. And don't ask why, seeking to cross a river, you'd choose to try it down here at Yuma where it's wide rather than up where's it narrow. It all may not make sense to you, but then you're not Neanderthal and you maybe aren't fond of crossing and letting others know you are doing so — "Hey, I be crossing again!" — assuming you had a language, which you wouldn't, being a caveman and all. Still....

* * *

It was great making fun of the Chamber of Commerce stuff from Yuma. Tyler seemed almost her old self. Still, it was vicious what we were doing. They were just trying to make it seem nice here, where it wasn't. I suppose people came because it was cheap, not because it was an artist colony or a center for scientific activity — sure as hell not because of the climate. But there were lots worse places, and we'd already been to some. The river was pretty and they had public parks, or so they said — I'm sure they did.

Seems to me most people live where you have to look hard for good points. But it's the same with bad points. It worried me that Tyler was so skilled at seeing only one way. It was funny and smart, but it didn't make her happy. But maybe it was just that freak who attacked her back in Felicity, except that the freak seemed to make her gentle for a bit and now she was back to normal. But I must admit I don't understand her too well. Let's say, don't understand her at all, nothing about her, nothing.

We spent so much time horsing with the Chamber materials that it was almost lunchtime when we set out to see for ourselves why so many were moving here, not to mention the swarms of winter tourists, drawn by the sunshine and tired of Miami Beach and Palm Springs. Sorry: Tyler's sarcasm is rubbing off.

Wendell & Tyler: We're Off!

Off to lunch, at a good Mexican place. I filled up on chips and salsa and had a salad. Tyler always has salads at these *cantinas*. I made the mistake of mentioning it.

"I figured you were right about salads, Tyler, so I got one, too."

"Did you just?"

"Huh?"

"That's the way refined folks talk, Wendell. Stick with me and I'll remove all those telltale white trash stains. Nobody'll ever know you are from trailer park stock, even though you're staying in a trailer park. I'll work magic!"

"You're in a trailer park too, fat girl." Why I called her fat girl I don't know. She blinked but ignored it.

"But who's gonna call me white trash, huh, Wendell?"

Oh damn. There were a lot of awful things to say, so naturally I chose the worst, just about: "Yeah, Tyler, they probably wouldn't."

"And just why's that, honky?"

"Tyler, why you doing this?"

She looked at me, maybe startled. I didn't want to hurt her, but I had this sense that maybe I could straighten things out: "Do you think I'm a racist, Tyler?"

"You have a subtle mind, Wendell."

"I know. I mean I know I don't. So tell me."

"No, I don't think you're a racist, Wendell. I just like raking your soft skin with my long nails. I'm a sadist, you know."

"I don't know. I don't think you are at all."

"You know me better than I do?"

"Yeah."

"Well fuck me."

"Okay!"

She looked shocked. For probably the only time this summer — I'd be willing to bet — I got her. And just to prove my point that she was nice, deep down nice, she laughed. I didn't say anything about her being nice, though, since maybe she would take her long nails — and they were — and rake my soft delicate skin — and it is.

The blunt truth, I'm afraid, is that Yuma has summertime attractions about like those in hell, once you loosen yourself from the fascinations of its history, which amounts to awful stuff about Indians, broken treaties, an army fort, and a vile prison. That's the main attraction, this prison dedicated to human misery, now The Yuma Territorial Prison State Historical Park, an attraction, if you can believe it.

The official pamphlet, Tyler said, would have made Adolf Eichmann blush. It goes on blandly about how twenty-nine of the 3,069 prisoners shut up there were women, how grand larceny was the most common crime, though polygamy was second. Then it sets loose the lies, without apology: "The prison was humanely administered, and was a model institution for its time."

This is prose better than the Yuma Chamber's. Notice how "humanely" tries to disguise the horror of that most grisly of human inventions, a prison, and how that misery is masked by the shameless idea of a "model institution." (I'm stealing some of Tyler's words here.) As we talked about it, we got madder. As the rank apologies go on, even the tortures are made to seem kiddie stuff: "The only punishments were the dark cells for inmates who broke prison rules and the ball and chain for those who tried to escape." Solitary confinement in the pitch black, balls and chains — hey, what's that amount to?

Here's the best, and then I'll stop: "During their free time, prisoners handcrafted many items." *Free* time.

Our guide through the state park, it turned out, agreed with us. We were the only ones on the tour, run by this kid not a whole lot older than us. After a few minutes of listening to the required spiel, Tyler let forth with some cynical comments. The kid then gradually altered his lines until he was saying things like:

"And here you see where the humane prison protectors ground the testicles of the falsely accused prisoners, mostly Indians, into fertilizer. Now, it was, mind you, very useful fertilizer that helped turn the countryside into the verdant paradise you now see. Right next to us is the treadmill, where merry residents could keep their waistlines trim while working off the effects of sumptuous meals."

Turns out he was a student at Arizona U who couldn't get any better work in the summer. He knew worse stuff about this prison and the lies being dished out by the state park system, but he was mostly interested in us and our trip. I think he was really interested in Tyler, though turns out I was wrong about that, as you'll hear.

This is kind of ugly, so I'll get through it fast. Why tell it at all? Just not to leave anything out, though naturally we're leaving lots of stuff out, so why not this?

Thorne — that was his name, "With an e," he said — told us there was nothing to do at night in Yuma. Nothing in the day either, but as he was working, that didn't matter so much. Ends up, he invites us to this party. I was flattered, figuring he thought we were college students, but I knew enough to let Tyler make decisions like these.

"Up to you, Wendell."

Why'd she choose now to give me power?

"Sure. Thanks, Thorne."

Thorne picked us up and took us to this house, where there were about seven other kids who looked a lot like Thorne, even the girls. We sat around for a while, drinking beer, which started out pretty bitter but improved. Then we smoked pot. I'd done it a couple of times before and got sick, so I pretended to suck, hold and blow out, then say, "Man!"

It was boring. Tyler was better at talking to older kids than I, but it wasn't that so much as not having anything to talk about. I've noticed that when other people are high or drunk they get uninteresting. I guess that's a dorky thing to say.

After a while, one of the girls suggested we "play old middle school games, like horny sixth graders!" Everybody treated it as a great idea, though it seemed to me kind of scary. I caught Tyler's eye, and I must say she didn't seem too thrilled either.

Before we knew it, we were in the middle of spin the bottle. People were kissing while they were off balance, tripping and falling. I wanted to find a way to go home, but I've been in that situation before, not being able to figure anything to do but stick it out.

I wasn't paying close attention, but it seems we'd moved to a new game, something like Post Office. It involved playing Rocks-Scissors-Paper; and whenever two came out the same, they went into this closet.

Took a while before there was a match, then some guy and Tyler did, and Tyler flat out refused, but nobody got mad. Next time around, I paired up with Thorne. I tried to do like Tyler, but it didn't work and I was dragged into a real dark closet. I tried to tell him I wanted out, but he was all over me, trying to kiss, his tongue working at my teeth. I was so startled I accidentally relaxed my mouth. One hand was holding my head, the other one diving down the back of my pants, doing gross things I don't feel like detailing. He kept moaning, finally took his mouth out of mine, so he could step back an inch and go at my zipper with his free hand.

"Oh Wardell, you're so hot! I want you so. Let me go down on you, Wardell; let me have your ass."

Gross as it was, I started laughing. "Wardell!"

That seemed to take him out of his trance: "Why the fuck you laughing?"

"Let me go! I'm not Wardell."

"Huh!"

"Get your hands off me, you bastard!" I was twisting hard, trying to get away; but he was bigger than me, stronger, and had me trapped against the closet wall.

"C'mon, let me go!" I repeated. "You'd better!"

The threat wasn't very clear, but I guess it made its way through his fog and he stopped: "Okay, bitch, don't call the cops!"

Not like I was going to do that. It was embarrassing enough as it was.

Tyler didn't ask what had happened, but I mentioned it later. She was incensed, wanted to go back and get Thorne, beat him up. But I talked her out of it.

"It seems like this whole country is packed with assholes ready to pounce on us. Jesus, Wendell, maybe we'd better get us guns or something. That really pisses me off, that miserable son of a bitch. What'd he do to you exactly?"

"Oh, Tyler."

"I'm sorry. I didn't mean it that way. I'd just like to cut off his balls and stuff them up his nose."

"I thought it was you he was interested in, Tyler."

"I think he'd be interested in anybody, the fucking loser."

"You think so?"

She seemed to imagine she'd hurt me: "I don't mean that you're ugly, Wendell."

"That's okay, Tyler. Not like I'd be flattered that old Thorne wanted to do me."

"Thorne's a walking hornball. He'd probably go after a house cat."

I thought that was funny: "Or even me."

"Yeah, Wardell, when he's *real* high."

Tuesday — To Gila Bend

Day 13

I got up a little before Tyler and dressed fast, tip to toe, right there in the open, by gum. She was upset last night, and I should have told her it didn't matter that much to an experienced being-pawed-at guy like me. But maybe that's not what she was upset about. Hard to tell. I think it was.

I'd picked up some "country cured ham" at a deli in Yuma, a town that shouldn't have had a nice deli but did. My mother loved this salty, tough ham from Kentucky or Virginia, and the woman there said this was just like it. To tell the truth, I didn't enjoy the texture — stuck in your teeth — but the taste is great and naturally I loved all the salt. I made pancake batter, heated up the syrup, got the pancake skillet real hot, had the ham in another skillet — and still Tyler slept on. Just as I was seriously considering waking her, she woke up on her own.

She was awful quiet and I couldn't think of anything to say, so I just served stuff up. Tyler came out of the bathroom with nothing on at all and got dressed, not fast like me. I didn't keep my eyes on her, more worried about how she was feeling.

"Wendell, this is ham my people don't ever eat, and you know why?"

"Really?"

"Yeah, but you want to know why?"

"Yeah."

"Because it was introduced by the Confederate Army, and it's known to this day as Rise-Again Pork."

"Like in 'The South's Gonna Rise Again'?"

"Exactly."

There's limits to how stupid even I am. "Oh sure. Up yours, Tyler!"

"Up mine? Well, you're one — sorry, Wendell."

Why was she apologizing? She seemed confused.

"Really, Wendell, this is terrific."

"Thanks. The pancakes aren't as awful as before, maybe?" (I should have said that the first time I tried, the pancakes turned out soggy and bad colored. The lady at the deli told me, when I asked, I didn't have the pan hot enough and was using too much oil.)

"I mean the ham. It's great. So's the pancakes. Really they are, Wendell. Thanks. Sorry I slept in, made you do all the work. I'll clean up."

This was not Tyler I was with but some nice person.

"Tyler, what's wrong?"

She didn't change expression, but it's like she had. I can't explain it too well.

"I want to talk to you about something, Wendell. I don't know why."

* * *

That was candid: I truly didn't know why. I'd gone to bed last night wanting to talk to the last person on earth I should want to talk to about the one subject I never wanted to bring up. Figured I'd sleep it off, but I woke up with the same itch. I guess it was because Wendell'd been mauled twice now by assholes, the last one even worse than the lunatic. Thorne didn't have that excuse; he was just selfish, dog-dirty mean! But why confess to Wendell? I don't want to know.

I told him about Rafael and DeShauwan, abusing their trust. I was so anxious to get to the humiliating part, I rushed over what I did that probably helped them.

"They weren't but little kids, Wendell, big as their bodies were. They relied on me too. I don't think I'd meant to put them in a vulnerable spot, but I hadn't *not* meant to. There they were, and I treated them terrible. It was like that lunatic might have done and Thorne did; it was that bad. Not sexual, but otherwise not at all unlike Thorne in being selfish. I guess that's why I felt like I had to tell you. That makes no sense."

Wendell was listening but he didn't say anything. I guess I didn't want him to.

The next thing I said was so surprising, it was like

somebody else said it. That's happened to me before, but not like this: "I think I wanted you to know what a fucked-up lousy person I am."

Wendell was looking at me in a way I couldn't read. Now I did want him to say something. For a while he didn't. Of course he soon did.

"No you aren't. I done worse."

Something about the "I done" touched my heart. I'm sure Wendell didn't intend it, but it was so cornball sweet I could have kissed him. I don't know why I didn't.

Ninety-nine out of a hundred kids would have done some one-upping, confessing to something themselves in the name of consoling. Wendell didn't.

We cleaned up together. Then we took off for Wendell's choice for a new stopping place, Gila Bend.

Gila Bend wasn't very far and promised even less than Yuma, so we were easy prey for anything likely to kill a little time, even a bowling alley. Didn't seem likely we'd run into Thorne there.

We didn't, but the place was bustling, ten of its twelve lanes swarming with little kids. Some kind of league, I guess. There was one empty lane — the other being occupied by a Mom and Pop bowling at the speed of paint drying — and the woman at the desk, Indian I'd guess, rented it to us for $5 dollars, unlimited games, and threw in the rental shoes for nothing. She said the lane wasn't being used anyhow, but how many people would do such a thing?

It was a nice place, clean and minus high-tech stuff: just a pinch beyond pin boys. The absence of automatic scorekeeping meant you could have as many do-overs as you wanted, and we wanted plenty.

The kids in the next lane, ten of them, were supposed to be fighting it out for trophies, ripping at one another in competitive fury. They had about as much interest in that as I had in outscoring Wendell, less. Within ten minutes they were invading our lane and we there's. Wendell started it all, kidding with them in his amazing way with kids. True to his heritage, Wendell was an accomplished bowler, a hundred times better than the rest of us, me being not quite the worst. He went over and bowled for some of the kids, pretending on the score sheet to be "Sarah," then "Kevin," then "White Horse." I guess some things in the town are integrated — the kids, naturally.

One of the kids turned to me.

"How old are you, Tyson?"

"I'm sixteen, Veronica, and you?"

"Me?" Veronica — what a loser name for a pretty kid! — needed some help.

"I mean, how old are you?" I had a plan, stolen from one of Wendell's routines.

"I'm ten, like all of us."

"No you're not."

It worked!

"I'm not ten?"

"Of course not, you lying shit. You can fool your parents and teachers, who are stupid, but not me. You're thirty-seven, and you make people think you're ten."

"How can I do that?"

"By being a lying shit, like I say. Also, you're a midget, tells people she's ten so they'll give her candy."

I shouldn't have said "shit," of course. Wendell wouldn't have and I think Veronica noticed, but she wasn't going to let anything screw this up. I may not have been any Wendell in this game, but I wasn't bad.

I suddenly thought of DeShauwan and Rafael, for some reason, but without the horror, the guilt. Maybe that burst-out with Wendell had washed me clean, just maybe. Wendell was no magic potion. He is a nerdy kid playing to type, sweet because he has no options. It may be pathetic, but that's the most you can say for it. And why did I want to pursue such a thin, cynical line? To keep from — what?

As soon as the three lines were bowled, we ended up with the whole league at the snack bar, tended to by the same expressionless woman who did the shoes. Our treat, of course. They charged only eighty cents for a huge Coke and gave us a discount for quantity. The woman running things was missing a chance. Hell, she could have unloaded some of that fry bread. But she didn't — gave away the store. Indians never learn, Wendell said later; they keep treating us as if we were human. No wonder generous-hearted Indians ended up on reservations, suffering the indignity of teams calling themselves "Redskins" and fatass fools like Jane Fonda doing the tomahawk chop.

We told the kids we were rich, to get anything they wanted, but they were so polite: some of them shared a single drink and nobody got anything but a soda. I forced some fries on Veronica. She did the loaves and fishes, spread them amongst the ninety. When the parents came to grab their kids, Wendell became a hunk of flypaper, kids hugging bye-bye. Preparing something nasty to say, I felt a hand curling up inside mine, pulling me down, for a hug of my own. Right then, I knew what Wendell must have felt.

We got free at half past two, close to our lunchtime. As soon as we reached Tacna, described by the guidebook as a "flyspeck ranching community," we were ready to tuck in, as my mother says when she's anxious to imagine herself white. Tacna was more "flyspeck" than "community"—a contradiction in terms if you thought about it— but it harbored what the same guidebook called "a great place to eat," especially for lamb chops and hamburgers. Quite a menu range.

* * *

I love lamb chops and would have ordered them, but Tyler had forgotten her winning ways and, back inside meanness, would have ripped into me about eating baby animals. Just to be safe I ordered a tuna salad.

"You know, buttfuck, that they just put down nets and pull in whatever comes up, including dolphins and sometimes the smaller whales even. Why don't you just eat chimpanzees or Costa Ricans?"

"Dolphins and whales?"

"Everybody knows that — those prick fisheries don't care what they put in cans."

"Tyler, you are so full of poo."

"I'm shocked at your language. Brutal! Like your way with the environment."

"Full of shit, then, right up to your kinky hair!"

She did look shocked, but only for a second. Then she laughed. That was good, but I hated what it cost to get her there — and she never stayed very long.

We stuffed ourselves so I didn't suggest stopping for the "delicious date milkshakes" available at Dateland, a smaller flyspeck, it looked, about a half hour east.

"Damn, Wendell. I almost missed that sign. Pull up!"

"Didn't mean to control your diet. You want a date milkshake?"

She looked at me in a way I couldn't decipher.

I pulled up at the first stop in the town, a town that seemed to be all gift shops, setting out to prove that dates can, alone and in combination, provide a complete and healthy breakfast, lunch, snack, supper, and bedtime tastie: copied from their brochure. On top of that, there were dates made into jewelry, petrified I guess. Date paperweights, date belt buckles, date hair scrunchies, date rearview mirror danglers.

Odd thing was they didn't sell things that were *about* dates; they only handled authentic actual date things. There were no T-shirts with pictures of dates, bumper stickers, carvings, dolls, books. I think they'd have upped sales with such tourist-pleasers. I decided to risk Tyler's sarcasm by raising the issue with the guy manning the cash register.

"Do you have T-shirts?"

"Sure don't. Don't have no panties neethur," he cackled, leering at Tyler.

I knew Tyler was up for that: "No panties? Oh I was going to try some on right here. I'm sooooo disappointed, Goober!"

Imbecile didn't get the Goober line and couldn't think of anything to say, just laughed while sucking in. He had something wrong with his throat that made the sound worse. He had plenty wrong with lots of him, I imagine, inside and out.

"Okay, well thanks a lot," I tried as an exit. But Tyler wasn't moving, at least not very fast, and the guy finally came up with a line:

"You wanna try on some panties, how bout trying mine?"

"You got a real purty mouth," Tyler mocked.

"So's you!" slurped idiot.

"Why don't you wrap them sweet lips round Wendell's dick, you sister-fucking maggot? We'll pay you two bucks, double your usual fee."

"Huh?"

Poor pathetic moron. I figured the only thing left to him was the "n" word, but he didn't use it. He wilted, didn't make any sound at all. His face was as close to expressionless as any I've seen, an utter blankness. He'd next to no brains but enough to feel vacuumed out, having used up the one script he had.

I was driving, which meant Tyler had nothing to do but pretend to read and stew. I should have let her do that without interrupting, but it wasn't ten minutes out of that sad town that I brought it up. I was mad I guess. I'm mad so seldom I hardly recognize the feeling, not that I don't know that's a defect. Nobody's bragging.

"You really showed him, Tyler."

"Up yours, Wendell."

"I don't know why you'd go after a poor pathetic moron."

She didn't say anything. I should have stopped right then and didn't.

"You get a kick out of that? Why do you do it?"

"Oh just fuck yourself, goody-good asshole."

In a little bit she added, "Sanctimonious cunt!"

Again, I should have kept shut up but I didn't: "Ouuuuuuuuuu, Tyler, that smarts. A cunt? You really know how to hurt a guy, Ty-Ty."

She sat quiet for a second and then exploded, leaped on me and started hitting and scratching me. I took my hands off the wheel to protect my face but then had to put them back fast, and she got in some good punches, making no noise at all. I let her, figuring it was better than ending up with this deluxe mountain on top of me. I didn't think that way at the time, of course; I just did what I did and supplied reasons later.

As quickly as it started, it stopped. Not before Tyler had scratched me some on the neck and smacked my nose twice, so hard it brought tears to my eyes. Tyler got off me, straightened her shirt, and slid back over to her seat.

I drove for five minutes not thinking of anything at all, except my nose. There was stuff going on in my mind, pictures and words, but disconnected. Nothing up there could be called thinking. When my brainstorm (not the good kind of brainstorm) quieted, I did try and think about what had just happened. I'll skip over the being mad part and the telling myself how right I was and how wrong Tyler was part.

Then, I tried to think different about why Tyler got so furious she'd hit me. I wondered if it was me Tyler was after. I had a class last semester, psychology, which said violence was almost always misdirected, exercised against a target that was merely convenient. Often people found it easier even to attack themselves, whatever was close, instead of a meaningful target, if there even was one. I liked all that.

However, I couldn't see how it applied here. Tyler was attacking me and she was attacking me because I was both the target and the cause. Let's say that. How come? I had mocked her, made light of her anger at the date store doofus. Maybe it wasn't that. She didn't seem to care what I thought of her. Maybe it was because she did think the date guy was important somehow and was mad that I didn't see that. Maybe that was it. I didn't know, and it didn't seem like more thinking would help.

Then I started to remember all that had happened to us in the last few days: the crazy in California and then Thorne and then this guy. I thought about her siding with me against Thorne, being incensed, putting herself in my place. How could I have forgotten that, which I didn't really forget, more like ignored?

Then she'd told me, right after, about those two kids she was helping. I figured she was helping them a lot, but she feels terrible anyhow, thinks she took advantage of them, used them so she could feel good. And she told me about it. That's what I should have kept in mind, that this painful thing is what she told me.

And she was a girl. I thought about that, how girls had to take stuff that hurt them, just because males are so blind. Most males aren't maybe meaning to hurt girls, but they do, one way or another, putting them in terrible spots. My mom told me some of this, but once you started thinking about it, looking around, it was obvious as hell.

Turning over all this, gumming on it, I watched as Tyler took on a whole new shape inside my head. The wonder wasn't that she'd hit me but that she'd stopped.

What I'm saying is that it all tied together and made sense, made sense in a way that started to make me feel rotten. Tyler hated people hurting other people, hurting the feelings or the bodies of those hardly able to defend themselves. Maybe the date guy, taken by himself, wasn't a big deal. Maybe he was, talking to Tyler that way because she was a young woman and because she was black. He didn't exist by himself but inside a string of abuses. Tyler had been bashed over and over, and I was treating it as a big joke. Another goon insulting women — so what? And Tyler also saw herself on the other side a little bit, as that guy, as part of the machinery grinding up the helpless. Like with the two boys she was mentoring. No wonder she wanted understanding and had a right to expect it after the way she'd been so good to me. All she wanted was some fucking decency.

I thought it over another minute, just to be sure I wasn't doing what I so often do, beat up on myself so I could solve a problem or avoid it. No, I wasn't.

"I'm so sorry."

"Wendell, I'm really sorry."

We said it at exactly the same time. On cue of some sort, we turned and talked on top of one another. The only difference was that Tyler put her pretty hand on my arm and I kept mine on the wheel.

It was a good thing and what followed was good too. We didn't vow eternal friendship and Tyler didn't dissolve in tears. Tyler was not a dissolver-into-tears type, and as we talked she didn't disagree with my analysis of my own insensitivity. But she did say that the whole psychology-class business about striking out at the wrong target did absolutely apply. I don't see how it applies. I didn't see what she meant in general, and she didn't do a lot to explain. But that's okay.

I don't know if we knew each other better after our tornado, but we thought we did. Anyhow, I was starting to see that Tyler was a person, corny and dumb as that sounds. She knew that about me all along.

* * *

I don't want to talk about what happened. Wendell went way beyond even Wendell's usual self-abasement. Had he hit back, screamed, justified his ways, I could have respected that, and we would have sailed forward happily.

All of which is bullshit. I don't know how I feel, why I went on a rampage, how I regard Wendell's apology and his analysis. Things had changed between us. One thing that had changed is that the idea of "between us," ridiculous as it had seemed, is now inescapable. Wendell was different; I was different; we were different.

I'd rather bury all this in the little shit-pit I keep in my head to hold what's confusing or annoying. This is both. Wendell, I imagine, has no shit-pit, probably does some of his "thinking" about the toughest stuff. He told me that. Maybe I'll ask him about it some day, if I stay interested, which is certain.

So off we go to Gila Bend. On the way, Wendell suddenly pulled over and asked if I'd drive. Didn't even say why. Wendell was wearing a shrunken tee shirt that rode up and showed skin, nice skin, if you like it babyish, perfectly smooth, and on a more or less grown boy. I found myself staring at his back and side as he slid himself out of the driver's seat. Had this impulse to touch him. Jesus Christ! But it was like the impulse you might feel to touch the velvet ropes in a fancy theater, nothing personal.

"Your undies are showing again, Wendell."

"Ah, Tyler!"

"If I bought you boxers would you wear 'em — and — ?"

"And what?"

"Try to keep them invisible?"

"I'm getting used to this, you know, Tyler? Pretty soon I won't mind you talking about my underwear."

"That'll be a step forward. So will you? I could go into the kiddie section at J. C. Penny's, which I happen to know from direct evidence is your store of choice, and get some superior boxers, size 6X. Would you wear them?"

"No."

"No?"

"No. You deef? You a big deefy?"

"That's a big step forward, Wendy. Stick to your guns. Stick to your underoos."

"Okay."

"Why we switching places?"

"We're changing places cause I feel like it and I'm the boy here."

This was getting unnerving, so I let it drop, took over steering our huge clumper down the road. Turns out Wendell wanted to read about Gila Bend

"Tyler, all I can find out about Gila Bend is that it claims to be the hottest place in America. Not hot like in 'cool' but hot like in makes-you-sweat. It's so keen on that title it's been caught several times lying about the temperature, inflating the statistics."

"That's beyond pathetic."

"Maybe we could stay there and not use our air conditioning — test their claims."

"Sounds like the one thing it has to offer. Misery."

"Tyler, did you notice that my vocabulary is growing?"

"Yes, I have. I had no idea you had the word 'vocabulary' in your arsenal."

"Thank you, but I was speaking of the unusual way of saying somebody likes something, which is to say they are 'keen on' it."

"I see. 'Keen on' means your pecker is throbbing and about to spurt."

"Tyler!"

"Sorry, Mom. British, is it?"

"What?"

"'Keen on.'"

"I thought you meant 'throbbing pecker.'"

"You keep surprising me, Wendell."

"I know I do."

"You're not altogether witless."

"I make the most of what I got."

"I'm afraid you do."

"That's admirable."

"It's also sad. It's not going to get any better. You're at the top of your game. And you will never win."

"Well, Tyler, some of us are happy just to play."

"No, you ain't. God, Wendell, it's got to bother you that you never win."

"It does."

"Maybe you haven't found the right game yet."

"Thanks, Tyler."

Why I said that, why I let the conversation go there, I don't know. I didn't want to feel sorry for Wendell. That'd be the worst. I couldn't let that happen, and I had.

Gila Bend introduces itself with a sign somebody thought was funny and nobody else had nerve enough to say wasn't. Let's hope there wasn't unanimous agreement. That sign, affixed to cute boards with jagged edges made to look Olde Weste, said:

GILA BEND

Welcomes You

Home of 1700 Friendly People

And 5 *Old Crabs*

Elev. 737 Ft.

You ready for this? The "*old crabs*" number was attached to a removable shingle, suggesting that the number changed daily as temperaments altered or murders were committed.

Anyhow, Wendell thought it was as bad as I did. "Embarrassing" was his term, whereas mine was "idiotic," and there you have the difference between us. Near as I could see, there was nothing but eye pain everywhere you looked between the sign and the campground. But we got a spot, choice, with a tree of our own, a picnic table and a grill.

One eye-opener, added to my list of you-learn-something-valuable-every-day, was that campsites were nice. I can hardly believe I'm saying that, but it's so: Campsites were nice, our camper was nice, the people next to us were, every one, nice.

I was once worried about life after 70, but now I look forward to retirement, enjoying the trailer parks kind hearted people establish. I know some kids start worrying about old age, once they realize there is such a thing in store for them, but not me, even if I'm not as spry as now, even if I am, say, dying of boredom — or just dying.

This Gila Bend KOA had an inviting pool. I'd noticed it, along with an equally inviting cafe, attached to a Best Western, called "The Outer Limits Coffee Shop."

Wendell had information on it. It was, he said, named after a popular sci-fi TV series from the sixties, which explained the flying saucer theme of the coffee shop and the motel. Flying saucers, Wendell knew, were what very old-timers called UFOs. You think about it, "flying saucers" has an unpretentious, campy feel, much better than the fake officialese of UFO. That's just my opinion, of course, so adopt it.

We ate before swimming, but not before discussing it.

"Nice pool, Wendell."

"And people have their bathing suits on."

"That's a plus."

"You wanta swim? We're all hooked up."

"I'm hungry."

"Yeah, that too."

"Which means?"

"Want to eat?"

"Eventually. No, sorry Wendell. Yes, I'd like to eat right away, if you would. Do we have anything?" I knew the answer, so why did I ask?

"Not really, Tyler. I could run out and get stuff while you swim."

"That's nice of you, Wendell."

"Oh sure."

"No, I mean it. But why don't we both go eat at the flying saucer place?"

"That's good. What sounds appealing to you?"

"Bouef bourguignon."

"Me too. With chilli fries."

They had peach pie. I talked Wendell into getting some. It was so fucking good. We'd both had salads, so we were justified in adding pie. In fact —

"Want more, Tyler?"

"Yeah."

"Me too. I've never had that much pie, but gee!"

"That's what I say. Gee! Also Holy Rim Job!"

"Tyler, you probably don't want to do this, but how about sharing a piece?"

I did want to do it and we did. You really get to know what a fella's made of when you dive into a big hunk of peach pie with him while sitting in a red vinyl booth in a room decorated with space ships, bad drawings of fake planets, and cartoon images the waitress told us were of *The Jetsons.*

We did go swimming after dinner. Plunged right in. Didn't wait the required two hours, reckless youth that we are. Of course we changed first. Wendell went into the bathroom, which was fine by me, since at least he wasn't peeking. Wonder if I cared?

He came out in a neon blue suit, which was okay, and it was tight, which was less okay, and it was a skimpy Speedo, which somehow made it so awful it was like watching your mother take a shit.

"Wendell!!!"

"You look nice, Tyler."

"Thanks. But, Wendell, I don't want to — well, don't you think, you know, that you might — you know?"

"Tyler, you talk like me. What is it? Slurp it out. You can tell me."

"It's your suit, Wendell."

"Yeah, surprise! Mike suggested I get one. You don't like it? I look funny? I know I'm pretty skinny and all."

"It's not that."

"What is it?"

"Do you think it's decent?"

"Is this you talking, Tyler?"

"That's not what I mean."

"It covers me, doesn't it? All that sticks out is my legs and stuff."

"It's so tight."

Wendell got all red, not just his face. He did that when he was embarrassed, but I'd never seen him or anybody else blush all over. But why did I care? It wasn't like I was staring at his pecker, but I guess I was and didn't want other people to do so, and my God what was wrong with me?

"Should I change? I got the old one, all baggy."

"Wendell, I'm sorry. I don't know why I said anything. You look pretty, Wendell, and I can't believe I just said that and I don't mean to insult you. I guess I'm just not used to seeing you — like that."

I had no idea what I meant, but Wendell looked as if he did. For some reason, I wasn't too irritated, as his out-of-nowhere aplomb made it so I didn't have to say anything and we could sashay off to the swimming pool, only a few people there. I touched Wendell a few times while we were swimming. Couldn't help myself. Tried to make it seem accidental, but it was pure molestation. Wendell was, of course, cool about it.

We returned to our rolling home, and I suggested we change back into clothes and watch *Waiting for Guffman*, a movie doubtless way over Wendell's head. And why do I say that? Getting harder to abuse my friend.

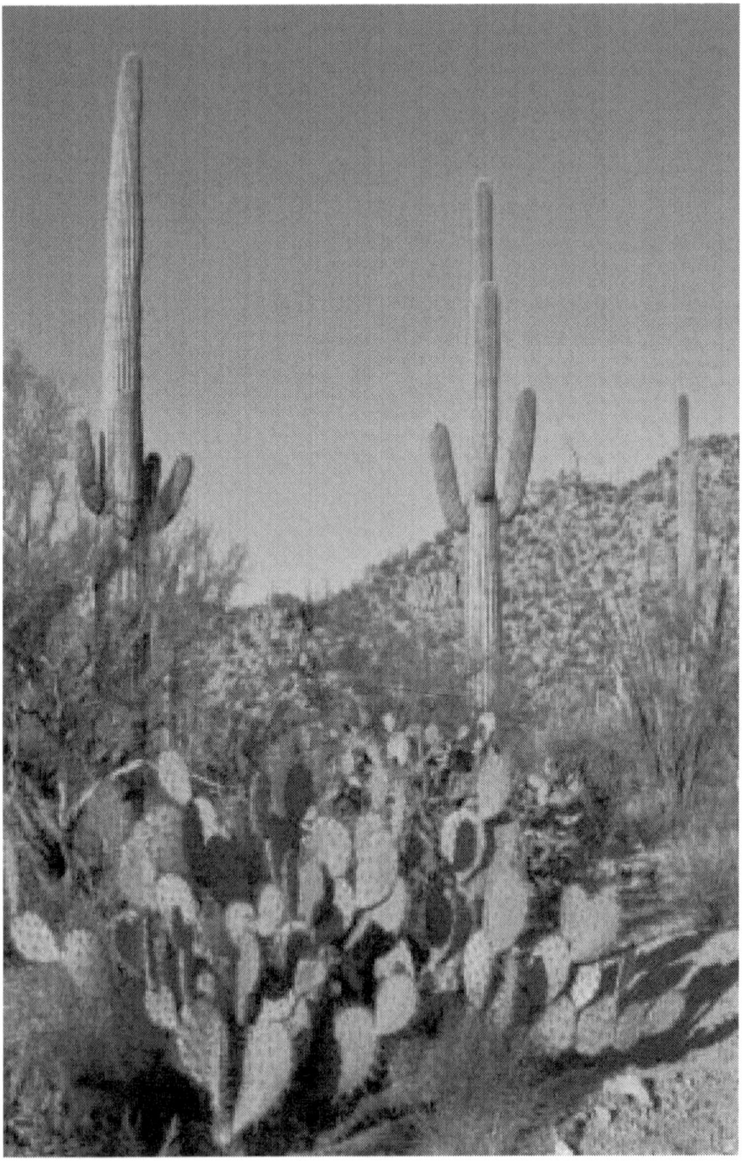

CHAPTER 8

Wednesday through Saturday — Tucson

Days 14 through 17

"Hello, Mike?"

"No."

"It's not?"

"You deaf?"

" Sorry. No Mike there?"

Silence.

"Well, good-bye.... Wait, is this Mike's cell phone?"

"Who are you?"

"My name's Wendell, a friend of Mike's. His uncle and aunt or something invited us to come up...."

Muffled sounds at the other end of the phone:

"Who's... Let me have... C'mon, Blake...." Finally: "This is Mike."

It was real clear, real fast, even to me.

"Hi, Mike. This is Wendell."

"Wendell!"

"Tyler and I are down here in Gila Bend."

"Where's that?"

"Never mind. You and Jenny still up for a visit?"

"Fuck yes!" Muffled sounds: "Yeah, Jenny. Wendell and Tyler! They're coming. I don't know." Then back: "Sorry, Wendell." More muffled sounds: "I know. I'm finding out, if you'll shut up." Then back: "So where are you?"

"Close by, I think. Just give me directions."
"Yeah — wait a second."
"Oh, Mike...."
"Yeah."
"Was that Blooper?"
"Oh yes."

We got directions but figured we would kill some time first so we didn't show up at lunch and start right in mooching. Besides, this Blake character seemed unwelcoming. Tyler said we could incite the other three kids to kick his butt, which was a plan. Not to be a woos — as if I had a choice — but kick-butt was not my idea of fun.

We saw signs going into Tucson for lots of things. It was the first big city we'd gotten to, apart from Felicity, and it was nice to have these billboards, cheesy as they might have been, telling us we could have fun: greyhound racing, a Titan Missile Museum, something called a Queen Mine Tour, Justin's Water World, Funtastics Family Fun Park, and many other experiences I'd like and Tyler wouldn't.

"So, Wendell, which sophisticated adult attraction should we choose?"

"How's that museum strike you?"

"I didn't see that sign. What museum?"

"Kinky Sex, exhibits change daily, interactive, nobody over sixteen admitted."

"What's today?"

"Wednesday. Not the most popular day so they have to try hard."

"Which means?"

"Going-down-on day."

"It's called cunnilingus."

"You and me know that, but not the general public, which is more likely to come in for plainly-labeled exhibits."

"And demonstrations."

"Workshops."

"Choose a member of the staff or someone from your own party."

"A family member."

"Wendell, you're going to hell. So where do you really want to go?"

"The university."

"Okay."

"Really?"

"Sounds good. It'll be interesting, maybe, though I know you had your heart set on some power plant tour."

"The university'll have a bookstore and we can get some stuff for Martin."

"That's nice, Wendell."

"Thanks."

"Stop it."

"Okay."

It was easy finding the university, once we asked about five people; and the parking guy told us we didn't have to pay. They have about thirty museums right there: we chose Indians and photography. There weren't many students around, it being summer, but those that were seemed friendly. A good many said hi to us and eyed up Tyler, too.

I was impressed by the bare landscaping, all natural desert style. No, I wasn't, until a kid at one of the museums explained it to us. You see, down here in Tucson, the progressive, leftist part of the state, Terry's sort of place, everyone believed in preserving scarce resources, of which the scarcest was water. Unlike some cities, characterized as "right-wing piss-holes." Did we know what cities he meant? "Up North," we ventured. Not quite, not Flagstaff and canyon country, which were more like "us." That left only one city in the state I'd ever heard of, "Phoenix?"

That turned out to be the very right-wing piss-hole: home of fake lakes, golf courses, and other marks of contempt for the planet. He was a nice kid, asked if we were thinking of coming there when we went to college.

"Should we come here?" Tyler wanted to know. Turned out he loved it, told us how serious the school was and about his major. I was thinking he'd talk about parties and football, but he didn't. I liked him. So, it turned out, did Tyler, which was the first thing we agreed on since we left home. That's not true. Wonder why I said that?

It was getting on toward four o'clock, but we were having fun walking around. We found the bookstore and got Martin a tee shirt, pencils, and a beer mug. I wanted to get more, but Tyler said we could pick up little bits as we went and send it, which would keep things coming to him and lighten our load.

Just as we exited the bookstore, we were blocked by some giants.

"Are you two students here?" This from a heavy-set man, accompanied by a bigger wife, and an even bigger, though younger, version, a daughter. Mom and Dad were smiling; daughter wasn't.

"Yes, we are," Tyler said with a great smile, fake, but dazzling to them — me too. "Just finished our sophomore year. Can we help you?"

"That's very nice of you. We were in the neighborhood, weren't we, Jessica?"

"Fuck no!"

Tyler and I exchanged glances, conspiring?

"Are you looking at colleges, Jessica?" Tyler purred.

"I'm not. My dad is."

Tyler ignored this real well. "I think you'd really like it here. There's nobody breathing down your neck. You can do anything you want, anything at all."

That seemed to hit Jessica right in her oversized breast — sorry to put it that way.

"Yeah?"

"I don't mean anything wild or dangerous, of course."

Tyler was now chirping and glancing winningly at Mum and Dad.

"It's being on your own and running your life. You control your own time, balancing hard work and hard play. It's really a valuable learning experience," I piped in.

The adult pudgies looked slightly alarmed, but Jessica was now bright and smiling. I decided to run with it; Tyler even gave me what I thought was a nod. Damn!

"Living in the dorm is required your first year, but Monica and I now live off campus, don't we Monica, in an apartment of our own. It's even cheaper than the dorm," I added, a god-blessed inspiration, as it made the adults look a lot brighter.

"Jordan's right," Tyler said, "and the dorms themselves are really nice too — and private. I know I never had so much fun. But they are also set up well for working. There's study sessions every night, with graduate students running them. Free too."

"Are these dorms co-ed?" Jessica had moved closer to Tyler, who was giving signs of friendliness I hadn't seen in her since the nudist colony.

"I think all college dorms these days are co-ed," Tyler said, "but that doesn't mean what some parents fear — and a lot of freshmen hope for!" Tyler managed somehow to get even the parents laughing at this. They seemed anxious to like the place and like me and Tyler and get their demon daughter to like it too, so they were willing to pretend they weren't as scared as they sure were about drugs and sex and the unknown.

We went on to talk about Jessica's probable major, art history, college costs, scholarships, the faculty, and social life. By the time we were done, there was no chance she would go anywhere other than good ol' U of A. Her parents were relieved that it was uncostly. Of course we had no idea what we were talking about. But we didn't mislead them on purpose. Tyler seemed well informed in a general way, and I followed her lead. I know I was convinced by us.

The only bad thing was breaking away.

"Well, we've really enjoyed talking with you lovely people, but Jason and I need to get back and do some studying for our computer class. It's a summer class."

"I thought his name was Jordan."

This was Tyler's game, and she didn't miss a beat: "You know what, Jessica? I sometimes call him Jason, or Jordan, or Scott, or Sean, or Tyler — just to make fun of pop names. His real name is — you'd never guess."

"What?" Mockery was clearly right down Jessica's alley and she was smirking.

"It's Baldwin. Honest to God, Jessica, it's Baldwin."

"Fuck you!"

"No, it is, Baldwin Caldwell III."

"What a dorky name! I had a name like that I'd slit my wrists."

"Jessica!" both her parents hissed.

I tried to laugh, but I was hurt. "Maybe I will, Jessica, now that you suggest it."

"Fuckin' should."

"I agree, Jessica," Tyler sang, "but he won't. I've hinted and hinted, hope he'll smother himself in the night or drown in his tears; but every morning there he is, eating his Count Chocula."

Good job, Tyler. Got us away, though I was still stinging at the insults to Baldwin Caldwell III, who could not help his name and was doubtless a good guy, down deep. I did like Tyler slipping in her own name with the list of stupids, admired her all over again, but kept myself from saying so.

We called ahead, and there were Mike and Jennifer and another kid, probably not Blooper, at the end of the driveway, waiting for us and then jumping up and down like 6-year-olds and waving when they saw us.

Mike, Jenny, Tyler, and I took up where we left it, gabbling. I went over to talk to Brandon, just a touch older than Jenny, I'd say, but without her great looks. Brandon had funny sticky-out ears, about six freckles that looked like they were painted on, and sparkly eyes that didn't seem ever to agree on what they were looking at. He was probably what you'd call ugly, but he had this way of bouncing when he talked, grabbing randomly at his ears and hair, leaning in close and squinting at you. He had no sort of self-consciousness or whatever it was that'd make people vain, which was a good reason why nobody'd ever insult him or otherwise hurt him.

I lack the words, a common occurrence with me, but I'd really like to be able to tell you about Brandon, as there's something about people like him that makes you forget what they look like.

It's what you often see in married people when one's pretty and the other's ugly, and people who know them for a while don't even see it. Brandon was that way.

* * *

That night after dinner Wendell and I took a walk. The kids had some chores to do, and the parents of Blake and Brandon told us to clear out or the kids would never get them done. They said it nice, but they meant it. The parents seemed invisible when they had to occupy the same space with us. Good!

"Where do you suppose that Blooper character is, Tyler?"

"You suppose they made him up?"

"Probably. No, they didn't; he answered the phone when I called. Maybe they sent him to camp or something."

"Military school."

"Jail."

"Ask Mike."

"I will."

"You leave Mike alone now, Wendell. He's an innocent

and you're not. Don't corrupt him with your worldly ways."

He laughed, which surprised me. "I was thinking more of Brandon."

"Looks like Alfalfa from the old *Our Gang*. Before your time, Wendell."

"I remember. Alfalfa, the one who sang real high in all the shows they put on and was in love with Darla, who puts me in mind of you, Tyler. You want to be disgusted?"

"I'm not entering in, Wendell."

"I was thinking you and me could get married and then adopt these three kids and settle in here in Tucson and have a good life."

"Now, there's a dream."

We got back and played outside games, variations on hide-and-seek that I'd never played before and can't now remember the rules, largely because I couldn't follow them at the time. You can imagine Wendell's state. None of our mess-ups seemed to matter, though, as the games all involved random hiding, tagging, pairing-up, home base, and lots of flailing about.

Inside, we were invited to down the most colossal ice-cream sundaes I'd ever seen, dished up by the grown-ups. They also gave each of us a can of our own personal aerosol-packed whipped cream and then beat it, leaving behind an open invitation to a very messy, then smelly fight outside in the back yard.

Planning for the next three days followed, originated by our host kids. Next day, from Jennifer, an amusement park, called somebody's Funtastic Family Flopfest; then, day following, from Brandon, Justin's Water World; then, day after that, from Mike, a scheme that included riding up into the wild mountains on goats, sleeping out under the stars, and walking back the next day, whereupon, we insisted, we would leave. We *had* to, we said, leaving unstated what was calling us so urgently.

First thing next morning, Jenny came sidling up to me: "Tyler, I gotta tell you something about Blake."

"Ummm."

"He's coming back in a little bit — from the hospital. He's been sick. Well, he's always sick. He has this condition, makes him really odd. Mike says he's just an ...."

"What? Some disease?"

"Maybe. Mike says he's just an asshole."

"That's sort of a disease. What kind of asshole?"

"Developmentally disabled. Mike says that means he's dumb. Also, attention disabled something. Mike says that also means he's dumb. And something else as a condition which name I forget which Mike says means he's an asshole, a mean asshole, a dumb mean asshole. You don't mind me saying asshole."

"All my friends say asshole. So why's Blake been in the hospital?"

"Treatment."

"I see. Will he be doing all this stuff with us?"

"Yeah. He's real fat."

"Maybe that's why he's mean."

"Maybe he feels bad for being fat?"

"Yeah."

"Maybe. Mike says he's just fat, too mean not to be."

"Mike has him pegged, I'll bet. Is he nice to you, this Blake?"

"No."

"Maybe I can get Wendell to beat him up?"

She giggled, whether because she liked the idea or because she didn't think Wendell could beat up anybody I couldn't tell.

I told Wendell about Blake, why I don't know. Want to know his response?

"Poor guy. All these disabilities.... Maybe if we're nice to him...."

Within twenty minutes of Blake's arrival, even Wendell

had been converted to Mike's view. Blake was, as Mike said, fat, dumb, and mean. He was about the age of me and Wendell, much bigger than either of us in all the wrong places, and had a blotchy liver-colored face. He talked constantly, had a terrible laugh, and was angry if anybody else got attention. He seemed especially annoyed by Wendell.

"What kind of name's Wendell, anyhow?"

"I don't know, Blake. Just a name. I think my uncle ...."

"It's a pussy name."

Wendell, being a sticks-and-stones kinda guy, said, "Okay, it's a pussy name."

Mike, not being a sticks-and-stones kinda guy, said, "Shut the fuck up, Blake, you fat shithead!"

That timely defense of Wendell had the effect of spreading Blake's nastiness everywhere, except to me. You can imagine how honored I felt. Resenting my exclusion, after a while I made my bid for attention.

"Hey Blake, how come you are ignoring me?"

He blushed and mumbled.

Mike picked it up right away: "Blake's hot for Tyler. Jesus Christ Almighty. You think a girl like her's gonna look at you, you fatass ugly stupid?"

Blake thereupon hit Mike in the shoulder, swinging hard but not managing much, as Mike was quick, able to dodge. Up to this point, Blake was no more than a jerk, a predictable psycho with a mean streak, Cartwright Princeton having more than its share. Products of social adaptation, this variation of the dweeb species substituted being rotten for video games.

A kid like Wendell, small and gentle, became a wounded kitten to a coyote: members of the Blake species just followed their demented instincts and flipped ears, tripped, snapped asses. There were ways of explaining these types: trying to get by, just wanted attention. It's just that their strategies were defective. And the more mistaken their tactics were, the more vigorously they employed them.

About a week ago, Wendell had started on this line with Evan Monroe, a Blake sort at school, as if understanding him made him better. I kept telling Wendell that exercising acute analyses on guys like Evan Monroe was worse than useless: just because you could explain why a skunk was a skunk didn't make him stink less. Wendell's brand of kindness wasn't inaccurate; he was just playing the wrong game.

And anyways, Blake turns out to be something beyond the garden variety mean asshole. After half-hitting Mike, he stands there all red in the face, his pig eyes narrowing, wanting to hurt somebody. Evan Monroe would have called his tormentor a "fuckface," made a threat or two, and beat a lame retreat. But Blake's need to hurt wasn't going to be drained. The only person close was Jenny, so he grabbed her arm, and reverse-twisted the skin on it real hard. That hurts like hell. Jenny was no sissy, but she yelped and tried to pull away, which gave Blake a chance to twist and hurt some more.

Jenny started to cry. "Why are you so mean, Blake?" She didn't want to cry, you could tell, but the pain was too much for her.

Mike started to run at Blake but stopped, reformed his plan, and then picked up and threw a handy stone, hard, catching Blake in the bony front part of his leg. Wendell, unequipped with Mike's quick thinking, substituted his body for the rock and got smacked around pretty good. Finally, Blake was finished, Wendell on the ground and soon out of range of Blake's kicks. Jenny was now crying out of anger rather than pain.

Blake snarled, "Pussy motherfuckers," and went into the house.

We joined together, the four of us, regathered our resources, and wondered what was going to happen now.

Not for long. Ten minutes later, the parents came out of the house, Blake in tow, ready to cart us all to the Fanastic Family Funpark, no clue to what had gone on. Somehow, there didn't seem any way to protest, much less snip off slowly Blake's private danglers, so we got into the shitty SUV and headed off.

Blake acted as if nothing had happened, was quiet for a short bit and then went back to what for him was normal because he had no imagination and couldn't figure out a way to go on with his temporary decent, or quiet, act. Normal was bragging, telling wild lies about what a hotshot he was, mixed in with lame jokes and sadism. Everybody alive has had to put up with this, and there's no need to illustrate Blake's version, so I will:

"This dick at fucking summer camp tried to arm-wrestle me, the stupid dick. Said he'd bet fifty bucks on it. I said, 'Make it 200, pussy!' so he did, like he fucking had to then. I mean, he was huge, three times as big as me and about twenty-five, so he thought he could beat me. Plus he was pissed at me because of Jacky, his hot girlfriend, or used to be his before I came along and she got a look at what a real guy could...."

Mike tried mockery, but it was hopeless. Blake ignored him, probably didn't understand Mike's sarcasm. The parents sat oblivious in the SUV cockpit. Wonder if they did anything to protect Brandon from his psychotic brother. I looked over at Brandon, who grinned, looking like a screwy, cross-eyed mongoose. How did he stand it? I decided to ask, keeping my voice real low, riding below Blake's braying.

"Brandon honey, how do you deal with him?"

He didn't pretend to misunderstand. "I stay out of the way, Tyler."

I couldn't think of anything to say. Brandon must have thought I figured he should have solved the problem on his own. His goofy grin disappeared:

"I tried fighting him, Tyler, I really did; but you know." He looked truly lost. I felt the same impulse that would have gripped Wendell: taking the kid along with us, saving him. What the fuck chance did he have? Maybe I was jumping to conclusions. Maybe things weren't this bad and maybe the parents did help him and maybe Jesus dropped down out of the clouds as needed and intervened

One thing about Blake's monologue was that he required no response, probably never got one so took being ignored as par for the course. He just went on, leaving the rest of us free to pursue our own devices, in this case, forming a plan to get back at Blake.

Mike suggested tipping him out of the log ride at the top so he'd get caught under the boat and dragged down backwards, ripping up his skin and forcing water into his lungs until the pressure got so great they'd explode. Beautiful, long-haired Mike wasn't kidding. That's not to say he would really rip Blake to shreds, but it's not to say he wouldn't. What he felt for his cousin ran a good deal deeper than loathing.

Short of exploding innards, suggested tortures for Blake ran all the way from tying him to a tree and beating him with "splintery" sticks (Brandon), to paying the cotton candy people to throw him into the sugar-spinner (Jenny), to stripping him stark naked in the middle of the park (pervert Wendell), to my plan, best of all and the one adopted.

First, we asked Blake to handle the money for us, and to take charge of reading the map, planning the rides. Any nitwit would have smelled a rat, but the half-ounce brain Blake did have was so drunk with fear and rage, and now with power, that he was a perfect set-up. Flattering Blake didn't take subtlety; subtlety might have backfired. Blake would never wonder why people who hated him would put themselves in his hands, no questions asked; he was incapable of thinking outside his own brutal delusions

We weren't fifty yards inside before Blake had managed to pinch, slap, or gouge every kid in our group — except me. I was the one punching him, friendly as hell — in a good cause. Blake was sucking it up, and with great fanfare drew up a plan to coordinate our day's amusements here at Funland, one that had us bouncing from one end of the park to the other in a zigzag that probably represented the misfirings of the neurons in Blake's brain. We all dragged along behind him, submitting to his power, egging him on, lowering the defenses he needed to live as usual, surrounded by those wishing him harm.

Meanwhile, had we been subject to any unwelcome creepings-in of mercy, Blake's ongoing maliciousness would have firmed us up. Even Wendell was steeled.

"Hey Jennifer, you pussy!" That was Blake's characteristic way of addressing his little cousin, a way he may have thought was witty, were he given to thought.

"Hey, Jennifer, you pussy! I saw you! You were playing with yourself! I saw you! God, that's disgusting. Playing with yourself out here in public! Jennifer's playing with herself! Look, she's doing it again!"

This was on top of earlier claims that Brandon was playing with himself, that Wendell was a pussy with a pussy name, and that Mike had no pecker at all. Somehow, though, this attack on Jenny, carried on pretty near at the top of his braying nasal voice, was beyond anything this moron had come up with yet.

Blake was leading the way, talking without turning his head (imagine how loud), so I could signal and shush and restrain the members of our party eager to attack, Mike and Wendell and comfort a little those most recently hurt, Bra~ nd Jenny.

ke. Can we do the Free Fall? Can we?"

nitation of an eager girlie and he did his of a
ure, why not? It's a pussy ride, but if you

The Free Fall was the first of our ideas, and the one least likely to work. It involved bribing or distracting the kids working there so that we could drop Blake to the ground before he was buckled in. As I say, not likely we could do that, but we had a back-up, which was that I'd ride with him in the adjacent seat and seduce him into thinking it was manly to pretend to be hooked in and not be. We understood that keeping the safety bar unclicked might give us more than we bargained for in the way of injury, might possibly give Blake a broken back, fractured skull, a happy termination to his life. I don't know that we outright wanted to kill him, at least I didn't. But I hadn't been included in the list of those assaulted.

Sure enough, the bribery idea turned out to be impossible. The kids running the machine looked nice but official, didn't appear to be drooling morons (our model for that particular look being Blake) and would no way do something so stupid.

So, we were left with the fallback, me convincing Blake that he could win my favor by faking the hook-in and falling through the sky like a real man. I figured it wouldn't be easy to make him understand this, much less persuade him, so I started on it while we were still in line. I carried this on for a good ten minutes, but it was worse than the ten minutes I once spent getting a rotten splinter extracted from deep under my fingernail with a needle shakily wielded by my blundering dad.

"Hey, Blake, can we sit together on the Free-Fall?"

"Huh? Yeah, you scared?"

"Well, duh! I just know you'll protect me."

"Fuckin' yeah I will — honey."

Why were we concocting plans? Why didn't we just castrate this motherfucker with a pair of rusty pliers?

We stood in line for about four hours — maybe not four hours, but try talking to a pinheaded version of Jeffrey Dahmer for as long as I had to. When we got close enough to where I calculated Blake would hold firmly in mind what I said until we fell. I tried it:

"Blake, you know what my ex-boyfriend did?"

"That pussy!"

"Jesus, asshole; you didn't even know him!" Oops.

"He is a pussy!"

"Yeah, he is. You're dead right. A certified pussy! But you know what he did on the Free-Fall back in L.A.?"

No point in letting him blurt out his "That pussy!" again, so I hurried on: "He pretended to lock himself in and didn't, just put his hands over where the bar clicks so it looked like he was locked in, and then did the Free-Fall without any support."

"Huh?"

"No support at all, just fell."

"That pussy!"

Was there a brain there at all?

"Bet you wouldn't do that, Blake."

"What did you say?"

"Shhhhh." He was screaming. "If they know you're going to try it, they'll check and buckle you in."

"Oh yeah. Anyhow, anything that pussy can do, I sure as fuck can, the asshole."

Got 'im!

It was touch and go. Blake was a sneak, but he was also incompetent, and the two traits did battle as he tried to hide his fake buckling. To be fair, it turned out to be harder than I thought it was gonna, as there was a huge mechanism with two sections that came clanking down over our heads with great clamps ready to whomp into place.

"Just shove 'em down," said the unsurprisingly bored kid running things; "shove 'em down till they both click. Okay. Got it?"

"Got it," says I.

"They both clicked?"

"They both clicked," I said, and so did Blake, after I

nudged him hard. He was holding his tee shirt out over the mechanism, about as obvious as you could get, only the Free-Fall handler was luckily paying no attention.

Then, without warning, we shot downward, "shot" being the right word for it. I got an instant wedgie, as the clamping machine held my upward-pushing, downward-plunging body, putting cloth and butt cheeks in a fierce competition.

Blake got no wedgie, I expect, as his body wasn't held in, moving upward as we fell, and then slamming back, whack, when we hit, at which point, he made a gratifying piglet scream. I was worrying about myself, but as the cart got to the end of the chute and came up against the padding, I looked over at Blake. Yes: face contorted with pain, whimpers, blood around the mouth, one hand wrapped around the other and shaking it. Turned out, it was his finger, broken, he was howling over. Turned out also that Blake was minus a good part of two teeth. His head had snapped forward hard when the chair had hit, smacking into something and giving him lovely snaggles, cut lips and gums, and what we all hoped was pain never before experienced by humans.

"What happened, Blakey? You crying? Oh boo-hoo, Blakey? Crying little pussy pisshead blow job!" That from Mike.

"I'm glad you got hurt!" That from Brandon.

"God, Blake, you okay? I guess not." That from Jenny.

"You'll be okay, Blake. Stop acting like a sissy and tell us where the next ride is." That, if you can believe it, from Wendell.

Up until Wendell's comment, Blake had clearly been finding some pleasure in his pain, plunging into self-pity, untroubled by Mike's routine abuse. But something Wendell said, or just Wendell saying it, ignited him, turning the sniffles into rage. He made a move to get at Wendell but caught his finger on something and stopped short, grabbing it and barely stifling a scream. He did have a certain kind of toughness, I guess, or maybe just the hysterical focus of a psychopath. We'd heard all that in psychology back at old CPA, and here it was being acted out right before our eyes.

Blake didn't attack, but I've never seen anybody look on another with such hatred as he directed toward Wendell, the only one of us being cool. Jenny and Brandon were alternating between empathy and mockery. I was trying to find a face for the occasion. Mike was next door to hysterical with happy anger. Only Wendell stumbled onto the right thing to do: get Blake mad by insulting his manhood. That way, it'd never occur to him to get us in trouble with the authorities; he wouldn't even make us miss the rest of the rides on our list because of an inconvenient trip to the Emergency Room.

We made it through the rest of the day, all of us trying not to smirk, excluding oddly, Wendell. I don't know what it was with him, but he was cold and serious, not like I'd ever seen him. It was as if he wanted somehow to extract more hurt from Blake.

As soon as Blake headed for the men's, alone, Wendell let us know what he wanted. He talked like he was in charge, had a plan — all of this so un-Wendell-like I thought I was with a stranger. Anyways, his plan, sure enough, was to keep it going on Blake. Wendell and Attila the Hun!

"So we ditch him," he said. "We set him up to check something out for us, then we ditch him, hide, stay away from him, doing stuff, and let him walk around stewing."

"He'll tell," said Brandon.

"Leave that to me, buddy. I can make it seem like his fault. He's supposed to be in charge and he let us all get lost."

That seemed to do it — and it did. You'd think maybe Blake would have located us, just wandering about; but it was a big place, and anyway he didn't. Of course, he could have used the park announcing system, forever blaring out messages, one every minute or two, telling the misplaced to go somewhere, where someone was waiting for them, ready to turn the lost into the found. But such obviousness would never occur to a fool, which is, oh yes, just what Blake is.

* * *

We gathered by the entrance at the right time and there was Blake. He'd cleaned up and wasn't bloody. His finger was in a splint; I guess he'd gone to the First Aid. He didn't say anything, which was spooky. He stood there pretending he was alone and fine. You could tell in his face that he was hurt pretty bad and in pain. I didn't care.

The parents showed up on time and were real upset about Blake's teeth. Turns out his two front ones were only half there. I didn't see them, as he never looked at any of us, except Tyler.

I don't know if the parents thought we'd done this to him. Blake didn't say anything in front of us and I don't know if he knew Tyler had set him up. My own opinion is that he didn't tell the parents and also that he realized we'd planned the injury ride. But who knew? He was an awful kid, but he was sick in some way. Even if he hadn't been sick, what we'd done was lousy.

Nobody wanted to talk about what had happened. We'd had a good time after we ditched Blake, but it was different now in the car, seeing him and having him there all silent. That night, we made popcorn and watched a movie. Blake wasn't there.

And he wasn't there the next day either, when we went to the water park.

I was wondering about Blake, so I turned to my old buddy, Mike. I know he was younger than me and I hadn't known him long, but he was a friend for sure.

"Mike, what's really going on with Blake?"

Mike was wearing the rattiest clothes I'd seen outside of the homeless shelter my mom took me to when she thought things were getting too cheery. He had on jeans with holes everywhere, including the butt. His tee shirt was all stretched out and hung down from his neck in a way that would make anybody other than Mike look awful.

I expected a joke about how much he loved Blake. I was always underestimating:

"It's sort of like he's sick and he's mean," Mike finally said. "You can say he's mean because he's sick, I guess. That's the thing. What do you think?"

"If he's mean because he's sick, then you could say we hurt him, pretty bad, and then ditched him too, embarrassed him, only because he's sick."

"Is that what you think we did?"

"I don't know."

"Fuck my mother, End-All, I know you don't know. What's in your head?"

"Different things at different times."

"Yeah, and when we did that stuff to Blake, what was there? You knew what you wanted to do. Why?"

"Because he was so mean to you and to Brandon and, most of all, to Jenny."

"There you have it. What was in your mind was getting at Blake because he was a mean fucker."

"Yeah, but—"

"Ain't no buts."

Not a bad way to think about things, I guess. Seemed honest.

I spent the day at Water-Wings, or whatever it was, with Brandon hanging from my neck, arms, shoulders, anything he could grab. He was a great kid, once liberated from his sicko brother. And he wasn't some peewee genius like his cousin Mike, so it was relaxing. Jenny joined in too, and Mike often.

Here's the topper. Tyler too! Playing some kind of "blind monster" game, I was startled to feel a different body attached to my back. Tyler, every bit of her front pressed into me, squealing. I would never have thought it possible.

Late in the afternoon, well into the "fifteen minutes more" we had tacked onto our reasonable quitting time, set up so we could meet the parent car, Jenny came flying at me from the side of the Jacuzzi pool, slapping into my back with such force, even from her teeny body, that I fell forward, flipping her into a somersault.

I tried to grab her as she catapulted by, managing only to deflect her from where she was heading — right for the concrete side. As it was, she hit the shallow water next to the side only inches ahead of the wall. The water broke her fall some, but not enough. She came up spitting water, laughing, and bleeding almost as bad as Blake had yesterday.

Turns out it was just her nose, a big mean scrape on the outside and enough of a smack inside to cause a nosebleed I didn't think would ever stop. It did. And Jenny continued to treat it as a joke, wanted to keep the game going.

I suppose it wasn't all that big a deal, but on top of yesterday and the general bad treatment of this little kid by Blake, it was just awful.

I was so upset I must have shown it, since Mike and Brandon, even Tyler, spent as much energy consoling me as soothing poor little Jenny.

When the parents came, though, they weren't interested in consoling me. They were so mad they could hardly contain themselves.

"What happened *now*?" The tone was really sort of like the one the DA uses in those TV shows when there's a real rat on the stand.

After we explained, the parents still were mad, glaring hard at Tyler and me, me mostly. Not like I'd done anything on purpose, but I didn't blame them.

Jenny did, though, and so did Brandon, doing everything little kids could — and that was a lot — to let me know their adults were dicks.

"They're just all screwed up about Blake, right Brandon?"

"Yeah, Jenny. That's right. They treat him special and think they have messed him up. Then it's like they were the ones ditching him. Only that's real dumb."

Only it wasn't dumb. Tyler was nice to Brandon about that, told him how smart he was and gutsy too, putting up with Blake and still being such a cool kid.

* * *

Off to the mountains we went next day, on flea-infested goats, especially big goats, all lumps and bones. They stumbled and lurched up the hill, asshole goats, rubbing close to trees so as to mash our legs, going straight for the lowest branches.

All of us includes Blake, now sullen and slit-eyed. I decided to — what do they say? — make an intervention in this kid's psychic life. Stupid! Fixing Blake wasn't a challenge, it was a dive into futility. I could make things worse or I could do nothing at all. Could be the influence of Wendell, who has an unerring instinct for causes that are not only lost but lethal.

"Hey Blake, can I ride by you?"

Silence.

"You look like you can manage these donkeys. I can't."

"Goats, fuckface."

"I don't do face fucks, Blake."

He laughed, mean but a laugh.

"Goats, huh?"

"Yeah, that's the big deal. They're some sort of special goats."

"Big goats, huh? I think they're produced by regular goats fucking with horses."

"Fucking with elephants!"

"Right."

"Fucking with whales!"

"Right."

"Fucking with tyrannosaurs rex!"

"Right." Was this dimwit ever going to stop?

"Fucking with that asshole, asshole, asshole Wendell, that asshole pussy!"

"Right."

"What a cocksucker asshole!"

"Blake, what do we do when we get up the mountain, to the top?"

"Asshole pussy! You in love with him?"

"No!"

"I thought you were married or something."

"No. I was just so bored back in L.A. I came along with him. I thought I might run into neat people, you know?"

"You fucking him, though, right?"

Why was I in this conversation? "No I'm not, Blake. I'd rather do it with that donkey you're riding, goat I mean."

"Me too. God, what a pussy!"

"You like sports, Blake?"

"No! God!" He screamed so loud, everybody turned round to see what was going on. It was as if I'd asked him if he wanted to go down on Wendell.

"Okay. Sorry. You like music?"

"Fuck no."

Who didn't like music? I was making progress here!

"Look, Blake, I'm really sorry about what happened at the park. Are you okay?"

He looked at me with a depthless vacancy, unreadable or horribly empty.

"I mean it. Do you have any pain?"

"Fuck no."

"I apologized, Blake. You forgive me?" What was wrong with me?

"It's not you, Tyler. It's that suck-cock Wendell."

"You know, Blake, you got Wendell right. He's a pussy."

He laughed. Not that he relaxed at all but he seemed a little less psycho-looking. I should've been satisfied with abusing Wendell, Blake having no saturation point there. Anyways, I didn't keep to that same safe dry road, but strode right off into the deep mud:

"So, he's a real pussy, like a bunny or something, not worth you thinking about."

He muttered something I didn't catch. Odds were good it was "Fucking pussy!"

"Put him out of your head, Blake. He doesn't matter."

"Fucker!"

"He's really harmless, like a kitten."

Big mistake. Something I said put him right back where he was. He returned to slit-eyed misery, silent except for some grunts. I kept trying, but the pattern was the same. I could get him talking by attacking Wendell, but it was less "talk" than bazooka fire. Anything else I tried was met with stares, fucking pussy sputters. Did I feel guilty about adopting Blake's view of Wendell? Very. Finally I gave up and dropped back with Jenny, who never once called any person or animal a pussy.

The summer-job college kids leading the goats were less phony than those we'd run into generally. They seemed to know what they were doing and were very polite without pretending to be cheery or particularly warm.

There were about twenty people along, all of them but us doing a return after the big steak and beans dinner. Wendell had attached himself to a funny-looking family, all with red hair and glasses and big loud laughs. Mike glommed with them too, probably because Wendell was there. One of those mysteries of life, Mike's attachment to Wendell, but there it was, cool and uncool joined at the hip.

It was about four o'clock when we made it to the flat place where we got to stand around while the guides built the campfire, set up the campstools and tables, started dinner, and tried to get us singing, which we did — not well. It's one thing to campfire-sing in the cool of the evening; it's something else when it's sunny and dusty. The redheaded family did know some good lyrics to songs, kind of off-color:

> *Someone's in the bedroom with Dinah*
> *Someone's in the bedroom with the ho*
> *Someone's in the bedroom with Diiii-naaaahhh*
> *To hell with the old banjo!*

> *She'll be comin round the mountain when she comes*
> *I'll be comin with her comin when she comes*
> *I'll be comin with her comin*
> *I'll be comin on her cousin*
> *I'll be comin on her cousin when she comes!*

You had to have been there. One thing made it fun was the reaction of most of the other people on the trip. There were three other families along, all with kids. They didn't seem fond of the lyrics, but were too awkward and shy to protest. The kids, of course, thought it was hilarious, even the ones who didn't know what "comin'" meant and maybe had no idea what Dinah might do in the bedroom minus the banjo.

Finally the fun-lovers saddled up and we five were left there with our bedrolls and packed sandwiches and a night without singing, I hoped to hell. Thanks to Brandon, who knew all kinds of outdoor games, variations on tag and hide-and-seek, we spent a couple of hours chasing each other all around the mountain clearing and into the trees. It was really pretty there, and, after it got to sundown, very nice out, not so burning hot. The moon was full, bright, and seemed very close to us, so it was easy to keep playing.

Blake took part in games, didn't really subtract from

the hilarity. There was something spooky about the way he played, but nobody paid any attention.

Finally, we built our own fire and tried some scary stories. Brandon had a whole bunch, but he tended to get them confused, so that werewolves turned into flesh-eating maniacs. Mike had a good one, less scary than obscene, about the child-molester who lived on the hill and came down into the village at night, testing all the windows to see if anybody had neglected to lock them. If they had — and here Mike lowered his voice to a whisper and put a flashlight under his chin — if they had — do you know what? Do you know what would happen? Can you imagine? Why, this child-molester would slowly open the window — you sure you want to hear this? He'd open the window real real slow— creeeeeeeeeeeek.

Then he'd put one crummy old scabby leg up on the window ledge and then he'd — real slow — put the other crummy old scabby leg up, and then he'd lift his crummy old scabby belly up. Reeeeallll slooooowwwww.

His belly was big and scabby — almost as big as Wendell's, though not quite so scabby. Then he'd shove his pimply big-eared face into the room and look around for kids. Reeeeeaaaallly slooooowwwww.

Then he'd slither into the room like a scabby old lizard and then he'd slither over to the bed — real slow. Then he'd put his scabby old hand on the covers, right on the covers. (He was barely whispering now.) And then, real real slow, he'd take his scabby old hand with the bugs crawling on it and the lice and the maggots and, real real slow, he'd lift up the covers, higher and higher and higher and higher. He'd be real quiet.

Then — real slow — he'd slip his scabby old fucking body right into the bed, all bugsy and maggoty and he'd crawl into the bed — real slow — right next to the kid. (You could hardly hear him).

And he'd get closer to the kid and closer and the maggots would be crawling and the bugs would be biting and he'd get his big scabby belly and big crawly body closer and closer and closer and closer and closer and closer. (Long pause). And then he'd – (long pause) – *Go To Sleep*! The last three words were screamed at the top of his voice and were so scary I screamed too.

It was late when we went to bed, almost two o'clock. I thought everybody went to sleep immediately, tired as we were. We all bunched together with our bedrolls, not because we were scared of the dark exactly, but because we were scared of something. I was on one side of Jenny with Wendell and Mike on the other, Blake next to me. He was the only one not very close, which didn't fill me with grief, though it should have.

I got shocked out of a sound sleep, we all were, by somebody shrieking, several somebodies shreiking, turns out two people, Wendell and Jenny. There was also a weird light and a terrible smell. Within seconds it was clear that two people were on fire. Brandon and Mike were trying to get stuff on them to put it out. Soon as I saw what was happening, I got my bedroll and covered Wendell with it, Mike taking care of Jenny.

I think everybody knew what had happened, more or less, but nobody said anything about it for a while. Wendell's bedroll was almost completely gone and his jeans had been burned, a few bright red areas on his calves. Jenny had gotten burned on the face and neck, even some of her hair. We had some cortisone cream for bug bites in our kit, and that seemed to help her a little.

Mike was the first to explode, partly because he was Mike and partly because he found a lighter fluid can, was holding it in his hand and waving it.

"You fucking psycho, Blake! You lousy bastard! You tried to kill my cousin and my friend and you're fucking going to jail. You're going to jail for fifty years!" He was shaking, he was so mad.

"What the fuck you talking bout, you pussy?" Blake tried to sound innocent, but he was as bad at that as everything else.

We got back to Tucson and tried to explain, but the adults were directing all their anger at Wendell and me.

"Why don't you two just leave? We were getting along fine before you came and now every day some serious injury happens. They aren't just *accidents*!"

We hadn't said they were, though this last attempted homicide, for sure no accident, certainly was not our fault. But there was no point in us saying anything in our defense. What could we say? We kind of were at fault. But then the real murderous horror wasn't inside us.

"Leave!"

I wish I could say we then said good-bye to the kids and left. Wendell even whispered to me something like, "Let's just go." But the little kids were so mad that we were getting blamed and were yelling at the adults with everything they had. The two smaller ones were most furious, but they weren't as colorful as Mike.

"You lousy bastards! These are our friends and they didn't do anything except be nice to us. Just ask Brandon. Why don't you ask Brandon, you lousy bastards!"

"Yeah, just ask me. Ask me. I'll tell you."

Of course the old folks spread their anger around, telling the kids they'd ask whomever they wanted when they wanted and didn't need advice from smart-mouthed kids and Michael you watch your mouth or—

"Oh just fuck yourself! Just fuck yourself!"

It truly was time to leave. We were making things worse for our friends. I did say my stupid part.

"Instead of yelling at Mike or at us, you ought to see what you're doing to your own kids by keeping Blake around. He belongs in an institution. He tried to kill Wendell and Jenny, for God's sake, and you're yelling at us!"

Of course it did no good. Wendell was right. We should have left right away—and finally we did.

Jenny didn't want to let go of me, and Mike and Wendell looked like they couldn't unhook. The little ones cried hard.

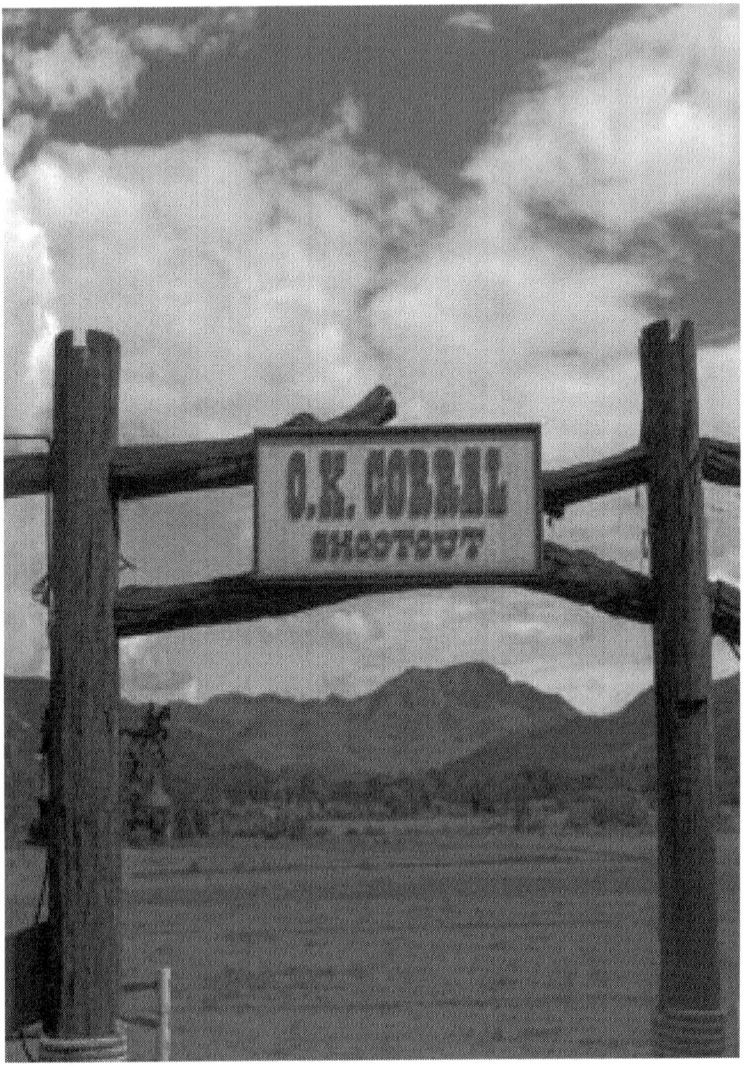
O.K. CORRAL
SHOOTOUT

CHAPTER 9

Sunday and Monday — Tombstone
Days 18 and 19

Tyler was driving, so I had nothing to do but ferret out the most magnetic spot lying ahead: Tombstone, the books said, a mustn't miss place. On the way there was a pile of attractions. I knew by now that, however bossy Tyler was, she didn't care where we pulled over, was game for all stops, even or especially tawdry stuff. Come to think of it, Tyler really wasn't bossy. Right up to this very minute, I thought she was. But she's not. She's sometimes bitchy, often, but that's not it. Meanwhile, I just told you nothing at all except that I'm trying to delay talking about what happened back in Tucson.

Neither of us was thinking about Tombstone or the caves we were going to stop at on the way. I didn't want to talk about Blake, and I figured Tyler wanted to talk about it even less, so of course I brought it up:

"We do seem to be trailing misery wherever we go, huh, Tyler?"

"Defiled with a sinuous trail of slime the dreamy and trusting country that by then had become nothing but dog-eared tour-books, postcards, old tires, and her sobs in the night — every night every night — the moment I feigned sleep."

"Huh?"

"*Lolita.*"

"I read that, but I didn't remember that passage. What a beautiful book."

She stared over at me so long I started to get worried about hitting a roadside cactus: "You think it's beautiful, Wendell?"

"Yeah."

"I'll be fucked."

"Me too. Someday."

"I expect so. Blake was eager to go at you. Too bad we maimed him before you two could work it out."

"Blake'd be enough to make me give up on girls forever."

"I suppose that'd happen anyhow if you got hooked up with Blake."

"He'd take care of the competition."

"But you're right, Wendell. This trip is like a return to the Old West, violence round every corner."

"Caused by us."

"Now there's where you're wrong."

"You think what we did was right?"

"Hell no. We almost got Jenny killed. You too, but Jenny'd been a loss."

"Yeah — and we also really messed up Blake."

"Left him worse than we found him, bad luck for Brandon. There's no good news there, Wendell. We messed up one sick kid and hurt some good ones. Nice job."

"But we made friends, Tyler."

"We did that."

I thought Tyler was being sarcastic, but she was looking at me with a little smile.

"So it wasn't all bad," I said, not very confidently.

"Mostly it was — bad."

"So we learn from our mistakes."

"Anyhow, we roar past em. Go on to new adventures, Wendell. Not likely Tombstone will have another Blake for us, but that's how it is. Good friends come along and you mess 'em up."

"That's what my mom had in mind for us, learning about the true life, the tough life, the look-em-in-the-eye-and-fuck-em life."

"Wendell! — Yes it is."

"Tyler, what's your fancy, a monument to something or a cave?"

"My fancy?"

"I was going to say 'What strikes your fancy?' which is more like it, but I don't want to go past your range."

"You're a surprise a week."

"The phrase is 'a surprise a minute.'"

"Which you aren't. I'll choose the cave."

Good. I was driving and didn't know where the monument was or what it was to. Can't see everything. We're trying, but there comes a time when....

"Actually, there's two caves, Tyler."

"In the state? The continent?"

"On Route 80."

"I say we choose one for initial viewing."

"Wet or dry?"

"Closest. Hope that's dry. 'Wet cave' sounds something like 'running sore.'"

"'Dry' is closest to us. We should see both. The guidebook recommends both."

"In that case, we'd be idiots to pass em by."

"The book says — here, you read it so I don't wreck us. Start right there."

"Yassuh. 'Avid cavers will appreciate comparing Colossal Cave, which is a dry cave, with the newly opened Kartchner Caverns, a wet cave, where the humidity will have you dripping with perspiration.' I'm not sure I want you dripping with perspiration, Wendell, stuck as we are in this phone booth."

"I know where you're going, sissy girl. You're trying to avoid the wet cave; but I'm the man here and I'll protect you."

"Okay."

Okay? Didn't sound sarcastic even.

Colossal Cave welcomes the tourist for $7.50 — $3 bucks for parking.

You can't wander, have to follow this guide, who tells you not to touch things, elaborates the difference between uppies and downies, and calls your attention to lumps that look like Dwight Eisenhower or high-button shoes. Tyler kept saying things like, "Resembles a small cock!" The family on tour with us ignored her. One interesting thing we learned was that robbers had escaped to the cave from a train heist they'd pulled, hid their money here, $62,000 big ones, which has never been found, to this day.

"Any questions?"

"How do you know the money's still here?" Thank God it wasn't me asking that dumb question, but a kid dragged along on the tour by his parents.

"Oh, that's been authenticated."

Tyler let loose. "How in hell can you authenticate something that's lost?"

The guide, another college kid, looked nervous and didn't say anything. Pathetic. Anybody else would have let up. Not Tyler.

"So, some official certified that the money's here, only lost? The Secretary of Lost Money?"

"Oh, it's authenticated all right."

"Tell us how it could be? We're eager tourists and want to know."

The guide looked pleadingly.

"C'mon, ace, don't leave us in the dark."

Finally guide boy lost it:."I don't know. Okay? I don't know — asshole."

He tried to hold back the "asshole" but couldn't. It came out strangled but it came out. I hope the family didn't turn him in. I laughed, which made Tyler glare at me.

The wet cave was hard to find, and we almost didn't get included in the tour:

"Do you have reservations?"

"Sure don't," said Tyler

"Oh my. People make reservations months in advance. You really need reservations. You can't just show up."

"So the tours are all filled?"

"As it happens, you're in luck; but next time you must get reservations."

"We'll make 'em for 2035. Just give us the tickets."

It really was swampy. The sweat kept stinging my eyes, so I was anxious to get back to the camper where it was not 100 percent humidity, which the guide said they kept this place at, for some reason I didn't catch, to keep the lumps growing, I guess.

It was the most boring tour I've ever been on and almost as bad as church. The guide seemed enthused about there being thirty different types of something and also the second longest soda straw growth. It seemed like the tour lasted for six weeks. At least Tyler didn't ask many questions to humiliate this guide. Just one, really.

"Excuse me, Kent, but can you tell me where the really long soda straws are?"

"Well, I really don't know."

Thank Jesus she let it drop before it got even more embarrassing.

So I artfully moved us to new pastures.

"There's a lot between here and Tombstone, Tyler. Want to see a museum?"

"Of what?"

"You don't want to see it."

"You're right. What else is designed especially for young singles?"

"The museum features Navajo and Apache cultures, since this was the territory of famous warriors like Cochise and Geronimo. But you don't care."

"Jesus screw your aunt, Wendell. Those places make me feel guilty. Would you, too, you weren't such a hard ass."

"Doesn't bother me. There's a museum of lynching and minstrel shows up ahead." Whatever possessed me to say that? Here it comes!

But she laughed.

Tyler didn't go for extended jokes. I'd tried a few dozen times with the same disasters coming as surely as snot after sneeze. I knew enough not to throw bad money after good, or whatever that saying is, so I moved on to a new subject.

"See those signs, Tyler?"

"Rest stop ahead? We have our own plumbing, bladder boy."

"That one there."

"Come See The Thing? That one? There's been about fifty of these signs today, every half-mile. I want to see The Thing, Wendell. Can we, huh?"

"You promise to behave? Last time we stopped to see a Thing you threw a tantrum cause you couldn't take it home. No more of that, young lady."

"That it? Looks like a gas station."

"It's the inside stuff that counts."

Inside was a car they said once belonged to Adolf Hitler, a lot of posters and crudded-up things in cases. We bypassed all that and headed right for this mummy model, The Thing, not a model, I guess, but a genuine mummy.

"That was worth the money, Wendell. Not every day you can see a smelly old corpse for seventy-five cents. Beats anything in Egypt, though they do have first-rate cave soda straws there. Now, we're off to the OK Corral."

"You've been peeking at the guidebook, which is my job."

Tombstone is one of those places you think might be okay and then surprises you by being terrible. Of course I hadn't given it a chance. We got in about eight o'clock at night and only had time to look for the KOA, like all of them very nice, and a chain grocery store, like all of them very much like all of them. We got stuff to make fajitas, Wendell's latest kitchen marvel, hooked ourselves up to the air-conditioning charger—it was about 112 degrees — and settled in next to some old folks with some young kids. I was afraid Wendell would strike up a friendship.

Actually it was me did it.

"We're with our grandparents. Can you imagine anything worse?"

"Being with Wendell here."

They laughed, which was a good sign. So did Wendell.

* * *

"You guys married or what?"

"Just on a summer exploration, Wendell is. I signed on for the ride. And no, we're not boyfriend and girlfriend."

"Shaggin it up with no commitments. That's cool."

These kids were getting annoying. No point in responding. Even Wendell stayed mum. Probably had no idea what "shagging" meant.

The boy had been doing the talking, but the girl took over now. I figured she couldn't be any worse.

"That sounds like fun, a summer exploration, just the two of you." She was trying hard to be chummy. "Just the two of you — as friends," she added, a little too pointedly, though I could see what she was trying to do.

"How about you?" Wendell fatally asked, having no defenses against the sort of appeal the girl was making or the girl herself, who was really very handsome, not pretty but what my ass mom calls "striking." She had dirty yellow hair and very dark eyes and she was skinny, the right kind of skinny.

"Rex and I are with our grandparents, who take us every summer, so our parents can do their work."

"So our parents can get the fuck rid of us," Rex added, grinning.

"That's true," the girl said.

"They don't like you much?" I said and then got flustered at what I'd said.

"Nope," the girl said. Rex nodded.

"Bet you return the favor," Wendell said.

"Oh, we love them deeply, tragically; but they remain indifferent, no matter how hard we try. I think I'll just run off with the nearest druggie and live on the streets."

"Me too — or end it all."

"It could be, worse, " Wendell said, beating me to the punch; "Tyler's parents exhibit her for money and my mother makes me her sex slave."

"You got a picture of your mother?" Rex asked.

Just then this one half of the ancient pair stuck his head out of their Winnebago and yelled. We were only about ten feet away, but he yelled as if we were in the next county: "You kids stay close, goddam it!"

Rex and his sister (?) pretended not to hear, and gramps finally pulled his beaky turtle head back into his shell.

"So, that's an improvement on Mom and Dad?" I asked.

"It's different," the girl said.

"It's abuse," said Rex, "but it's attention."

"It must be hell for you to go around with them all summer." Wendell looked concerned, as if we'd just run onto a troupe of blind orphans.

"You can't imagine. If we didn't have one another—" the girl started.

"Without incest, where would we be, Megan?"

"So your name's Megan?" Wendell's ability to disrupt a sweet tempo with stupefying bluntness was unmatched in my experience. The kids were up to anything, though.

"You see right through us. No, it's not. You think we'd use our real names, when we're taking such risks. Incest's a capital crime in Mississippi."

"And if this isn't Mississippi, I'd like to know where is," I said.

Again, the Old Man of the KOA stuck out his ugly head: "Get in here now!"

"Did you call, Grampy?" Rex trilled. "Was that you a-callin'?"

"How about we have five more minutes, or how about five hours?" Rex didn't lower the pitch or the sweetness of his voice.

"What did you say?" The old guy really did look terrible, with a bald head way too skinny for his body, for any body past its fourth year. It was a face more like a claw, now red and pulsing.

"Just wondered if you'd like to go fuck yourself with the toilet exhaust hose."

The old guy said some stuff we couldn't make out and shut the door, kind of quiet. Odd thing was he didn't seem mad. Rex and Megan acted as if nothing unusual had happened, which maybe it hadn't.

Turns out Rex and Megan were twins — didn't look it — and seventeen — didn't look it even more. They were headed the opposite direction from us, toward a whole series of National Parks. They said they spent most of their time on computers.

"Playing video games? Facebook?" Wendell, not unreasonably, asked — not unreasonably given his interests. Were he honest, he'd have added "porn sites."

Rex and Megan both looked embarrassed. "No, we're taking classes, distance-learning from University of Washington. Worst of all, we don't have to. We signed up for the hell of it."

"Might as well admit it, Rex, now that you've let the shit out of the bag. We signed up because we're interested. Taking eight hours of classes."

"What in?" I was drawn to these kids.

"Philosophy, Eng. Lit.," Rex said.

"And Spanish — just two extra units," Megan said, as if she'd just admitted she loved going down on old dogs.

"I'll be damned!" Wendell said, probably for the same reason I would.

"Don't hate us!" Rex said, only half mockingly.

We proceeded to make plans. These kids didn't seem to have options, and hanging out with us might be better than going around Tombstone with grandpa buzzard and his wife, doubtless well matched.

The upshot of our council was that Wendell went over, knocked, introduced himself, and disappeared inside. We'd sent him on a mission to convince the oldies that it was safe to trust their charges with us and in everyone's best interests. Wendell was very good at these sorts of missions, being just the boy responsible grown-ups would be sure to trust. Plus he was polite, make that kind, and not above taking a genuine interest in the doings of losers, even nasty losers like these old coots.

Rex and Megan said it'd be better if we stayed outside — I had suggested going to our camper for cocktails. Wendell and I had abandoned the alphabet, skipped ahead to martinis, which we drank dutifully without enjoying them, and manhattans, which we loved. For some reason, we never got drunk, never had more than one or two; but they sure made our evening — board games and movie watching — slip by smooth.

Wendell emerged about thirty minutes later. It hadn't seemed so long, Rex and Megan being fun to talk to. They were much better looking than I had thought at first, Rex, I'll admit it, being hotter than hell. Anyhow, here comes Wendell, smiling.

"Your grandparents are really nice."

"They're fucking saints, Wendell. What happened?" It was a little funny to hear Megan say "fuck" so much, but I guess I did it too. She just seemed prissy, apart from that — maybe just that she was starched and neat, her clothes anyhow.

"They said okay."

"You're good, Wendell. Thanks, man." Rex seemed to like Wendell.

"They said you could spend the night tomorrow night — if you want."

"Fuck your mother! Really?"

"Yeah, only I ain't sending for Mother. You'll have to make do with Tyler."

Wendell! I was set to be snotty, but Rex took it in stride, rushing at me and giving me a hug, not sexy but friendly — not meant as sexy, though it sure as Jesus was.

"I convinced them that you two could protect us and help us out, as we're all on our own and need responsible friends to protect us and didn't they see that and wouldn't they please help out two immature kids by letting their very mature grandkids watch over them for the day and tomorrow night even, though I knew they'd miss their grandkids but we'd only ask for the one day please and one night please it would be very nice of them and they said yes. I told them we were fourteen, me and Tyler."

So there it was. We agreed to meet at ten tomorrow morning. I asked them to breakfast, but they said they needed to do their classes early in the morning and would get coffee and rolls there with Granny and Gramps, so we'd be all set to hit the town at ten, not miss a thing. Wendell and I retired to our trailer for fajitas and a movie, but not before they both kissed us. It wasn't a peck and it wasn't a passionate prelude to a fuck either, closer to the first, I guess. I bet Wendell had never kissed such a beautiful girl. As for me, of course I'd made out with dozens of guys much hotter than Rex. Yeah, and Donald Trump is staying right here at the KOA, next row over.

First thing in the morning, we got ourselves a Tombstone Adventure Pass, one each, which set us up for four extraordinary experiences at a considerable saving. I was worried Wendell would try to pay for everybody, but he didn't. Then I got pissed that he hadn't. I recognize my own inconsistency, a trait I intend to cultivate.

Halfway through the day, after Wendell had indeed bought us all lunch, two things became clear: Rex and Megan were smarter even than we'd thought; this town was genuinely interesting. It was interesting because Rex and Megan knew so much about it. Tombstone was more than a vile spot where the gunfight at the O..K. Corral took place. For instance, this tourist trap, population now about a thousand, all employed running attractions, was once the biggest city between St. Louis and San Francisco, the most remarkable boomtown in the 1880s.

Silver mines and claims everywhere, along with whores, guns, and lice. Megan had done a report on life in the gun-slinging West. She said it must have been as close to hygienic hell as anything since the 11th Century: nobody bathed, nobody brushed teeth, nobody did a thing about the vermin crawling over and into all the flesh in sight. Indians, she said, were clean; but not Europeans, whose level of what anybody would call cultivation was miles lower.

Of course this prettied-up version of Tombstone gave no hint of any of that. There were two good spots: the newspaper museum and The Bird Cage Theatre. In both, we shuffled away from the tour group and listened to our buddies. The newspaper, *The Tombstone Epitaph*, was big during the boom times and still is published now and then. Rex located exhibits the tour ignored, exhibits where the original write-up of the O.K. Corral gunfight was there to be read, along with other neat stories: "Virgil Earp Shot," and "Geronimo Surrenders." Turns out this place is free, and it's the best thing in town, in my opinion, which is also that of Rex and Megan, who have views that count.

The other place, The Bird Cage Theater, is authentic as hell. The tour assholes say so, but so does Megan, and she knows. The place was closed in 1889 and boarded up, some flood, I think. It was opened fifty years later as a museum. The birdcages were like they used in go-go clubs in the '70s only here back in those times there were whores on exhibit in them. And I thought the Miss America Pageant was a meat-market! Also, the building has lots of bullet holes. There were sixteen big-scale gunfights in this saloon in the 1880s, where a good many shots found their target. Megan says, though, that lots of these famous gunfighters were more famous for shooting than hitting. Wild Bill Hikock once drew on a man across a poker table, fired at him from a distance of four feet, and missed. I love stuff like that.

Everything else in town was shitty. The hoked-up reenactment of the O.K. Corral Gunfight was all too close to the one back at Barstow. We dragged our way through a lot of stuff, but after a while it was just a matter of using up our tickets.

We got groceries and went back to our place. Simple stuff: a salad I made with blue cheese, walnuts, and crisp little bacon; and Wendell's spaghetti sauce over little pasta tubes. Stuffed mushrooms for an appetizer. No dessert. Instead, some manhattans.

We just sat around talking. I almost always do enjoy talking, for some reason. I used to enjoy talking to my parents, even — and Wendell. These kids, though, were inside a lot I wish I knew about. They made me want to read and think more. Wonder how they survived in school, what with the usual level of triviality you get hammered with? Acting like leak-mouth Wendell, I just asked, "How do you guys stand it at school?"

They didn't pretend to misunderstand. "Probably the way you do. You find kids. And we have fun too at dumb stuff — football games and dances. It's you and Wendell make us all serious. We don't have kids like you where we go to school, do we Rex?"

"Christ, no. You two are intense. It's not that you're smart. I don't mean you're not smart, but lots of people are. It's that you listen and think. You're not dying to say something smart, so you just do."

"And you don't try to one-up whomever has just talked. That's the way a lot of conversations are fucked up, right Rex? I mean, people get competitive and don't think; they just show off. You two don't. That's terrific."

I don't know about Wendell, but I never felt so flattered.

"How do you stand these summers being shuffled off with granny and gramps?"

Megan picked it up. "It's a long story, Wendell. You really want to hear it?"

"Duh, Megan. What do you suppose they're going to say? 'No, we'd rather hear about your bowel movements?'"

"Rex tries to compensate for his dubious gender identification by talking fourth grade potty mouth. It's ever so tough."

"So, as to Gran and Gramp?" Wendell was visibly uncomfortable.

"Sorry, Wendell. Though what a rude fuck you are! Anyhow, we've done it the last two years, a month last summer but all of this one, if they make it. You see, our grandparents were great to us when we were little. Maybe all grandparents are, but ours were as kind as it's possible to be. Not just money and hugs but sensitive ways of helping, small things but important to both of us. They gave Rex and me our first condoms, if you can believe it."

"Old hippie swingers?"

"No, Tyler, not at all. I know it sounds like it, but they just like us better than they like their own views. We both went to them with every problem under the sun, not just sex. They studied up so they could do the new math, and they read the novels and poems we read. They took us to

Peru and into the rain forests so we could see for ourselves what was happening. There's no end to it."

I looked over at Rex as Megan was talking and saw that he had tears in his eyes. How could the people we saw be the ones Megan was describing?

Megan paused for a minute.

"They both are dying, Tyler — and Wendell. They have cancer, different kinds but both advanced. They're dying." She paused again. For a long time, so Rex took over:

"That stuff about me saying 'Fuck you.' I know how that sounds and how they sound. Partly it's a game, partly it's because my grandpa is in so much pain he can't stand it." Rex was about to cry. Megan tried to help him out by talking, but she couldn't do it, which seemed to be what Rex needed to let loose with the tears. He did.

I couldn't think of anything to say. Neither could Wendell, so he said it.

"I'm really sorry. We didn't mean to joke. I think it's great that you two are being with them as they die. You two are about the finest people I've ever met."

Rex and Megan seemed eased. They didn't climb all over Wendell, but you could tell he'd drained something for them, let them slide out of a grief that was about unbearable. Wendell was right about one thing: these two were about the best people we'd met.

Rex and Megan got us fast back to other stuff. It was so stimulating and moved so quickly we talked until three o'clock without realizing it. All those hours, and it seemed like twenty minutes. Finally, Megan looked at her watch:

"Oh fuck. We need to be back by ten or so in the morning, just to check on our grandparents. They're right next door, of course, but they'd never bother us, even if something bad were happening. Better get to bed. You guys have a nice setup here."

"What a sweet way of asking where in this flophouse

is everybody going to sleep, Megan. Well, just you watch while Wendell pulls out his magic swantz and waves it around and the whole ass-end of the camper opens up and we have plenty of room, a partition too, so there's two separate sleeping quarters. Privacy assured."

Rex started to say something, stopped, and then giggled.

Wendell was doing his aw-shucks routine, and I felt equally flummoxed. How were we going to do this? Boy-boy/girl-girl, of course. Maybe not?

"Well, we're way beyond same-sex, right buddies? I mean, I trust you two like nobody I've known years longer. That's dumb. You know what I mean."

"How would they know what you mean, Rex? He means, do you mind if I sleep with Wendell and he sleeps with Tyler? I won't say we won't cuddle, since that seems natural. But you can trust us — mostly." She laughed so sweetly it'd taken youths more resistant than me and Wendell to have resisted, assuming we wanted to resist, which I guess I didn't. I had no idea. I didn't know about Wendell but can honestly say I was at least as confused as Wendell must have been — oh hell.

"Unless you're gay. In that case, we'd be glad—"

"Nope, we're not gay," Wendell jumped in. "We'd love to do that — what you say. Right, Tyler?"

It was like he was agreeing to go roller-skating. I'll admit it wasn't too clear what we were agreeing to. That made it that much more exciting and scary.

Wasn't too long before I knew. I'm going to include this, since I'm trying to report the important stuff, which doesn't mean it wasn't also embarrassing (or should be, probably will be some day) or that I can quite believe it happened the way it did and didn't happen another way — and happened at all.

We had four single beds, in two sections, with a partition between the sections. Not much of a partition but at least it made peeping tough. I got into my pajamas in the bathroom and got into bed, not knowing what Rex was doing, not looking to tell the truth. Nothing happened at all for a minute or two. I was just about to close my eyes and try to sleep, when I felt this hand on my shoulder. Rex.

"You mind if I crawl in. I'm littler than I look and I'm a real good cuddler."

Yes he was. That and probably a lot more — I hoped, or dreaded, or something.

He scrunched in, pulled me close to him, my back to his front, and right away began nuzzling my neck and rubbing both hands up and down my sides. That's all it took for me to feel prickly and nervous and, I don't know, hungry. That sounds so corny, but I'd better stop worrying about how it sounds or I'll never get this told.

He seemed to sense what I was feeling. I know he was feeling that way too by the erection pressing into my butt. I'd felt that before, but never in bed and never with just my pajamas and whatever he had on separating it and me. Turns out what he had on was pajamas too. I found that out next morning, when I finally worked up courage to look, if courage was what it was, which it wasn't. I kept expecting Rex to do something else, but he didn't, just kept rubbing my sides and then my temples. Before long, the horniness I was experiencing seemed to change, without me knowing it, into the warmest, most secure feeling ever. I suppose it was a feeble substitute for outright sex, only I don't believe that. It was what it was, and what it was made me feel happier here in this strange trailer than I had ever felt at home.

I got so relaxed it made me understand what cats feel when they purr. I didn't purr. What I did was, I fell off the bed. I rolled over, thinking I'd get closer to him and went the wrong way, I was so befuzzed, and found myself in empty space. Rex caught me and rearranged us both. Not exactly spontaneous, but nothing was fractured.

So there we were, back in cuddle-land. I remember thinking just that, wishing I could stay there forever, never do anything that would get me evicted.

"You okay, Tyler?"

"Okay? " Where was this going?

"Me too," he said.

"Yeah."

"Good night, dear."

"Good night, Rex — dear."

* * *

I wasn't the least bit self-conscious, shut up in about three square feet or something with this beautiful older woman. One year older, but still .... I had managed much tougher situations, all the time. This was nothing.

Actually, I was hoping I'd die or she'd fall down and hit her head and go all unconscious. Anything to get me through this. How was I going to undress? What would I say? At least I wanted the light off. It wasn't really bright — some kind of night-light, but it was on. And she was between it and me. The very worst thing that could have happened did: Megan just stood there looking beautiful, waiting for me to give directions. I stood there too, not looking beautiful. Finally, Megan took pity. She talked anyhow, though she couldn't have said anything worse.

"Could we leave the light on, Wendell? Do you mind a lot?"

"All night?"

She laughed. "No, I'm not scared of the dark — not with you holding me."

"Oh."

"You'll hold me, won't you?"

"Okay."

"Wendell, can I watch you undress?"

"Oh God."

"You mind?"

"No, it's not that."

"Great. I think it's so sexy. And you're so pretty, Wendell. I don't know when I've seen such a hot guy. I'm not just saying that to get you in bed either."

"You're not?"

"Well, yes. I'm hoping to get you in bed, that's true; but what I said is even truer, if that makes any sense; it's dead true."

"Dead bed, she said."

She didn't laugh. Why should she? She actually looked, not scared, but a little like she had been shut up with a loony, which sort of she had.

"Can I watch you undress too, Megan?"

"If you want."

"Oh yeah."

"I know, Wendell. Let's do it real, real, slow, like a striptease. Make it a game. If we both do it together, we won't get embarrassed." She understood a lot about me.

That seemed to make it better; I don't know why. I wish I'd let it go at that, but if there's a way to keep yammering when there's no need, I'll find it: "What are we taking off, real slow like you say?"

"Huh? Our clothes."

"And?"

"I'm sorry, Wendell. I don't follow you. We take off our clothes."

"All of them?"

"Oh, I see. What do you usually wear to bed, honey?"

"It varies. You know, sometimes I ...." I trailed off. This was pathetic.

"It varies? That's interesting, Wendell. Most people, I'll bet, get into a rut about bedtime wear."

"I wear my underpants. You know, my underwear."

"Well, tonight you're going to wear — you ready for this?"

"Yeah." I thought she was going to say I had to wear *her* underpants.

"Not one thing, *nada*, bare-assed and happy."
"Okay."

Then she started to take off her shoes, which she did slow. Then she pretended to take off stockings, peeling them down real sexy and unhooking garter belts, only of course she didn't have them on. Then she started ooching up her shirt, sometimes pulling it back down a little. Then she turned her back to me, looking over her shoulder, licking her lips and making her eyes real narrow. She pulled her shirt up and down real slow, and then unbuttoned her jeans in front, turning back around to face me, as she slid her pants up and down, near the top, and kept her shirt going too, a little higher each time until her bra started showing and I almost had an accident in my pants.

Meanwhile, I was trying not to move too fast. I had my shirt hanging from one arm, spinning it and trying to be sexy or at least not too much of an ass. I hadn't unbuttoned any on my pants yet, paralyzed by Megan's dance. She was now without a shirt, having flipped it over my head. She turned her back to me again, reached round, and unhooked her bra. Then she squirmed her jeans down a little, showing the tops of her bikini panties. Mine, not bikini-style, were still hidden, but that couldn't last.

I unbuttoned the top button on my pants and tried to imitate her skidding them up and down, which I had to manage without rubbing against my dick. It couldn't take much more. Finally, I worked my jeans down a little, turned round and pulled them down my butt, wiggling it and trying to imagine I was a stripper from back at Exotic World, working the crowd, showing teasing glimpses.

When I turned around and stopped thinking about my own moves, there was Megan, holding her hands in front of her breasts, with her jeans down by her knees. Then, real slow, she moved one hand, then the other, upward under her breasts, jiggled them slightly, not gross, slid her hands, rubbing her belly slow and sexy, down to her jeans. She took them all the way off and then did some grinding wiggles with her hips, bare breasted and only her panties on.

I wanted to catch up in the clothes-off race, but this was getting to be more fun than embarrassing, even my part in the dance, though naturally watching her was the best. I got this idea of trying to dance my pants off and almost fell down, tripping about six times. But Megan didn't laugh, seemed sort of mesmerized by my legs and butt. She was flushed and was breathing hard. You can imagine what state I was in.

She turned around again, back to me now, and started sliding her panties down, finally showing her butt crack and then her whole naked butt. Then she faced me and kept her panties on their slow way southward, looking at me right in the eye and smiling. I'd stopped doing anything. She was even prettier this way, a lame thing to say, but that's what hit me. Also, I realized that, apart from Mom and porn sites and peeks at Tyler, this was the first time I'd seen a woman naked. I'm glad it was Megan.

I lowered my J. C. Penny's slow, my back to her and my head turned around the way she'd done. That way I could keep staring at her. Not much of me was worried any more about the tent I was making in front. No use postponing it. I turned round, wiggled my hips the way she had, and slid my underpants out over my mini-ramrod.

"Wow!" Megan said, as my personal best came into view. That was pure kindness, I'm sure, as I knew from gym class that my dong was no record-setter. Average, maybe a tiny bit above, but not a wowser, I knew. I'd take it, though.

"I hate to stop looking at you, Wendell, but maybe we should get into bed now, turn off the light?"

"Okay. That was fun."

"Yeah, I'd say that, Wendell. I wish I had a video of you stripping. I'd make millions — only I'd keep it for myself."

"Ha! You're the most beautiful thing I've ever seen, Megan."

"Thanks," she said, but she laughed.

She came over and held my face in both her hands and kissed me really nice. I figured that was good night and got into the smaller of the two beds."

"Move over, fatty."

God, there she was! She twisted me round so we were facing each other, and she started kissing me again — and me, her.

Next thing I knew, though, she was somehow behind me, kneading my neck and nuzzling, but not with her tongue. I was busy doing I'm not too sure what, mostly kind of humming, to tell the truth. We settled in to a state of squirming, slower and slower and slower. It wasn't that I went to sleep, not right away, but pretty soon I did.

* * *

Just before drifting off to the sweetest sleep in my life, two thoughts snaked into my head: there were strange singing noises coming from about eighteen inches away where my little companion and Megan were; the noises Rex and I were making, I was making, must have formed a kind of geeky harmony to Wendell's lilting melodies. You suppose he heard? Worse, do you suppose he and Megan ...? Why do I care? But I sure do, care a lot. What's wrong with me?

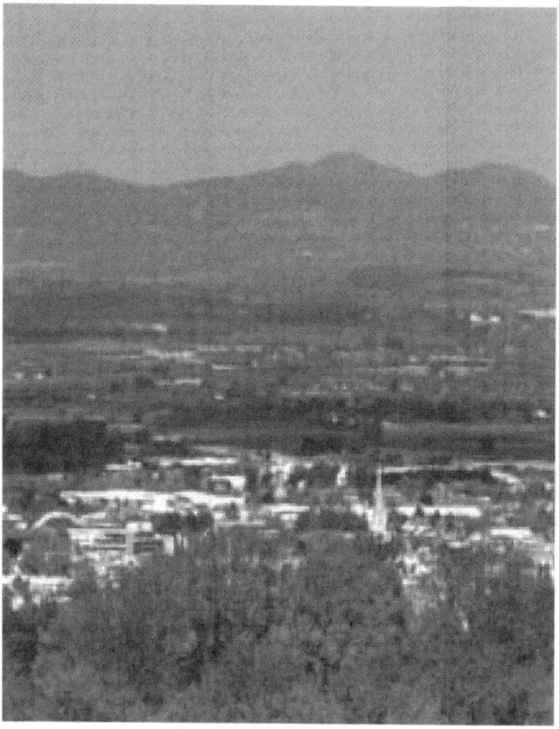

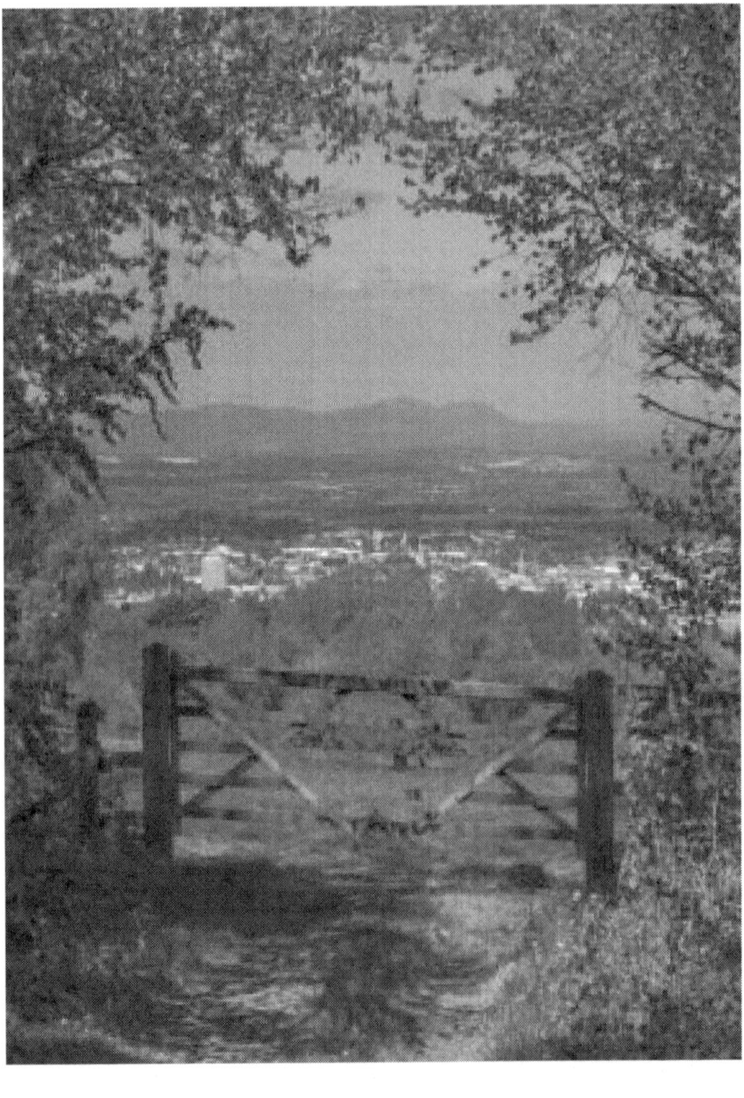

CHAPTER 10

Tuesday — El Paso

Day 20

Wendell and Megan were making breakfast when I woke up, with Rex just about where he must have been all night, curled up behind me. I didn't want anything to change, but it had to: I woke him up gently and didn't make any aggressive moves. What virtue! Of course our being within touching distance of our companions had something to do with it. No it didn't.

Wendell went over and got the grandparents, who weren't the least bit crabby. They were dignified and soft-spoken and made the rest of us quiet. They did their best to appear interested in Wendell and me, and they made it clear to their grandkids, without saying it, that they were sorry for any rough talk yesterday, that they loved them as much as they loved the small bit of life they had left to them. I don't want to talk about the breakfast or saying good-bye. I guess that's what we did. Somehow it got to be clear that we weren't staying in touch. That was that. I won't pretend I was cool about it.

For the first time, we took off, Wendell driving, without having any idea whatsoever where we were going. It seemed important to move. I figured Wendell and I would never talk about what had happened, only I knew we would. But not just then.

"You know, Tyler, I never expected, when we set off, that I'd settle all my sexual confusions on this trip."

"Didn't you?"

"No. But I did. Well, I didn't, but I had fun getting more confused."

"Did you?"

"Yeah. I guess you could say that — well, never mind."

"What, Wendell?"

"A gentleman never tells, so they say."

"God damn you, Wendell, you lousy prick!" I couldn't keep the anger out of my voice. He looked over at me, I don't know, sort of gently.

"Tyler, I was kidding. And that's mean. We just cuddled."

"It's none of my business, Wendell."

"Sure it is, Tyler. Sure it is. I don't want to pretend. I kept my dorkiness just where it was — in — what's that word?"

"Intact, Dumbo."

"Yeah."

I was so happy. What an asshole I am. And I proved it by what I said: "Ain't you gonna ask about me and Rex, Wendell?"

"No."

"Don't you care?" As soon as I said that, I realized how unfair it was. But Wendell could be cool sometimes at the oddest times, and now was one of them.

"Tyler, I care so much — but I won't talk about that. What I mean is I care about you and think you are so — well, I want you to be happy."

I tried to stop him: "I know what you mean, Wendell."

"No you don't. Sorry, Tyler. What I mean is that I know I have no right to ask or to have it be any of my business whether you have sex or not."

"Wendell, I have to say this. I was caring about whether you did — have sex — and hoping you hadn't. I understand if you felt the same way. Sure I do."

"Yeah."

"And my intactness is also just like yours. One of many ways we two are.... And let's not say another fucking word about it now, okay?"

"Okay."

* * *

We got along real well on the road this morning, me and Tyler. Took off with me driving, all upset, but not as bad as we might have been because the talk we had. It was confusing, but that's okay. It was pretty terrible thinking and talking about what had happened, considering that these old people were leaving a life they had lived so brightly, and, as it closed down on them, were not even able to be nice always to their young grandkids who loved them so. But for a long time they were great to them, kinder than anybody; so I guess it evens out in a way. Rex and Megan were doing the best they could to help the old people say good-bye, and maybe the way they took to Tyler and me, getting in bed, was a desperate thing to do. They were rough talking to their grandparents, even mean, but they only wanted to revive them, give some of the life they had too much of to people losing the little they had left. Cuddling with us might have been a way of wishing they could help their old companions.

I read this line in a book I partly didn't understand, called *Young Men and Fire*, where people are out on a rescue party after a terrible fire that's killed some young smoke-jumpers. I won't get the line right but it's something like, "Humans do few finer things than go out to rescue others, even when they are rescuing the dead."

Tyler didn't want to talk any more about the night before and I didn't either, so we drove along gabbling about easy stuff. Tyler asked me again about music, about a book I was reading while we were sitting around sometimes, or while she was driving. It was a book on Debussy, and she wanted to know about it. Ordinarily, I'd figure she was getting ammunition to use against me, but now it seemed different. I didn't hold back.

"The part that interests me — here let me get it." I shuffled around. Here it is. It's about his, Debussy's, *Fantasie for Piano and Orchestra*. I don't know what that music sounds like, but I've heard it. I mean, I can't remember it the way you remember some stuff — Beethoven, or Berlioz, or your favorite group. So, it's not really about this piece that I want to tell you."

"Wendell?"

"Yeah."

"Just tell me. I can see why you'd be apprehensive, talking about something you know about, talking to me, but go ahead."

"Oh. Well, Debussy was visiting the Universal Exposition in Paris in 1889, and, while everybody else was climbing the new Eiffel Tower, Debussy was listening to a music group from Java. He spent hours listening to what were really strange sounds then, now, too. Here's what he said, 'If one listens to it without being prejudiced by one's European ears, one can find a percussive charm that forces one to admit that our own music is not much more than a barbarous howl of noise more fit for a traveling circus.'"

"What gets me is how extreme he is. At first I thought he was showing off, calling European music a 'barbarous howl,' but then I saw he was clearing the ground so he could do something strange: 'European ears.'"

"What do you mean?"

"Well, Tyler, imagine he's not just saying this music is different and we aren't used to it. What if he's saying our ears, our ears you know, the ears on our head ...."

"I'm following you, Wendell."

"What if he's saying our ears really can't hear, that our ears don't just grow up like corn but are more like prejudices or the way some countries like skinny and some like fat — or big breasts or eat snails."

"I sorta see."

"I chewed on that a long time. Isn't it interesting, Tyler? If ears and eyes are not natural, really, but social or cultural. Then it's not that we don't hear this Java music very well, or right; we can't hear it at all."

"That's fucking awesome."

"Fucking awesome. So Debussy listens and listens, trying to get new ears — or get his made over, plastic-surgeoned."

"Damn, Wendell."

"There's more. Debussy was trying to find a way to get out from under Wagner, who was dominating European music then, it says. Debussy gets away from Wagner by getting new ears, not by getting a new influence."

"Yeah."

"I also read somewhere, Tyler, that cats don't say meow in all parts of the world."

"Huh?"

"Think about it."

"Thanks, Wendell. That's nice of you, not to go on being teacher. I see what you mean. Cats don't sound the same to people because ears are different."

"Maybe."

"I see. Maybe cats are different too. Maybe it's not just ears that get formed by culture but voice boxes too."

"I never thought of that, Tyler."

"Yeah, maybe there are parts of the world where cats say 'Meow' and other parts where they say, 'Go fuck yourself.'"

"Those'd be the cats for you."

* * *

Turns out we were heading north, back to the main road east, toward our eventual destination and, I sure as hell hope, out of the desert and these ugly hills. There's this line in Housman, "those blue remembered hills." I wonder why hills are always supposed to be pretty? Of course Housman was thinking of English hills, which are ground down and don't try for much in grandeur, like everything else in that second-rate country, about which I know nothing, which makes it easier to have opinions. But these hills in Arizona aren't blue or memorable. I asked Wendell about it:

"That's interesting, Tyler. People can hide in hills."

"Yeah. And they can fix on them. Who remembers brushing her teeth on a particular day when she was thirteen? But hills are like special events, real or not, like the way we *want* to remember what the past was, wish it had been."

"Yeah, and...."

"Sorry, Wendell — I wonder why these hills are so depressing. I like the desert, but these hills aren't what hills ought to be. I mean, if these brown squatty things are the only elevation around, then it's like there's never going to be anything but brushing your teeth. So we retain the illusion that hills are blue and memorable, gotta be."

"Blue?"

"You remember that Housman poem, Ms. Barnes-Roman's class, about 'blue remembered hills?'"

"That's really a strange poem — about something so sharp in the past that something something 'cannot come again.' I think that's creepy, but yeah I remember. Old Housman. Yeah. What do you think that poem means, Tyler?"

"Housman doesn't seem to be — let me start over: the memory of beautiful blue hills makes it really awful to live in the present. The past paralyzes him. Those remembered hills form his only reality and it's gone. I don't know if that's clear."

"If Housman grew up around these hills he'd have an easier time of it."

"You think lots of old people, like our parents, need those hills, those blue hills, even if they've never seen anything like them, even if they bring 'an air that kills?'"

"Maybe. My mother never talks about the past, though I

think that's because she doesn't want the past to have anything to do with me. Your parents do?"

"Quite a lot. No blue remembered hills, though. I think that's a white thing."

"I don't."

"No, you're right."

Which was about enough of that.

We'd taken off early and zoomed along east on the fascinating Interstate 10, into New Mexico, the land of enchantment, coming up to the first big town, Los Cruces. Having skipped breakfast, which we never did, realizing it is the most important meal for growing teens, we were getting hungry.

"Tyler, what do them there guide books tell us about Los Cruces and what to do and where to eat?" I'd been paging through them off and on as we drove.

"I'll read directly to you, Wendell: 'Spreading not very picturesquely alongside the not very verdant banks of the not very attractive Rio Grande, Los Cruces is, like most towns in this state, best avoided altogether. It calls itself a prosperous agricultural center, which is only half right; and even were it prosperous, why should you give a rat's ass? The town's name, in English, "lotsa crosses," is an index to its combination of morbidity and insipidity. The best thing about it is its nearness to a more bearable place three miles south, called Mesilla, where nobody is buried, where Billy the Kid once escaped from the jail, and where there is a pastry cafe that has low-cal sweet rolls and Mexican breakfasts.'"

"What's a Mexican breakfast?"

"I'm surprised you don't know, Wendell — grilled dog with beans."

"You're a bigot, Tyler."

The restaurant was probably good, but we only had a roll and coffee, not wanting to dull our appetites for our regular four p.m. lunch.

Which we had over in La Mesa, at a highly recommended place called Chopes, a roadside diner, made of cement blocks, sporting two signs, one hawking Italian Swiss Colony wine and one 7-Up. Wendell thought the signs said it all, "Stay Out." I forced him inside with promises of Italian Swiss Colony, delivered too when the friendly waitress pretended to believe our IDs. Italian Swiss Colony probably had no alcohol in it; certainly it had no taste, none that was good.

"Tyler, everything on this menu is chillis."

"Chillis are like peppers, Wendell, a very versatile food, often stuffed with things or chopped up and mixed in with these same things."

"Hot?"

"When fried and served in a timely way, yep."

"I mean spicy."

"I thought you might. I won't mislead you, boss man. Some chillis are hot."

"Are the particular chillis on this menu hot?"

"My last visit to Chopes they were hot, but I think they vary by the season."

"Are the chillis all of them hot, I mean spicy?" Wendell asked the waitress, now hovering over us.

"I can recommend some things that aren't spicy, if you'd prefer that, honey," she cooed, actually sliding in next to Wendell and leaning close into him, jamming her tit into his arm while pretending to show him the menu.

Wendell turned fire engine red. I was trying to figure out some way to rescue him, when the pretty woman slid her ass out and got herself vertical again.

She sold us on chilli rellenos, on the basis of their non-spiciness. Tasted great. Chopes is something!

We got to our El Paso campground while it was still light, but barely. Not a KOA this time, and not up to our usual standard; but it had a discreetly located waste-disposal pipe, electricity, and water, so it'd do. Besides, we were tired and as ready to settle in as the 90-year-old fluffs around us.

Wendell popped round to the shops and picked us up some fresh fish, which he grilled with a little less butter than usual. Rice, tomato and avocado salad. No dessert. Two manhattans. We're getting good.

But as we were cleaning up, goddam shit Wendell, lurking behind me as I was doing the last of the dishes, put his hand on my shoulder. Turns out he was trying to put a bowl away, or so he said later and I knew later was certainly true, but it sure felt then like a, I don't know, caress or, just as bad, some buddy-buddy pat.

Quick as anything, I whirled around, swung my arm and caught him in the face. The bowl must have flown out of his hands. Anyhow, it struck the leathery table and bounced onto the floor, where it hit like a bomb, exploding into a million bits.

Wendell just stood there and I hit him again. I don't know how many times. He was quiet, but I wasn't.

"Don't touch me ever, you horrible asshole. You understand me? Do you?"

"What?"

I hit him again, really hard. He backed away a little.

"What?"

"You imbecile! What do you mean 'What?' I told you never to touch me! I told you. You pawed me, you prick."

He backed away, but just over to the closet to get the broom and pan. I was by this time only about half-furious but also half-dazed, and pretty soon I felt paralyzed, staring at him, all bleeding and stooped over, not looking at me.

I stood there, getting further out of the minute. Right then, I would as soon have hit the people next door as Wendell, like it was somebody else had been furious, propelling all that rage. I'd wanted to kill him, felt like I was inside a terrible fire. Maybe I wouldn't have killed him, but I was possessed by that impulse. Not for long, but how long do you need? Now he was all scrunched over, fussing away — pretty, so very small — and it didn't seem possible I'd wanted that boy dead.

He looked up at me, bloody and puzzled. Alluring almost, though that sounds sick. With all that blood he didn't seem pretty, just defenseless. I didn't feel a thing, certainly not remorse. Maybe I would in a while.

I went into the bathroom, closed the door. I thought something dramatic might occur, but the only thing I could measure was the change inside my head. The boy, the attacker, was slowly changing form and within a few minutes had become Wendell. It was then I realized that I had been ripping and tearing at somebody else, something else.

To be Continued...

ABOUT JAMES R. KINCAID

James R. Kincaid is an English Professor masquerading as an author (or the other way around). He's published two novels (*Lost* and *A History of the African-American People by Strom Thurmond* — the latter with Percival Everett). He is also the author of about twenty short stories, and ever so many academic and nonfiction articles, reviews, and books, including long studies of Charles Dickens, Anthony Trollope, and Alfred Tennyson, along with two books on Victorian and modern eroticizing of children: *Child-Loving* and *Erotic Innocence*.

Kincaid has taught at Ohio State, University of Colorado, Berkeley, University of Southern California; and is now at University of Pittsburgh.

Jim welcomes reader reviews in print or on line at Amazon.com, or GoodReads.com, orother social media sites. He invites your comments, be they words of praise or howls of execration.

You can friend him on Facebook or contact him at: kincaid@usc.edu

MORE BOOKS BY JAMES R. KINCAID

The Open Road Series

WENDELL & TYLER: WE'RE OFF, Open Road Series, Vol.1, by Jim R. Kincaid.

WENDELL & TYLER: ON THE ROAD, AGAIN, Open Road Series, Vol.2, by Jim R. Kincaid. (To be released.)

WENDELL & TYLER: FINAL DESTINATION, Open Road Series, Vol.3, by Jim R. Kincaid. (To be released.)

Single Titles

LOST, traces the reckless expedition undertaken by two adult couples, by James R. Kincaid

A History of the African-American People by Strom Thurmond, by James R. Kincaid and Percival Everett.

Made in the USA
Lexington, KY
26 November 2015